TELL TALE

JEFFREY ARCHER, whose novels and short stories include *Kane and Abel*, the Clifton Chronicles and *Cat o' Nine Tales*, has topped the bestseller lists around the world, with sales of over 275 million copies.

He is the only author ever to have been a number one bestseller in fiction (nineteen times), short stories (four times) and non-fiction (*The Prison Diaries*).

The author is married to Dame Mary Archer, and they have two sons, two grandsons and one granddaughter.

ALSO BY JEFFREY ARCHER

THE CLIFTON CHRONICLES
Only Time Will Tell   The Sins of the Father
Best Kept Secret   Be Careful What You Wish For
Mightier than the Sword   Cometh the Hour
This Was a Man

NOVELS
Not a Penny More, Not a Penny Less
Shall We Tell the President?   Kane & Abel
The Prodigal Daughter   First Among Equals
A Matter of Honour   As the Crow Flies
Honour Among Thieves
The Fourth Estate   The Eleventh Commandment
Sons of Fortune   False Impression
The Gospel According to Judas
(with the assistance of Professor Francis J. Moloney)
A Prisoner of Birth   Paths of Glory

SHORT STORIES
A Quiver Full of Arrows   A Twist in the Tale
Twelve Red Herrings   The Collected Short Stories
To Cut a Long Story Short   Cat o' Nine Tales
And Thereby Hangs a Tale

PLAYS
Beyond Reasonable Doubt   Exclusive   The Accused

PRISON DIARIES
Volume One – Belmarsh: Hell
Volume Two – Wayland: Purgatory
Volume Three – North Sea Camp: Heaven

SCREENPLAYS
Mallory: Walking Off the Map   False Impression

JEFFREY ARCHER

TELL TALE

PAN BOOKS

First published 2017 by Macmillan

This paperback edition first published 2018 by Pan Books
an imprint of Pan Macmillan
20 New Wharf Road, London N1 9RR
Associated companies throughout the world
www.panmacmillan.com

ISBN 978-1-5098-8410-0

1 3 5 7 9 8 6 4 2

A CIP catalogue record for this book is available from the British Library.

Printed and bound by CPI Group (UK) Ltd, Croydon, CR0 4YY

Visit **www.panmacmillan.com** to read more about all our books
and to buy them. You will also find features, author interviews and
news of any author events, and you can sign up for e-newsletters
so that you're always first to hear about our new releases.

TO PAULA

My thanks to

Simon Bainbridge, Henry Colthurst,

Naresh Kumar, Christian Neffe, Alison Prince,

Catherine Richards, Rupert Colley, Susan Watt,

Maria Teresa Burgoni and Vicki Mellor

FOREWORD

This is the first set of short stories I have written since the Clifton Chronicles.

Once again, some of them are loosely based on incidents that I've picked up on my travels from Grantchester to Calcutta, from Christchurch to Cape Town. These tales are marked with an asterisk, while the remainder are the result of my imagination.

However, after *Tell Tale* was published, I was given an idea by Rupert Colley for a short story that was so irresistible that I couldn't wait another ten years to write it. The result is 'Confession', which has been added to the paperback edition.

Since then I have turned 'Confession' into a one-act play, and along with 'Who Killed the Mayor?' they make up a double bill.

Jeffrey Archer,
March 2018

CONTENTS

* Inspired by real events
** Inspired by Rupert Colley

UNIQUE

A Challenge

Many years ago an editor from the *Reader's Digest* in New York invited me to write a hundred-word story with a beginning, a middle and an end. As if that wasn't enough of a challenge, he insisted that it couldn't be 99 words or 101.

Still not satisfied, he asked me to present the finished piece within twenty-four hours.

My first effort was 118 words, my second 106, and my third, 98. I wonder if you can work out which two words I had to put back in.

The result was 'Unique', which you will find on the next page.

It may interest readers to know, this is also 100 words.

Paris, 14 March 1921

THE COLLECTOR relit his cigar, picked up the magnifying glass and studied the triangular 1874 Cape of Good Hope.

'I did warn you there were two,' said the dealer, 'so yours is not unique.'

'How much?'

'Ten thousand francs.'

The collector wrote out a cheque, before taking a puff on his cigar, but it was no longer alight. He picked up a match, struck it, and set light to the stamp.

The dealer stared in disbelief as the stamp went up in smoke.

The collector smiled. 'You were wrong, my friend,' he said, 'mine is unique.'

CONFESSION

1

Nothing would have stopped them playing poker on a Friday evening. Even the outbreak of war.

The four of them had been friends – well, at least colleagues – for the past thirty years. Max Lascelles, a huge man who was used to throwing his weight about, sat at the top of the old wooden table, which he considered no more than his right. After all, he was a lawyer and mayor of Saint Rochelle, while the other three were only town councillors.

Claude Tessier, the chairman of Tessiers Private Bank, sat opposite him. He'd inherited the position, rather than earned it. A sharp, wily, cynical man, who was in no doubt that charity began at home.

To his right sat André Parmentier, the headmaster of Saint Rochelle College. Tall, thin, with a bushy red moustache that indicated what the colour of his hair must have been before he went bald. Respected and admired by the local community.

And finally, Dr Philippe Doucet, who was the senior physician at Saint Rochelle Hospital, sat on the mayor's right. A shy, good-looking man, whose head of thick black hair and warm open smile made several nurses dream about becoming Madame Doucet. But they were all to be disappointed.

All four men placed ten francs in the middle of the table before Tessier began to deal. Philippe Doucet smiled when he saw his hand, which the other three players noticed. The doctor was a man who couldn't hide his feelings, which was why he'd lost the most money over the years. Like so many gamblers, he tried not to think about his long-term losses, only rejoice in his short-term gains. He discarded one card, and asked for another, which the banker quickly replaced. The smile remained in place. He wasn't bluffing. Doctors don't bluff.

'Two,' said Max Lascelles, who was seated on the doctor's left. The mayor showed no emotion as he studied his new hand.

'Three,' said André, who always stroked his bushy moustache whenever he felt he was in with a chance. The banker dealt the headmaster three new cards, and once he'd checked them, he placed his cards face down on the table. When your hand is that bad, there's no point in bluffing.

'I'll also take three,' said Claude Tessier, but like the mayor, once the banker had considered his hand, he gave nothing away.

'Your call, Mr Mayor,' said Tessier, glancing across the table.

Lascelles tossed another ten francs into the pot, to indicate he was still in the game.

'How about you, Philippe?' asked Tessier.

The doctor continued to study his cards for some time

before saying confidently, 'I'll match your ten and raise you a further ten.' He placed his last two grubby notes on top of the mounting pile.

'Too rich for me,' Parmentier said with a shake of the head.

'Me too,' said the banker, also placing his cards face down on the table.

'Then it's just the two of us, Philippe,' said the mayor, wondering if the doctor could be tempted to part with any more money.

Philippe's eyes remained fixed on his cards, as he waited to see what the mayor would do.

'I'll see you,' Lascelles said, nonchalantly tossing another twenty francs into the centre of the table.

The doctor smiled and turned his cards over to reveal a pair of aces, a pair of queens and a ten, the smile remaining firmly in place.

The mayor began to turn his cards over one by one, prolonging the agony. A nine, a seven, a nine, a seven. Philippe's smile was still in place until the mayor revealed his final card, another nine.

'A full house,' said Tessier. 'The mayor wins.' The doctor frowned as the mayor gathered up his winnings without revealing the slightest emotion.

'You're a lucky bastard, Max,' said Philippe.

The mayor would like to have explained to Philippe that luck had very little to do with it, when it came to playing poker. Nine times out of ten, statistical probability and the ability to bluff would decide the final outcome.

The headmaster began to shuffle the pack, and was about to start dealing another hand when they all heard the key turning in the lock. The mayor checked his gold pocket watch: a few minutes past midnight.

'Who could possibly consider disturbing us at this time of night?' he said.

They all looked towards the door, annoyed to have their game interrupted.

The four of them immediately stood up when the door was pushed open and the prison commandant marched in. Colonel Müller came to a halt in the middle of the cell, and placed his hands on his hips. Captain Hoffman and his ADC, Lieutenant Dieter, followed in his wake. Another full house. They were all wearing the black uniform of the SS. Their shoes were the only thing that shone.

'Heil Hitler!' said the commandant, but none of the prisoners responded as they waited anxiously to discover the reason for the visit. They feared the worst.

'Please be seated, Mr Mayor, gentlemen,' said the commandant as Captain Hoffman put a bottle of wine on the centre of the table, while his ADC, like a well-trained sommelier, placed a glass in front of each of them.

Once again, the doctor was unable to hide his surprise, while his colleagues remained poker-faced.

'As you know,' continued the commandant, 'the four of you are due to be released at six o'clock tomorrow morning, having served your sentences.' Eight suspicious eyes never left the commandant. 'Captain Hoffman will accompany you to the railway station where you will take a train back to Saint Rochelle. Once you're home, you will resume your former duties as members of the town council, and as long as you keep your heads down, I feel sure no stray bullets will hit you.'

The two junior officers dutifully laughed, while the four prisoners remained silent.

'However, it is my duty to remind you, gentlemen,' continued the commandant, 'that martial law is still in force, and applies to everyone, whatever their rank or position. Do I make myself clear?'

'Yes, Colonel,' said the mayor, speaking on behalf of his colleagues.

'Excellent,' said the commandant. 'Then I will leave you to your game, and see you again in the morning.' Without another word, the colonel turned on his heel and departed, with Captain Hoffman and Lieutenant Dieter following closely behind.

All four of the prisoners remained standing until the heavy door was slammed shut, and they heard the key turning in the lock.

'Did you notice,' said the mayor once he'd lowered his heavy frame back down onto his chair, 'that the commandant addressed us as gentlemen for the first time?'

'And you as Mr Mayor, but why the sudden change of heart,' said the headmaster, as he nervously touched his moustache.

'The town's affairs can't have been running quite as smoothly without us, would be my bet,' said the mayor. 'And I suspect the colonel will be only too happy to see us back in Saint Rochelle. He clearly hasn't got enough staff to administer the town's affairs.'

'You may well be right,' said Tessier. 'But that doesn't mean we have to fall in line.'

'I agree,' said the mayor, 'especially if the colonel is no longer holding all the aces.'

'What makes you think that?' asked Dr Doucet.

'The bottle of wine, for a start,' said the mayor, as he studied the label and smiled for the first time that day. 'Not vintage, but quite acceptable.' He poured himself a glass before passing the bottle across to Tessier.

'Not to mention his demeanour,' added the banker. 'Not the usual bombastic rhetoric suggesting that it can only be a matter of time before the master race has conquered the whole of Europe.'

'I agree with Claude,' said Parmentier. 'I can always tell when one of my boys knows he's about to be punished but still hopes to get off lightly.'

'Once France is free again, I have no intention of letting anybody off lightly,' said the mayor. 'The moment the Hun retreat back to the Fatherland where they belong, I shall round up all the quislings and collaborators, and impose my own form of martial law.'

'What do you have in mind, Mr Mayor?' asked the headmaster.

'The whores who made themselves available to anyone in uniform will have their heads shorn in public, while those who assisted the enemy will be hanged in the market square.'

'I would have thought as a lawyer, Max, you would have wanted to conduct a fair and open trial before passing judgement,' suggested the doctor. 'After all, we can't begin to know what pressures some of our countrymen must have been under. I can tell you as a doctor that sometimes there's a fine line between compliance and rape.'

'I can't agree, Philippe, but then you've always been willing to give everyone the benefit of the doubt,' said the mayor. 'An indulgence I cannot afford. I shall punish anyone and everyone I consider to be a traitor, while honouring our brave resistance fighters who, like us, have stood up to the enemy whatever the consequences.'

Philippe bowed his head.

'I can't pretend I've always stood up to them,' said the headmaster, 'and am well aware that as town councillors we have often received preferential treatment.'

'Only because it was our duty to ensure the town's affairs are run smoothly in the interest of those who elected us.'

'Let's not forget that some of our fellow councillors felt it more honourable to resign than collaborate with the enemy.'

'I am not a collaborator, Philippe, and never have been,' said the mayor, thumping his fist on the table. 'On the contrary, I have always tried to be a thorn in their flesh, and feel I can safely say I've drawn blood on several occasions, and I'll continue to do so given the slightest opportunity.'

'Not that easy while the swastika still flies above the town hall,' suggested Tessier.

'And you can be assured, Claude,' continued the mayor, 'I will personally burn that evil symbol the moment the Germans depart.'

'Which might not be for some time,' murmured the headmaster.

'Possibly, but that's no reason to forget we are Frenchmen,' said the mayor, raising his glass, 'Vive la France!'

'Vive la France!' the four men cried in unison, as they all raised their glasses.

'What's the first thing you'll do when you get home, André?' asked the doctor, trying to lighten the mood.

'Have a bath,' said the headmaster. They all laughed. 'Then I shall return to my classroom and attempt to teach the next generation that war serves little or no purpose, either for victor or the vanquished. How about you, Philippe?'

'Report back to the hospital, where I expect to find the wards full of young men returning from the front, scarred in more ways than we can imagine. And then there will be the sick and elderly, who had hoped to enjoy the fruits of retirement, only to find themselves overrun by a foreign power.'

'All very commendable,' said Tessier. 'But that won't stop me going straight home and jumping into bed with my wife. And I certainly won't be bothering to have a bath.'

They all burst out laughing.

'Amen to that,' said the headmaster with a chuckle, 'and I'd do the same if my wife was twenty years younger than me.'

'But then, unlike Claude,' said the mayor, 'André hasn't deflowered half the virgins in Saint Rochelle, with promises of an overdraft.'

'Well, at least it's girls I'm interested in,' said Tessier, once the mayor had stopped laughing.

'And can I assume, Tessier,' said the mayor, his tone changing, 'you will then return to the bank, and make sure all our affairs are in order? I can remember exactly how much was in my account the day we were arrested.'

'And every last franc will still be there,' said Tessier, looking directly at the mayor.

'Plus six months' interest?'

'And what about you, Max,' responded the banker, equally sharply. 'What will you do after you've hanged half the population of Saint Rochelle, and shorn the hair off the other half?'

'I shall continue my practice as a lawyer,' said the mayor, ignoring his friend's barb, 'as I suspect there will be a long queue waiting outside my office in need of my services,' he added, as he refilled everyone's glass.

'Including me,' said Philippe. 'I'll want someone to defend me when I can't afford to pay my gambling debts,' he added without a hint of self-pity.

'Perhaps we should call a truce,' suggested the headmaster. 'Forget the past six months, and wipe the slate clean.'

'Certainly not,' said the mayor. 'We all agreed to abide by the same rules that applied while we were on the outside. A gentleman always honours his gambling debts, if I recall your exact words, André.'

'But that would clean me out,' said Philippe, as he checked the bottom line in the banker's little black book. He didn't add that while they'd been incarcerated, every night had become a Friday night, and Dr Doucet had come to realize for the first time just how much the mayor must have pocketed over the years.

'The time has come to consider the future, not the past,' said the mayor, wanting to change the subject. 'I intend to convene a council meeting as soon as we get back to Saint Rochelle and expect you all to be present.'

'And what will the first item on the agenda be, Mr Mayor?' asked Tessier.

'We must pass a resolution denouncing Marshal Pétain

and the Vichy regime, and make it clear that we consider them nothing more than a bunch of quislings, and in future will be supporting General de Gaulle as the next president of France.'

'I don't recall you expressing those views at any of our recent council meetings,' said Tessier, not attempting to hide his sarcasm.

'No one knows better than you, Claude, the pressures I've been under, attempting to keep the show on the road,' said the mayor. 'Which resulted in me being arrested and thrown in jail for collaboration.'

'Along with the rest of us, who did no more than attend the private meeting you'd called without notice,' said Tessier. 'Just in case you'd forgotten.'

'I offered to serve all your sentences,' said the mayor, 'but the commandant wouldn't hear of it.'

'As you never stop reminding us,' said the doctor.

'I do not regret my decision,' said the mayor haughtily. 'And once I'm released, I shall continue to harass the enemy whenever possible.'

'Which wasn't all that often in the past, if I recall,' said Tessier.

'Children, children,' said the headmaster, aware that six months locked up together hadn't improved their relationship. 'Let us not forget we're all meant to be on the same side.'

'Not all the Germans have treated us badly,' the doctor said. 'I confess I've even come to like one or two of them, including Captain Hoffman.'

'More fool you, Philippe,' said the mayor. 'Hoffman would string us all up without a second thought if he believed it would benefit the Fatherland. Never forget the Hun are either on their knees or at your throats.'

'And they certainly don't believe in an eye for an eye when it comes to our brave resistance fighters,' said Tessier. 'You kill one of them, and they'll happily hang two of us in revenge.'

'True,' said the mayor. 'And if any of them should fail to make it back across the border after the war is over, I'll be the first to sharpen the guillotine, so help me God.'

The mention of the Almighty stopped everyone in their tracks, and both the headmaster and the doctor crossed themselves.

'Well, at least we won't have a lot to confess after spending six months in this hellhole,' said the headmaster, interrupting the eerie silence.

'Although I feel sure Father Pierre would not approve of us gambling,' said Philippe. 'I'm reminded that Our Lord threw the moneylenders out of the temple.'

'I won't tell him, if you don't,' said the mayor as he refilled his glass with what was left in the bottle.

'That's even assuming Father Pierre will still be around when we get back,' said Philippe. 'When I last saw him at the hospital, he was putting in hours that would have broken a normal man. I begged him to slow down, but he simply ignored me.'

A clock in the distance chimed once.

'Time for one more hand before we turn in?' suggested Tessier, handing the cards to the mayor.

'Count me out,' said Philippe, 'before I'm declared bankrupt.'

'Perhaps it's your turn to win,' said the mayor as he

began to shuffle the pack, 'and you'll get everything back on the next hand?'

'That's just not going to happen, and you know it, Max, so I think I'll call it a day. Not that I expect to get much sleep. I feel like a schoolboy on his last day of term who can't wait to go home.'

'I hope my school isn't this bad,' said the headmaster, as he began to deal another hand.

Philippe rose from his place and made his way slowly across to his bed on the far side of the cell, before climbing up onto the top bunk. He was just about to lie down, when he saw him standing there, in the centre of the room. The doctor stared at him for a few moments, before he said, 'Good evening, Father. I didn't hear you come in.'

'God bless you, my son,' replied Father Pierre, giving the sign of the cross.

The headmaster immediately stopped dealing when he heard the familiar voice. They all swung round and stared at the priest.

Father Pierre was bathed in a shard of light shining from the skylight above. He was wearing his familiar long black cassock, white collar and silk bands. A simple silver cross hung around his neck, as it had done since the day of his consecration.

The four men continued to stare at the priest, but said nothing. Tessier tried to hide the cards under the table, like a child who'd been caught with his hand in the biscuit tin.

'Bless you, my children, I hope you are all well,' the priest said, once again making the sign of the cross, 'although I fear I am sadly the bearer of bad tidings.' The four of them froze like rabbits caught in the headlights, all of them assuming they were no longer going to be released in the morning.

'Earlier this evening,' continued the priest, 'a train travelling to Saint Rochelle was blown up by local resistance fighters. Three German officers were killed, along with three of our own countrymen.' He hesitated a few moments before adding, 'It will not come as a surprise to you, gentlemen, that the German High Command are demanding reprisals.'

'But three Frenchmen were killed,' said Tessier, 'isn't that enough?'

'I fear not,' said the priest. 'As in the past, the Germans are demanding that two Frenchmen are to be executed for every German killed.'

'But what has this to do with us?' demanded the mayor. 'We were locked up in here at the time of the bombing, so how could we possibly have been involved?'

'I did point that out to the commandant, but he remains adamant that if three of the town's leading citizens were to be made an example of, it would send a clear message to anyone who might consider taking similar action in the future. And let me assure you, no amount of pleading on your behalf would move him. Colonel Müller has decreed that three of you will be hanged in the town square at six o'clock tomorrow morning.'

The four men all began speaking at once, and only stopped when the mayor raised a hand. 'All we wish to know, Father, is how the three will be chosen?' he asked, a bead of sweat appearing on his forehead, although the cell was freezing.

'Colonel Müller has come up with three suggestions, but has decided to leave the final choice to you.'

'How considerate of him,' said Tessier. 'I can't wait to hear what he has in mind.'

'He felt the simplest solution would be to draw straws.'

'I don't believe in chance,' said the mayor. 'What are the alternatives?'

'A final round of poker, when the stakes could not be higher, if I recall the colonel's exact words.'

'I would be happy to go along with that,' said the mayor.

'I bet you would, Max,' said Claude. 'After all, the odds would be stacked in your favour. What's the final choice?'

'I hesitate to mention this,' said the priest, 'as it is the one that least appeals to me.'

'Do enlighten us, Father,' said the mayor, no longer able to mask his feelings.

'You will all agree to make a final confession before you face your maker, and I will be left with the unenviable task of deciding which one of you should be spared.'

'That would certainly be my choice,' said the headmaster, without hesitation.

'However, should you decide to go down that particular path,' continued the priest, 'there is a caveat which I insisted on.'

'And what was that?' demanded the mayor.

'Each one of you will be expected to confess to the worst sin you have committed. And you would do well to remember that I have heard all your confessions over the years, so there isn't much I don't know about you. And possibly more important, I have also been privy to the confessions of over a thousand of my parishioners, some of whom have considered it their sacred duty to share with me their innermost secrets. Not all of which reflect well on you. One of them, an unimpeachable source, says one of you is a collaborator. Therefore, I must warn you gentlemen, should you lie, I would not hesitate to strike your name from the list. So I'll ask you once again, which of the three options would you prefer?'

'I'm quite happy to draw straws,' said Tessier.

'I'll opt for one final game of poker,' said the mayor, 'and leave God to deal the cards.'

'I'm willing to confess to the worst sin I've ever committed,' said the headmaster, 'and face the consequences.'

They all turned to Philippe, who was still considering his options.

'If you agree to play one final game of poker,' said the mayor, 'I'd be willing to wipe the slate clean.'

'Don't listen to him, Philippe,' said Tessier. 'Take my advice and draw straws. At least that way you'd still be in with a chance.'

'Possibly, but with my luck, Claude, I don't suppose drawing straws would make any difference. No, I'll join my friend André and admit to the worst sin I've ever committed, and leave you, Father, to make the final judgement.'

'Then that's settled,' said Tessier, shifting uneasily in his chair. 'So what happens next?'

'Now all you have to decide,' said Father Pierre, 'is which one of you will go first?'

'Shall we leave the cards to decide?' said the mayor, who dealt four cards, face up. When he looked down at the queen of hearts he said, 'Lowest goes first.'

The headmaster left the group to join Father Pierre.

André Parmentier, the Headmaster

The priest blessed the headmaster as he knelt before him.

'Blessed are the merciful, for they shall receive mercy. May God, the Father of all mercies, assist you as you make your final confession.' Father Pierre smiled at a man whom he'd admired for so many years. He had followed André's career with considerable pleasure and satisfaction. Textbook, you might have described it. Young Parmentier had begun his life as a student at Saint Rochelle College for Boys, where he would end his days as headmaster, with breaks only to graduate from the Sorbonne in Paris and to spend a sabbatical year as a supply teacher in Algiers.

On his return to Saint Rochelle, André had taken up the position of junior history teacher, and, as the cliché has it, the rest was history. He had progressed rapidly through the ranks, and no one was surprised when the Board of Governors invited him to be headmaster, a position he'd held for the past decade.

Many of his colleagues were surprised that André hadn't deserted Saint Rochelle for plusher pastures, as it was well known that several other more renowned schools had approached him over the years. But he had always turned them down, however tempting the offer. Some suggested it was because of family problems, while others accepted his explanation that he had found his vocation and was happy to remain in Saint Rochelle.

By the time war broke out, Saint Rochelle College was among the most respected schools in France, attracting young and ambitious teachers from all over the country.

Recently the Board of Governors had begun to consider the problem of who would replace their respected head-master when he retired in a couple of years' time.

When the Germans marched into Saint Rochelle, André had faced new challenges and tackled them with the same resolution as he had always done in the past. He considered occupation by a foreign power was an inconvenience, not an excuse to lower one's standards.

André Parmentier had never married. He treated all his charges as if they were his first-born. He wasn't surprised to find that many of them who hadn't excelled in the classroom, shone on the battlefield. After all, this wasn't the first time he'd had to come to terms with a brutal and pointless war.

Sadly, many of his charges were destined to die in the heat of battle and, like a grieving father, he wept for them. Somehow André kept his spirits up, never doubting that in time this barbaric war, like the last, must surely come to an end. And when it did, he would be given the opportunity to teach the next generation not to repeat the mistakes of their fathers and forefathers. But that was before a German decree had ordered that three of them must be hanged at six in the morning. And he didn't need to be a maths teacher to know the odds were against him.

'Forgive me, Father,' said André, 'for I have sinned and beg your forgiveness. My last confession was just before I was arrested and sent to prison.'

Father Pierre found it hard to believe that André had ever done anything reprehensible in his life.

'I accept your remorse, my son, aware of the good

work you have done in the community for many years,' said the priest. 'But as this could be your final confession, you must reveal the greatest transgression you have committed so that I can judge whether you should be spared, or be one of the three who the commandant has condemned to death.'

'When you have heard my confession, Father, you will not be able to absolve me, as my sin is cardinal, and I have long since given up any hope of entering the kingdom of Heaven.'

'I cannot believe, my son,' said Father Pierre, 'that you are the collaborator.'

'Far worse, Father. I must admit,' continued André, 'I have considered sharing my secret with you many times in the past, but like a coward on the battlefield, I've always retreated at the first sound of gunfire. But now I welcome this final chance of redemption before I meet my maker. Be assured that death for me, to quote the gospel, will have no sting, and the grave no victory.' The headmaster bowed his head and wept uncontrollably.

The priest couldn't believe the words he was hearing, but made no attempt to interrupt him.

'As you know, Father,' the headmaster continued, 'I have a younger brother.'

'Guillaume,' said the priest, 'whom you have loyally supported over the years, despite a tragic lapse in his youth, for which he paid dearly.'

'It wasn't his lapse, Father, but mine, and it is I who should have paid dearly.'

'What are you saying, my son? Everyone knows that

your younger brother was rightly sent to prison for the grievous offence he committed.'

'It was I who committed the grievous offence, Father, and should have been sent to prison.'

'I don't understand.'

'How could you,' said André, 'when you only saw what was in front of you, and didn't need to look any further.'

'But you weren't even with your brother when he killed that young girl.'

'Yes, I was,' said André. 'Allow me to explain. My brother and I had been out earlier that evening celebrating his twenty-first birthday, and both of us had a little too much to drink. When we were finally thrown out of the last bar, Guillaume passed out, so I had to drive him home.'

'But the police found him behind the wheel.'

'Only because I'd careered onto a pavement and hit a girl, a girl I taught, who later died. Would she still be alive today if I hadn't run away but stopped and called for an ambulance? But I didn't. Instead I panicked and drove quickly away, purposely crashing the car into a tree not too far from Guillaume's home. When the police eventually arrived, they found my brother behind the wheel and no one else in the car.'

'But that was exactly what the police did find,' said Father Pierre.

'The police found what I wanted them to find,' said André. 'But then they had no way of knowing. I had climbed out of the car, pulled my brother across to the driver's seat, and then abandoned him with his head resting on the steering wheel, the horn blaring out for all to hear.'

The priest crossed himself.

'I made my way quickly back to my own flat on the other side of town, slipping in and out of the shadows, to make sure no one saw me, although there weren't many people around at that time in the morning. When I eventually got home, I let myself in through the back door, crept upstairs and went to bed. But I didn't sleep. Truth is, I haven't had a good night's sleep since.'

The headmaster put his head in his hands and remained silent for some time, before he continued.

'I waited for the police to knock on my door in the middle of the night, arrest me and lock me up, but they didn't, so I knew I'd got away with it. After all, it was Guillaume they discovered behind the wheel, only a hundred metres from his home. The following day, several witnesses confirmed they'd seen him the night before, and he was in no fit state to drive.'

'But the police must eventually have interviewed you?'

'Yes, they visited the school the following morning,' admitted André.

'When you could have told them it was you who was driving the car, and not your brother.'

'I told them I'd had a little too much to drink so walked home, and that was the last time I'd seen him.'

'And they believed you?'

'And so did you, Father.'

The priest bowed his head.

'The local paper had a field day. Photos of a pretty young girl with her whole life ahead of her. A headline that remains etched in my memory to this day. A crashed car, and a young man being dragged out of the front seat at two in the morning. The only mention I got was as the poor unfortunate brother, whom they described as a popular and respected young teacher from the local college. I even attended the girl's funeral, only exacerbating my crime. By the time it came to the trial, the verdict had been decided long before the judge passed sentence.'

'But the trial was several months later, so you still could have told the jury the truth.'

'I told them what they'd read in the papers,' said André, his head bowed.

'And your brother was sentenced to six years?'

'He was sentenced to life, Father, because the only job he could get after he came out of prison was as a janitor in the school, where I was able to pull a few strings. Few remember that Guillaume was training to be an architect at the time, and had a promising career ahead of him, which I cut short. But now I've been granted one last chance to put the record straight,' said André, looking up at the priest for the first time. 'I want you to promise me, Father, that after they hang me tomorrow, you will tell everyone who attends my funeral what actually happened that night, so that my brother can at least spend the rest of his days in peace and not continue to take the blame for a crime he didn't commit.'

'Perhaps Our Lord will decide to spare you, my son,' said the priest, 'so you can tell the world the truth and begin to understand what your brother must have suffered for all these years.'

'I would rather die.'

'Perhaps we should leave that decision to the Almighty?' the priest said, as he bent down and helped the headmaster back onto his feet. André turned and walked slowly away, his head still bowed.

'What can he possibly have told Father Pierre that we didn't already know about?' said the mayor when he saw André collapse onto his bunk and turn his face to the wall, like a badly wounded soldier who knows nothing can save him.

The priest turned his attention to those still seated at the table.

'Which one of you will be next?' he asked.

The mayor dealt three cards.

Claude Tessier, the Banker

'Forgive me, Father, for I have sinned,' said Claude. 'I wish to seek God's understanding and forgiveness.'

'Blessed are the poor in spirit, for theirs is the kingdom of Heaven.' Father Pierre couldn't recall when Tessier had last attended church, let alone confession, although there wasn't much he didn't know about the man. However, there remained one mystery that still needed to be explained, and he hoped that the thought of eternal damnation might prompt the banker to finally admit to the truth.

Claude Tessier had become chairman of the family bank when his father died in 1940, only days before the Germans marched down the Champs-Elysées. Lucien Tessier had been both respected and admired by the local community. Tessiers might not have been the largest bank in town, but Lucien was trusted, and his customers never doubted that their savings were in safe hands. The same could not always be said of his son.

The old man had admitted to his wife that he wasn't sure Claude was the right person to follow him as chairman. 'Feckless and foolhardy' were the words he murmured on his deathbed, and then whispered to the priest that he feared for the widow's mite when he was no longer there to oversee every transaction.

Lucien Tessier's problems were compounded by having a daughter who was not only brighter than Claude, but also honest to the degree of embarrassment. However, the old man realized that Saint Rochelle was not yet ready to accept a woman as chairman of the bank.

Claude's only other banking rival in the town was Bouchards, a well-run establishment that the old man admired. Its chairman, Jacques Bouchard, also had a son, Thomas, who had already proved himself well worthy of succeeding him.

Claude Tessier and Thomas Bouchard had advanced through life together, admittedly at a different pace on their predestined course. School, national service, and later university, before returning to Saint Rochelle to begin their banking careers.

It was Bouchard's father's idea, and one he quickly regretted, that the two boys should serve their apprenticeships at rival banks. Claude's father happily agreed to the arrangement, and got the better deal. After two years, Bouchard never wanted to set eyes on young Claude again, while Lucien wished Thomas would join him on the board of Tessiers. Nothing much changed as both boys progressed towards becoming chairman of their banks; that is until the Germans parked their tanks in the town square.

'May God, the Father of all mercies, help you when you make your final confession,' said the priest as he blessed Tessier.

'I was rather hoping, Father, that it wouldn't be my final confession,' admitted Claude.

'For your sake, let us hope you are right, my son. However, this might be your last chance to admit to the most grievous transgression you have committed.'

'Which believe me, Father, I intend to do.'

'I'm glad to hear that, my son,' said the priest. He leant back, folded his arms and waited.

'I readily admit, Father,' began Claude, 'that I failed to stand by my oldest friend when he most needed me, and I beg the Lord's forgiveness for this lapse, which I hope you will feel is out of character.'

'Should I assume you are referring to the fate that has befallen your closest friend and banking rival, Thomas Bouchard?' enquired the priest.

'Yes, Father. Thomas and I have been friends for so long, I can't ever remember when I didn't know him. We were at school together, served as young lieutenants in the army, and even attended the same university. I was also his best man when he married Esther, and am godfather to their first child, Albert, but when he most needed the support of a friend, like Saint Peter I denied him.'

'But how could that be possible after such a long friendship?'

'To understand that, Father,' said Claude, 'I have to take you back to our university days when we both fell in love with the same girl. Esther was not only beautiful, but brighter than both of us. To be fair, she never showed the slightest interest in me, but I still lived in hope. So I was devastated when Thomas told me that he'd proposed to her and she'd agreed to be his wife.'

'But despite the sin of envy, you still agreed to be his best man?'

'I did. And they were married in a local town hall on the outskirts of Paris, just days after we graduated. They then returned to Saint Rochelle as man and wife.'

'I well remember,' said the priest. 'And confess that at the time, I was disappointed not to have been invited to conduct the wedding ceremony. However, I only recently discovered why that would not have been possible, and admire you for keeping your friend's secret.' Father Pierre fell silent as he realized Claude had reached a crossroads, but was still unsure which path he would take.

'And be assured, Father, I have continued to do so, and was horrified when the Germans discovered Esther was Jewish and the daughter of a distinguished academic who had denounced the Nazis.'

'I was equally horrified,' said the priest, 'but did you keep your side of the bargain, and remain silent about Esther's heritage?'

'I did better than that, Father. I warned Thomas that the Germans had found out that Esther was Professor Cohen's daughter, and he shouldn't delay in taking his wife and children to America, and only return when the war was over.'

'Are you sure it wasn't the other way round?' said the priest quietly.

'What are you suggesting?' said Tessier, his voice rising with every word, causing his colleagues to look across in his direction.

'That it was in fact Thomas who confided in you that he was planning to escape before the Germans found out the truth about his wife, and then you betrayed him.'

'Who would consider accusing me of such treachery? I even offered to manage Thomas's affairs while he was away, and hand back the bank the moment he and Esther returned.'

'But if you were the only person in Saint Rochelle who knew Esther was Jewish, how could the Germans have possibly found out, if it wasn't you who told them?'

'It was covered by the national press that Professor Cohen had been arrested and disappeared overnight, which would explain how the Germans found out.'

'I don't think the professor would have informed the Nazis that he had a daughter and a grandson living in Saint Rochelle.'

'I swear on all that is sacred, Father, that I would never have told the Germans his secret. Thomas was my dearest friend.'

'That's not what Captain Hoffman told me,' said the priest.

Claude looked up, his face drained and chalk white, his whole body trembling. 'But he's a German, Father, who cannot be trusted. Surely you wouldn't take his word against mine?'

'No, I wouldn't in normal circumstances. But I would

take his word in the presence of Our Lord after he'd sworn an oath on the Bible.'

'I don't understand,' said Claude.

'What you couldn't know is that Karl Hoffman is a devout Roman Catholic, as are millions of Germans.'

'But he's first and foremost a Nazi.'

'The man who attends my church privately every Thursday to take Mass before making his confession is no Nazi, of that I can assure you. In fact, it was Hoffman who first warned me that the commandant was planning to arrest Esther and have her sent to a concentration camp in Poland.'

'He's lying, Father, so help me God. I did everything I could to help my friend escape.'

'But Hoffman warned me a week before Esther was arrested,' said the priest, 'giving the partisans more than enough time to organize a safe passage for the family to America. Esther's bags were packed and ready when the Gestapo turned up in the middle of the night, arrested her, took her to the station, and threw her on a train that didn't require a ticket.'

Tessier slumped down, burying his head in his hands.

'And something else you could not have known. Your friend Thomas also attempted to board that train so he could be with his wife, and only the butt of a German rifle prevented him from doing so.'

'But—'

'And because you betrayed your friend, he will spend the rest of his life only being able to imagine the abject horror and degradation his wife must be going through.'

'But you have to understand, Father, the Germans

were putting pressure on me,' pleaded Tessier. 'They were making my life hell.'

'Nothing compared to the hell Thomas is now experiencing while you sit and watch his whole life crumble in front of him. Even some of his customers have begun to cross the road and transfer their accounts to Tessiers, for fear of reprisals from the Germans.'

'That wasn't what I intended, Father, and if you'll give me a chance, I swear I'll make it up to him.'

'I think it's a little late for that,' said the priest.

'No, no. If I get out of here alive, I'll merge the two banks and make Thomas the senior partner. And what's more, I'll donate a hundred thousand francs to the church.'

'Would you be willing to make a will confirming this, whatever my decision?'

'Yes,' said Claude, 'you have my word on it.'

'And the Almighty's,' said the priest.

'And the Almighty's,' repeated Claude.

'That's most generous of you, my son,' said the priest. 'If you do keep your word, I feel sure Our Lord will be merciful.'

'Thank you, Father,' said Claude. 'And perhaps you might mention my offer to the commandant,' he added, as he raised his head and looked directly at the priest.

'You have given your word to Our Lord,' said Father Pierre, 'which should surely be more than enough.'

Claude got off his knees and, not looking totally convinced, bowed to the priest and returned to join the mayor and the doctor.

'How did it go?' asked Max.

'I simply told him the truth,' said the banker, his poker

face back in place, 'and am content to await the Almighty's decision.'

'I have a feeling it won't be the Almighty who makes that decision,' said the mayor, as he dealt two more cards.

The doctor stared down at the five and said, 'My turn, it seems.'

'Be warned, Philippe,' said Tessier. 'If you bluff, he'll catch you out.'

'I think we're all agreed that I'm not much good at bluffing.'

But then Philippe knew exactly what he was going to tell Father Pierre.

Philippe Doucet, the Doctor

When Philippe Doucet knelt in front of the priest, Father Pierre had never seen him looking more at peace with himself. The priest had often witnessed that same contentment when the old finally accept they are going to die, and almost welcome it.

Father Pierre gave the sign of the cross, touched the doctor's forehead and pronounced, 'Blessed are they that mourn, for they shall be comforted. May the God of all mercies assist you when you make your final confession.'

There was little the priest didn't know about Philippe Doucet. After all, he was a regular churchgoer, and made his confession at least once a month. His idea of sin rarely demanded more than half a dozen Hail Marys.

Philippe was an open book, and the only chapter that the priest hadn't read was the first one. No one could explain how he'd ever ended up in a backwater like Saint Rochelle. Unlike the mayor, the banker and the headmaster, he hadn't been born in the town, or attended its only college, although everyone now accepted him as a local.

It was common knowledge that he'd been educated at Paris Sud Medical School, and graduated with honours, as the several certificates and diplomas hanging from the walls of his surgery confirmed. However, it remained a mystery why a man who was surely destined to become the senior partner of a large medical practice had ended up as a hospital doctor in Saint Rochelle.

Was Philippe Doucet about to turn the first page?

'Forgive me, Father, for I have sinned. My last confession was on the Friday before I was arrested.'

'I am not expecting this to take too long, my son, because as long as I've known you, your life has been an open book.'

'But there is one chapter you don't know about, Father, that was written before I came to Saint Rochelle.'

'I feel sure that Our Lord will forgive some youthful indiscretion,' said the priest. 'That could hardly compare with being a collaborator.'

'What I have done is far worse than being a collaborator, Father.' Doucet was clearly distraught. 'I have broken the sixth commandment, for which I must suffer eternal damnation.'

'You, a murderer, my son?' The priest was stunned. 'I don't believe it. Every doctor makes mistakes . . .'

'But this was not a mistake, Father, as I will now explain. After leaving university,' Doucet continued, 'I began my medical career as a junior doctor in a large and prestigious practice in my home town of Lyon. As over sixty other graduates had applied for the post, I considered myself fortunate to be chosen. When I wasn't working, I was reading the latest medical journal, so I would always be one step ahead of my contemporaries. Within a year, I was promoted, and already preparing to take my next step on the medical ladder.'

'Which surely can't have been as a junior doctor at Saint Rochelle Hospital,' suggested the priest.

'No, it was not, Father,' admitted Philippe, 'but Saint Rochelle was the only hospital that offered me a job at the time.'

'Why was that?' asked the priest. 'When you'd already proved to be a shining light among your contemporaries?'

'It was a Thursday in November 1921 when I fell off the ladder,' said Philippe. 'I had been working at the practice for just over a year when one of my colleagues, Victor Bonnard, a doctor not much older than myself, asked me if I would visit one of his patients. He explained that she was an elderly lady who suffered from the illnesses of the rich, and once a week liked to while away an hour or two with her doctor. Victor explained that an emergency had arisen at Saint Joseph's that he considered far more pressing.

'I readily agreed, not least because Victor always seemed to have time for the practice's latest recruit. I grabbed my bag and headed for the Boulevard des Belges, an arrondissement usually only visited by senior doctors. When I arrived outside a magnificent Palladian mansion, I stopped to catch my breath. An experience that was to be repeated moments later when the front door was opened by a beautiful young woman whom I assumed must be an actress or a model. She had long blonde hair and deep blue eyes accompanied by a captivating smile that made you feel you were an old friend.

'"Hello, I'm Celeste Picard," she told me, offering her hand.

'"Philippe Doucet," I replied. "I'm sorry that Dr Bonnard can't make it, but he was held up at the hospital," I explained. Although in truth I wasn't at all sorry.

'"It's not important," Celeste assured me as she led me upstairs to the first floor. "No one pretends Great-aunt Manon is ill, but she does enjoy a weekly visit from the doctor. Especially the younger ones," she said with a grin.

'When she opened the bedroom door, I found an old lady sitting up in bed waiting for me. It didn't take a very thorough examination to realize there wasn't much wrong with Great-aunt Manon that holding her hand and listening to her endless stories wouldn't have taken care of. I realized that it was no wonder the practice was so successful with patients like this.'

The priest smiled but didn't interrupt.

'When I left the house an hour later, Celeste rewarded me with the same disarming smile, and if I hadn't been so shy, I might have attempted to strike up a conversation, whereas I only managed "Goodbye", as she closed the front door.

'It was about a week later that Victor told me the old lady had asked to see me again.

'"You're clearly in favour," he teased. But my only thought was that I might see Celeste again. After I'd examined the old lady a second time, her niece invited me to join her for tea, and when I left an hour later, she said, "I hope you'll come again next week, Dr Doucet."

'I floated back to the surgery, unable to believe such a goddess would even give me a second look. But to my surprise, tea was followed by a walk in Parc de la Tête d'or, an evening at l'Opéra de Lyon, and dinner at Le Café du Peintre, that I couldn't afford, after which we became lovers. I couldn't have been happier, because I knew I'd found the woman I wanted to spend the rest of my life with.

'I waited for almost a year before I proposed, and was heartbroken when she turned me down. But Celeste explained it wasn't because she didn't want to marry me, but as she was the sole beneficiary of her great-aunt's will, she couldn't consider leaving the old lady until she died. I was shattered. Great-aunt Manon may have been eighty-two, but I couldn't see why she wouldn't live to a hundred.

'I tried to assure Celeste that I earned more than enough for us to live on, even though I knew it wasn't true. She did, however, agree to become engaged, but refused to wear a ring for fear her great-aunt would see it and dismiss me, and possibly even her.'

'And you went along with the deception?' said the priest.

'Yes, but it wasn't until Celeste said, "Don't worry, darling, she won't live forever," that the idea first crossed my mind, and I considered using my skills not to prolong life, but to shorten it. I didn't share those thoughts with Celeste.'

'How did the thought become the deed?' asked the priest.

'It must have been a few weeks after we'd become engaged that Great-aunt Manon complained about not being able to sleep at night. I recommended a course of sleeping pills, which seemed to do the trick. But whenever she complained about not having a good night's sleep, I found myself increasing the dosage, until finally she didn't wake up.'

Philippe bowed his head, but the priest said nothing as he knew there was more to come.

'When I filled in the death certificate, I wrote that she had died of natural causes. No one questioned my judgement; after all, she was eighty-four.

'I assumed that after a suitable period of mourning, Celeste and I would be married. However, when I attended the old lady's funeral, she turned her back on me. I tried to convince myself this was only sensible, as she wouldn't want to attract any unnecessary gossip.

'Some weeks later I was working at my desk when I heard laughter and raised voices coming from the corridor outside. I poked my head around the door to see Victor surrounded by doctors and nurses, who were warmly congratulating him.

'"What's the cause of the celebration?" I asked the receptionist.

'"Dr Bonnard has just got engaged."

'"Anyone I know?"

'"Celeste Picard," said the receptionist, without realizing how painful her words were. "You must have come across her, doctor, when you looked after her great-aunt."

'What a naive fool I'd turned out to be, Father, as it slowly dawned on me what role the two lovers had chosen for me to play. I started to drink, often arriving late for work, and began to make small mistakes at first, but then bigger ones that are unforgivable for someone in my profession. So when I came to the end of my trial period, it was hardly a surprise that my contract wasn't renewed.

'On the day of Victor and Celeste's wedding, I even considered committing suicide, and only my faith prevented me from doing so. However, I knew that I had to get as far away from Celeste as possible if I hoped to lead a normal life.'

'Which is how you ended up in Saint Rochelle?'

'Yes, Father. When the vacancy for a junior doctor was advertised in the medical journal, I immediately applied for the post. The hospital's supervisor admitted he was surprised that such a highly qualified doctor had even considered the position, and he didn't hesitate to offer me the job, even though the references from my former employer weren't exactly overwhelming.

'I have practised my profession in this town for over twenty years,' continued Philippe, 'and not a day goes by when I don't fall to my knees and beg the Almighty to forgive me for cutting short the life of an innocent old lady.'

'But your record during your time at the hospital has been exemplary, my son. Don't you think by now Our Lord may feel you have served your sentence?'

'The truth is, Father, I should have been struck off the medical register, and sent to prison.'

'Jesus told a sinner on one of the other crosses at Calvary that he would that night sit on his right hand in Heaven.'

'I can only hope Our Lord will show me the same mercy.'

'Have you considered, my son, while the war continues unabated, Saint Rochelle will need the skills God gave you as never before?'

'No more than the headmaster,' said Philippe, 'who

will be responsible for teaching future generations that war can never be the answer.'

'Bless you, my son,' said the priest, as he gave him the sign of the cross. 'I absolve you of your sins and pray you will enter the kingdom of Heaven.'

Philippe Doucet rose from his place, a look of serenity on his face, no longer fearful of facing his maker. He bowed and left the priest without another word and rejoined his colleagues.

'You look very pleased with yourself, Philippe,' said the mayor. 'Did Father Pierre promise you anything?'

'Nothing,' said Philippe. 'But I could not have asked for more.'

The mayor placed the cards back down on the table and looking at the banker said, 'Shuffle the cards, Claude. This shouldn't take too long, so there should still be time for another hand.' He sauntered across to the priest, trying to recall when he'd made his last confession.

Father Pierre was well prepared for the mayor, and suspected he would not display the same humility as his colleagues. But Our Lord would not have expected him to make a judgement before the lawyer had been allowed to admit to what he considered his worst sin. Where would he begin, wondered the priest.

Max Lascelles, the Mayor

'Blessed are the meek, for they shall inherit the earth,' said the priest, giving the sign of the cross. 'Are you prepared to make your final confession, my son?'

'No, Father, I am not,' responded the mayor. 'Not least because it is not going to be my final confession.'

'How can you be so sure it will be you that the Almighty spares?'

'Because it is not going to be the Almighty who makes that decision, but the commandant,' said the mayor, 'and I can assure you, Father, Colonel Müller is not on his knees at this moment seeking guidance from above because he's already decided that I am the chosen one.'

'But you were the one arrested for sedition. You even admitted that you'd arranged the meeting, and that your three colleagues were innocent of any charge.'

'True, but then it was the commandant who suggested I should set up the meeting in the first place, and during that conversation we also agreed on a six-month sentence and regular reports that I was being treated badly.'

'But that still doesn't explain why Colonel Müller would consider your life more important than that of a headmaster, a doctor or even a banker,' said Father Pierre.

'Because he knows none of them, even Tessier, would be willing to fall in with his long-term plans.'

The priest paused. 'So you are the collaborator.'

'I consider myself a realist, which is why my three colleagues will be hanged in the morning, and not me. However, you can be assured, Father, that as the town's leading citizen, I shall attend all three of their funerals and deliver glowing eulogies emphasizing their service to the community and how much they will be missed.'

'But if the Germans were to lose the war, the partisans wouldn't hesitate to string you up from the nearest lamp post,' said the priest, trying not to lose his temper.

'That's a risk I'm willing to take. But then I always try to make sure the odds are in my favour, and if I have to back the Germans or the British to win this war, I still consider it a one-horse race.'

'Mr Churchill may have something to say about that.'

'Churchill's nothing more than a foghorn on a sinking ship, and once he's been replaced, Hitler will quickly take control of the rest of Europe. By which time I will no longer be mayor of Saint Rochelle, but the governor of one his new provinces.'

'You seem to have forgotten one thing, my son.'

'And what might that be, Father?' said the mayor, raising an eyebrow.

'The intervention of the Almighty.'

'That's another risk I'm willing to take,' said Lascelles, 'as he's certainly taken his time over the Second Coming.'

'May God have mercy on your immortal soul.'

'I'm not interested in mortality, only in which one of us will be on the train back to Saint Rochelle in the morning, which I can assure you, Father, will be me.'

'Unless the partisans were to find out the truth,' said the priest.

'I don't have to remind you, Father, that if you utter one word of my confession to anyone, it will be you who will be condemned to spend an eternity in hell.'

'You're an evil man,' said the priest.

'At last we've found something we can agree on, Father,' said the mayor as the priest fell to his knees and began to pray.

The mayor gave the sign of the cross, before saying in

a loud voice, 'God bless you, Father.' He smiled and returned to his seat at the top of the table.

'That didn't take too long,' said Claude.

'No, but then I've led a fairly blameless life, and had little to confess other than my desire to continue serving my maker.'

'That's noble of you,' said Doucet, looking down at the priest. 'He was clearly moved by your testimony.'

'Possibly, but then I did make it clear to the good father,' continued the mayor, 'that I was content to let the Almighty decide which one of us should be spared, stressing that all three of you were far more worthy of his beneficence than I was.'

Tessier raised his eyes to Heaven in disbelief.

'Do you think Father Pierre has made his decision?' asked Philippe.

'I've no idea,' said Lascelles, as he turned to face the priest, who was still on his knees praying.

The mayor raised his glass and said, 'May the Lord guide you in your deliberations, Father.'

The other three raised their glasses and said in unison, 'May the Lord guide you—' but before they could finish, the mayor's face drained of all colour and he began to tremble. He dropped his glass and it shattered on the table as he continued to stare in front of him.

His three colleagues turned to look in the same direction, but the priest was no longer there.

2

They all counted the chimes as they rang out: one, two, three, four. Two more hours before they would discover their fate.

'What are you doing, Claude?' asked the mayor as he sat back down in his seat.

'Writing my will.'

'Would you like me to draw it up for you? After all, you wouldn't want there to be any disputes or misunderstandings after your death.'

'Good idea,' said Tessier. 'Then I'll be able to say it was drafted by a lawyer, should I live.'

'Touché,' said the mayor.

Claude tore half a dozen pages out of his little black book, and handed them across to the lawyer.

The mayor spent some time studying the banker's efforts at making a will before he settled down to write.

'You've been extremely generous to your sister and your friend Thomas Bouchard,' he said, after he'd turned the second page.

'As I had always intended,' said Tessier.

'And your young wife?' said the mayor, raising an eyebrow. 'Is she to get nothing?'

'She's young enough to find another husband.'

The lawyer turned another page.

'And I see you've left a large donation to the church. Was that also something you'd always intended?'

'No more than I promised Father Pierre years ago,' Tessier replied defensively.

'I also made promises to the good father that I intend to keep,' said the mayor, before adding, 'should I live.'

The lawyer continued to write for some time before he presented the testament to his client.

Once Claude had read the document a second time, he asked, 'Where do I sign?'

The mayor placed a forefinger on the dotted line. 'You'll need two witnesses who are conveniently on hand at no extra charge.'

Tessier looked across at the doctor, who could have been in another world. 'Philippe,' he said, interrupting his friend's thoughts. 'I need you to witness my will.'

The doctor blinked, picked up the pen and turning to the last page added his signature.

'Are you still awake, André?' asked the mayor, looking across at the headmaster's back.

'I haven't slept a wink,' came the weary reply.

'I need a second witness to Claude's will, and wondered if you'd do the honours.'

André heaved himself slowly up off the bottom bunk and placed his feet on the cold stone floor before making his way across to the table.

'Do I need to read the document before I sign it?' he asked.

'No, that won't be necessary,' said the mayor. 'You're simply witnessing Claude's signature.' He watched as

André Parmentier scribbled his name below that of Philippe Doucet. The lawyer placed the will in his battered briefcase.

Tessier jumped up from the table and began pacing around the cell as he thought about the document he'd just signed. If he was to die, it made sense for Thomas Bouchard to merge the two banks and allow his sister to play her part. He didn't doubt that, between them, they'd make a far better fist of it than he'd managed. He only wished he'd taken his father's advice and put Louise on the board years ago.

The mayor was taken by surprise when André didn't return to his bunk, but said, 'I would also like to make a will, Max.'

'I'd be delighted to assist you,' said the lawyer, ripping some more pages out of Claude's little black book before picking up a pen. 'Who will be the main beneficiaries?'

'I want to leave everything to my brother Guillaume.'

'Don't you think you've done more than enough for him already?'

'Not nearly enough, I'm afraid,' the headmaster replied. He extracted a sheet of paper from the pile and began writing a letter to his brother.

Dear Guillaume . . .

The mayor didn't have time to argue with his client, so set about preparing the headmaster's will. A simple exercise that only took him a few minutes, and once he'd double-checked each paragraph, he handed the single sheet of paper across to the headmaster.

'Thank you,' said André, who read it slowly, before signing on the bottom of the page and handing it to

Tessier and Doucet for their signatures. 'I'd also like this letter to be attached to my will,' he added, giving a folded sheet of paper to the lawyer before returning to his bunk.

Once again André closed his eyes, although he knew he wouldn't sleep. If he were among the three picked, at least Guillaume and his family would live in comparative comfort for the rest of their lives. And he hoped the letter would finally make it clear that his brother had not been responsible for killing the young girl – especially since Guillaume believed he was still the guilty party. When five chimes interrupted his reverie, André wasn't troubled by the thought of only having one more hour to live.

Once the mayor had placed the headmaster's will and his letter to Guillaume in his battered attaché case, he smiled at Philippe and said, 'What about you, my friend, have you thought about making a will?'

'What's the point,' said the doctor, 'when I'd have to leave everything to you just to clear my gambling debts, and that there still wouldn't be enough to pay your fee.'

'Prison visits are pro bono,' said the mayor with a chuckle.

Philippe leant on the table and placed his head in his hands as the lawyer began writing a third will. The doctor's thoughts drifted back to Celeste as they so often did when he was alone. She'd be middle-aged by now, and he wondered if she was still married to Victor Bonnard. Did they have any children? Had they migrated to their home in the country after the Germans had marched down the Champs-Elysées? Had the Palladian mansion been requisitioned by the German High Command? Not a day went by when Celeste didn't creep into his thoughts.

Once the mayor had completed a document of which he was the only beneficiary – not strictly legal, but who would know – he swivelled it round for Philippe to sign. Claude and André added their signatures without comment.

'Will you be making a will, Max?' asked Claude.

'That won't be necessary,' replied the mayor without explanation.

A strange and eerie silence descended on the cell. Four men lost in their thoughts as the seconds ticked by and they waited to learn their fate.

The mayor occasionally checked his watch, only to find time was something he couldn't influence as it progressed on its predetermined course, like a runner on his final lap. No one spoke when the first chime rang out, echoing around the cell. Long before the sixth bell had struck, they all heard the key turning in the lock.

'You can rely on the Germans to be on time,' said the mayor.

'Especially for a hanging,' added the banker as he stopped pacing and stared at the door. The mayor placed the deck of cards neatly back on the table. The headmaster sat bolt upright in his bunk, while Philippe continued to think about Celeste. Was he finally going to be released from her spell?

They all watched apprehensively as the massive door swung open and Captain Hoffman marched into the cell, a large smile on his face.

'Good morning, gentlemen,' he said. 'I hope you all had a good night's sleep.'

No one responded as they waited to find out which one of them would be reprieved.

'I have your tickets,' said Hoffman, before handing each of them a small green *billet*. 'We'd better get a move on, as the only train to Saint Rochelle today leaves in about half an hour.'

The four of them still didn't move, wondering if they were taking part in some elaborate Teutonic version of gallows humour.

'Can I ask,' said the doctor, the only one willing to voice what he knew was on all their minds. 'How many people were injured in last night's train crash?'

'What train crash?' Hoffman asked.

'The one that took place yesterday evening. We heard three German officers and three Frenchmen were killed by a bomb that had been planted on the track.'

'I've no idea what you're talking about,' said Hoffman. 'There hasn't been a bombing on the Saint Rochelle line for several months. A fact that the commandant is particularly proud of. I think you must have had a bad dream, doctor. Let's get moving, we can't expect the train to wait for us.'

Hoffman turned to leave, and the four men reluctantly followed him out of the cell.

André wondered if he was about to wake up.

Hoffman led his little band down a long dark corridor, up a steep flight of worn stone steps and out into a sharp morning light that the four of them hadn't experienced for the past six months. As they walked across the courtyard, their eyes focused on the gallows.

◄◦►

Colonel Müller and his ADC marched into the station and came to a halt in the centre of the platform. When the locals saw them, they immediately scattered to the far ends of the platform, as if the colonel was Moses, parting the Red Sea.

'I've allowed the mayor and the three councillors to travel back to Saint Rochelle first-class,' said the commandant. 'The occasional concession does no harm if we hope to keep things running smoothly.'

'Is the mayor still onside?' asked Dieter.

'For the moment, yes,' responded the commandant. 'But that man would switch sides without a second thought if it suited his purpose.'

Dieter nodded. 'And I fear I'm going to have to leave you to deal with the damn man, sir, because I've just received orders from Berlin instructing me to join my regiment in East Prussia. It looks as if the Führer has called off an invasion of England, and has decided to attack Russia.'

'I'm sorry to hear that, Dieter,' said the colonel. 'And I suspect it won't be too long before I'll have to join you, and leave the mayor in charge of Saint Rochelle.'

'Perish the thought,' said Dieter.

'I'd rather the mayor perished,' the colonel replied as Captain Hoffman marched onto the platform, his four charges in his wake.

Captain Hoffman walked across to join his colleagues beside the first-class carriage in the centre of the train, while the mayor and the three councillors kept their distance. Hoffman clicked his heels and gave the commandant a Nazi salute. 'The paperwork has been completed, sir, and as instructed, they've been issued with first-class tickets.'

'Don't acknowledge them,' said the colonel as he turned his back on the mayor. 'No need to give the partisans any reason to suspect we have someone on the inside.'

'Frankly, I wish I could send the mayor to the Eastern Front,' said Hoffman.

'Amen to that,' said Dieter as the three German officers boarded the first compartment in the first-class carriage.

'Say nothing,' whispered the mayor to his three colleagues, 'until we're on board, when no one else can overhear us.'

The four Frenchmen waited until everyone else had got into the second-class carriages before they climbed into the last compartment in first-class, leaving an empty compartment between themselves and the three Germans.

The mayor placed his briefcase on the rack above him, and settled down in a corner seat.

'Max, I've been thinking about my will,' said Tessier, who sat down opposite him, 'and I've decided I'd like to make a few changes.'

'Why?' demanded the mayor, staring innocently across the carriage at the banker.

'Circumstances have changed.'

'But you gave your word to Father Pierre—' The mayor stopped in mid-sentence, aware that he'd raised the one subject none of them wanted to discuss.

3

The two resistance fighters picked up the bomb the moment the sun disappeared behind a solitary cloud. They crept out of the forest, moved stealthily down the grassy slope and planted it in the middle of the track.

The older man began to walk backwards, unwinding a wheel of fuse wire, until they were once again safely out of sight. Once the correct length of wire had been cut and attached to the detonator they both slithered back down the slope and spent the next twenty minutes covering the exposed wire with bracken, stones and tufts of grass.

'Just in case an observant driver spots the wire glinting in the sun,' Marcel explained to his latest recruit.

Once the job was done to the older man's satisfaction, they clambered back up the hill to their hiding place and waited.

'How old are you, Albert?' asked the resistance commander as he lit a cigarette.

'Sixteen,' the boy replied.

'Shouldn't you be at school?' he teased.

'Not until I've seen the last German leave France in a wooden box.'

'Why made you so keen to join our cause?'

'The Germans came in the middle of the night and arrested my mother. Father says we'll never see her again.'

'What was her crime?'

'Being Jewish.'

'Then it's your lucky day, Albert, because my contact in Saint Rochelle has assured me that three German officers, including the prison commandant, will be on the train this morning.'

'How will we know which carriage to blow up?'

'That's easy. German officers always travel first-class, so we are only interested in the carriage in the centre of the train.'

'Won't some of our own people be injured, even killed by the blast?' asked Albert.

'Unlikely. Once it's known there are German officers on a train, the two second-class carriages on either side of first-class will be deserted.'

Albert stared at the plunger, his hands trembling.

'Patience, my boy,' said Marcel as the train rounded the bend and came into sight, billowing clouds of smoke into a clear blue sky. 'It won't be long now.'

Albert placed both hands on the plunger.

'Not yet,' said Marcel. 'I'll tell you when.'

The young recruit could feel the sweat pouring down his face as the train came closer and closer.

'Any moment now,' said the older man as the engine clattered over the bomb. 'Get ready.' It was only a few seconds, but it felt like a lifetime to Albert, before Marcel gave the order, 'Now!'

Albert Bouchard pressed firmly down on the plunger, and watched as the bomb exploded in front of his eyes. As the blast tore through the carriage, a ball of purple and blue flames shot into the air, mixed with shards of glass and debris. The carriage was blown unceremoniously off the track, landing with a thud on the far bank, a mass of twisted, molten metal embedded in the grass. Albert sat there, mesmerized by the scene. His only thought was that no one could possibly have survived. He stared at the other two carriages lying like abandoned children by its side, doors flapping and windows smashed.

'Let's go, Albert!' shouted the older man, who was already on his feet. But the boy couldn't take his eyes off the carnage.

Marcel grabbed his new recruit by his collar and yanked him up. He quickly disappeared into the forest with young Bouchard following in his footsteps. No longer a schoolboy.

-◄o►-

The guard who had been stationed in the rear carriage was among the first on the scene. When he came across the bodies of three German officers, including Colonel Müller, he crossed himself. He moved on and was surprised to find the bodies of three of his countrymen lying nearby. They must have been travelling first-class. But why, he wondered. Everyone had been briefed about the latest directive from the commander of the resistance.

Next on the scene was the driver, who'd been furthest from the blast.

'How many dead?' he asked.

'Six,' replied the guard. 'Three Germans and sadly three of our own.'

'And I passed several passengers lying by the side of the track,' said the driver. 'But none of them were badly injured. They got lucky, because there was a local doctor on the train, and he's looking after them.'

VIEW OF AUVERS-SUR-OISE

'IT'S LIKE making love for the first time,' said the chief inspector. 'A copper never forgets his first arrest.'

While all his chums at school wanted to be Han Solo or James Bond, Guy Stanford saw himself more as Sherlock Holmes. So when the careers master asked him what he wanted to do when he left school, no one was surprised when he replied, 'I'm going to be a detective.'

Guy's only problem was his father, who assumed that like him, he would train to be a barrister and later join him in chambers. Being English, they agreed on a compromise. And as with parents who are unsure their son is marrying the right girl, Guy agreed to a trial separation; if he still felt the same way about it after three years, his father would put up no objection to him joining the police force.

Guy spent the next three years at Exeter University studying the history of art – the second love of his life. He graduated with a good enough honours degree for his tutor to suggest he might consider returning to do a PhD thesis on Sorolla, the Spanish impressionist. Guy thanked his tutor, took the next train back to Coventry, and after a two-week holiday, joined the local police force.

Guy didn't take advantage of the graduate entry

scheme that guaranteed accelerated promotion because, as he told his father, he preferred to win his spurs on the battlefield. His four years on the beat before he became a detective turned out to be full of challenges. For example . . . no. This is not a story about the recently promoted Chief Superintendent Guy Stanford, but a tale about PC Stanford's first arrest.

It had been a particularly gruelling week for Guy, which had ended on Saturday afternoon with his having to accompany the visiting Cardiff City football supporters back to the station, after they'd lost to Coventry, 3–0.

Once the last train had departed, Guy decided not to join his mates at the pub that evening, but to curl up in bed with a good book. But he was so exhausted that he only managed a couple of chapters of *Duveen* by S. N. Behrman before he fell into a deep sleep.

Twenty minutes later his dreams were interrupted by an insistent ringing. But it was still some time before he managed to pick up the phone.

'Stanford,' said a voice that wasn't used to being disobeyed. 'Report to the station immediately. And immediately means you're already late.'

'Yes, sarge,' said Guy, suddenly wide awake. He leapt out of bed, took a two-minute shower, didn't shave and threw on his uniform. He ran downstairs and out onto the street, jumped on his bike and didn't stop pedalling until he reached the station.

Once he'd dumped the bike, he joined several of his colleagues who were charging up the steps into the nick.

'Downstairs, lads,' said the desk sergeant. An order Guy obeyed without stopping.

When he entered the large situations room in the base-ment, he joined thirty or forty of his colleagues who had clearly all been drafted in at short notice. Although none of them had any idea what they were doing there, they didn't have to wait long to find out.

When Chief Superintendent Dexter (crime) walked in, Guy realized it had to be serious, and when the chief con-stable followed only a pace behind, the whole room fell silent.

'OK, listen up, lads,' said the super, as he placed his hands on his hips, 'because I don't have time to repeat myself. A small inner group of senior police officers have been working for several weeks on a particularly sensitive investigation. However, I was unwilling to give the go-ahead until we were confident every piece of the jigsaw was in place. An hour ago, we received information from a reliable source that we wouldn't get a better opportunity than tonight to bang up Bernie Manners, along with a few other well-known villains.'

Several of the officers began to cheer and applaud. Although Guy hadn't come in contact with Manners, he knew only too well who he was. His photograph had become a dartboard in the crime room long before Guy had joined the force. He knew Manners was the local drug baron, who controlled a territory that stretched from Watford to Birmingham, and anyone who strayed onto his patch went missing. But far worse were the number of young lives he had ruined with the distribution of heroin and crack cocaine by his army of dealers. Thanks to a cadre of expensive lawyers, Manners had never been con-victed or seen the inside of a prison cell. Even when they'd found a rifle in the boot of his Mercedes, Manners was able to prove he was on the way to a pheasant shoot, and that the gun was registered. The jury didn't seem to understand the difference between a shotgun and a rifle.

'My informant tells me,' continued the super, 'that Manners is holding a party in his home tonight to celebrate his fiftieth birthday, and among his guests will be some of the biggest rogues in Christendom, so we'll never get a better opportunity to give him an unexpected birthday present.'

This time the cheer was even louder.

'All of you will now be divided into three groups with a senior officer in charge of each section. Group one will be under my orders and will act as the lead unit. Group two will consist of twenty-one officers under Chief Inspector Wallis, who will surround the house, and if you find as much as a half-smoked joint on anyone trying to beat a hasty retreat, arrest them, bring them back to the nick and lock 'em up. Group three, you're the search party and will be led by Chief Inspector Hendry. Once you get the signal from me, you will enter the house, where you will each be allocated a room, and then I expect you to take the place apart. Any drugs you find must be listed, bagged and handed over to Inspector Hendry.'

Guy looked around to see that most of his colleagues couldn't wait to get going. This was the reason they'd joined the police.

'And don't forget. Every ounce of heroin or coke you find is another year in jail for Manners, and it's a life sentence if we can prove he's a dealer. Right, report to your group commanders who will brief you more fully.'

There was almost a stampede towards a large notice board where every officer was listed in alphabetical order, showing which group they had been allocated to.

Guy knew he wasn't senior enough to be a member of the command unit, but he still wanted to be in the search party, and not left standing outside the house hoping someone would try to do a runner.

He let out a muted 'Yes!', when he saw the number 3 by his name, and quickly made his way back upstairs and out of the nick. He climbed into a black patrol van, marked only with the number 3, and took a seat near the front. Once the door of the van slid shut, Chief Inspector Hendry began to brief his group.

'Right, pay attention. Like the chief, I'm only going to say this once. Our job will be to search the house from top to bottom, making sure we don't miss anything, and I mean anything. If you come across any drugs, even marijuana or poppers, bag them up and bring them straight to me. Don't expect to find everything stacked and labelled neatly on shelves. Manners will have stashed them in places you won't even have thought of, so make sure you do a thorough job, because we're not going to get a second chance.'

Guy looked out of the window as the convoy moved off. He was in the third of three unmarked vans, with two patrol cars in front leading the way, and another two behind bringing up the rear. They were clearly expecting a lot of guests at the party.

The convoy drove silently out of the city, ignoring drunks and vagrants who quickly disappeared down unlit alleys the moment they saw them. And once they'd crossed

the city boundary and began to drive through neighbour-
ing villages, Guy noticed that few lights were still on, as
most civilized people were already in bed, sound asleep.

With about a mile to go, Hendry stood up, turned to
face his group and said, 'Look lively, lads, it won't be long
now.'

As they swung off the main road, the two police cars
in front turned off their headlights and parked down a
narrow lane. Guy looked out of the window to see a vast
Georgian mansion lit only by the full moon. In fact the first
thing Guy noted was that there wasn't a light on in the
house. If Bernie Manners was holding a party to celebrate
his fiftieth birthday, he found it hard to believe the guests
had already gone home.

When the convoy came to a halt, Guy and his colleagues sat waiting impatiently for the off. But in which
direction, wondered Guy. He assumed the senior officers
sitting in the first van were discussing whether to go ahead
with the operation or slink back to the station, tails
between their legs and admit they'd been sold a bum
steer. In Guy's opinion that would have been the most
sensible thing to do. But he knew Chief Superintendent
Dexter only had a few months to go before he retired, and
no doubt that was also being weighed in the balance. What
a scalp to end his career with.

And then it became obvious what decision had been
made, because the two police cars in front switched their
headlights back on and began to move slowly up the drive
towards the house. Guy watched as his colleagues poured
out of the vans and began to surround the building, while
Hendry led his team off the third van and onto the front

lawn. He raised an arm and his group stopped, just yards from the front door.

No one moved when the super banged a clenched fist on the door. Moments later, a light shone from a second-floor window, followed by another on the stairs, and finally one in the hallway, before the front door was opened to reveal the massive figure of Bernie Manners framed in the doorway, adorned in a purple silk dressing gown.

'What's the meaning of this intrusion, Chief Superintendent?' demanded Manners.

Guy's immediate reaction was, why wasn't Manners surprised when he saw Dexter standing on his front doorstep? And why no shouting or bad language? Guy was beginning to wonder if the reliable source had always been working for the other side, but it was too late to turn back now.

'I have a warrant to search these premises,' said the superintendent, who handed over a court document for Manners to study, and he didn't wait to be invited in. Guy knew the warrant would have been issued by a judge earlier that evening, no doubt with a warning of the consequences if they didn't come up with a substantial cache of drugs that couldn't be described by a seasoned lawyer as recreational.

A few minutes later, the super reappeared in the doorway and waved a beckoning hand. The sign for the search party to join him in the house.

'OK, lads, let's get moving,' said Hendry as he led his men across the gravel courtyard and into the house.

Guy and two other officers were ordered to search the drawing room. To start with, they satisfied themselves with checking inside drawers, removing cushions from the sofas and chairs, and pulling books, CDs and DVDs from the shelves above the widescreen television. Inspector Hendry moved from room to room waiting for the first officer to report a find, while Manners poured himself a drink. An hour later the CO gave the order to move on to what he described as a more thorough search.

'You ain't gonna find a damn thing,' said Manners. 'Not that I have any idea what you're looking for,' he added as he poured himself another large whisky.

Guy believed the first statement, but not the second. The young constable switched his attention back to the job in hand, as a sergeant unsheathed a knife and thrust the blade deep into the sofa, causing feathers to fly in every direction. Guy started to remove the few books from the shelves and began to sift through the pages, but all he came up with was a fifty-pound note that had been used as a bookmark – not a crime.

The second hour also yielded nothing, except the downstairs rooms now resembled a council rubbish dump, and it worried Guy that Manners didn't seem to care. In fact he was beginning to wonder just who had planned this whole operation months in advance.

Manners put down his drink, checked his watch and made a phone call. It wasn't difficult for Guy to work out who he'd be calling at that time of night, but he was surprised how quickly the phone was answered.

In desperation, the super gave orders for everyone to change floors, and double-check their colleagues hadn't missed anything.

Guy was allocated the bathroom. He made his way

slowly up to the first floor, taking a moment to look at the paintings on the wall that were, with one exception, second-rate dross, probably bought from the railings on Piccadilly by an interior decorator who knew a sucker when he saw one.

He moved into the bathroom, which resembled a rugby changing room after a hard-fought game, and it only took him a few moments to realize his colleagues had done a thorough job, even removing the panels from the side of the bath and checking behind a medicine cabinet filled with drugs from Boots. But search as he might, Guy couldn't come up with anything stronger than an aspirin.

They all heard the whistle, the sign that the search was being called off. Guy came slowly back down the stairs to see the super looking as if he might be facing an earlier retirement than he had originally anticipated, but Guy now suspected that was all part of Manners' plan. Bang on cue, a black BMW came up the drive and double-parked outside the front door.

A moment later a tall, elegantly dressed man marched into the house, looking as if he hadn't been to bed.

'Michael,' said Manners. 'I wanted you to see what these bastards have been up to,' he added before he took his lawyer on a tour of the house so he could survey the carnage. When they reappeared, the man walked straight across to the chief superintendent and said, 'My name is Michael Carstairs.'

'I know exactly who you are, Mr Carstairs.'

'And I have the privilege of representing Mr Manners,' he continued as if he hadn't been interrupted, 'whose home you have ransacked for no apparent reason, especially as you must be well aware that my client is a respected local businessman, who has resided in the area for many years. So I'm sure you won't be surprised that I shall be making an official complaint on his behalf, but not before I've spoken to the chief constable.'

Guy watched carefully to see how the super would react. Dexter looked as if he couldn't be sure which of the two men to punch first, the lawyer or his client. At least if he had, he would have something to show for his troubles.

'If you're not going to charge my client with any offence,' continued Carstairs, 'perhaps it's time for you and your thugs to get out.'

The chief superintendent was about to give the order for his men to leave the premises, when Guy stepped forward.

'And what have we here?' said Carstairs, staring at the fresh-faced young constable standing in front of his client. 'Are you by any chance the arresting officer?'

'Yes, I am,' said Guy.

Manners burst out laughing, while the lawyer added contemptuously, 'On what charge, dare I ask?'

'Possession of stolen goods.'

'No doubt you're able to substantiate your wild claim, Constable,' he said, making no attempt to mask any sarcasm.

'I most certainly can,' said Guy, before he began to climb back up the stairs while his colleagues watched nervously. He stopped halfway, and removed an oil painting from the wall before coming back down to the hall.

'Do you recognize this painting, Mr Manners?' asked Guy, holding it up in front of him.

Manners just stood there, looking at his lawyer.

'It's a Cézanne,' said Guy. 'He was one of the most influential artists of the early twentieth century.' Guy paused to admire the painting. 'Never signed or dated, because the artist considered *View of Auvers-sur-Oise* unfinished, but more interesting is that the painting was stolen from the Ashmolean Museum in Oxford the night before the Millennium.' Guy turned to face the lawyer. 'I wonder if you have any idea of its value, Mr Carstairs?'

The lawyer didn't offer an opinion.

'Sotheby's valued it at a little over three million, but that's possibly a conservative estimate, as Sir Nicholas Serota, the director of the Tate, described the painting as a national treasure, and irreplaceable.'

The chief superintendent nodded, and two of his senior officers stepped forward, handcuffed Manners, read him his rights, and led him out to a waiting car. Guy reluctantly handed over the painting to the chief superintendent.

As Hendry caught up with Guy on his way back to the van, the chief inspector remarked, 'It's like making love for the first time, lad. A copper never forgets his first arrest.'

A GENTLEMAN AND
A SCHOLAR

WHEN SHE entered the lecture theatre for the last time, the entire faculty rose and cheered. She progressed up the steps and onto the stage, feigning to be unaffected by their warm reception. She waited for her students to resume their places before she began to deliver her final lecture.

She held her emotions in check as she looked up at the assembled audience for the first time. A lecture theatre that held three hundred and was rarely full was now so packed with professors, lecturers and scholars she had taught over the past four decades, that some of them had spilled out onto the steps at the sides, while others stood hugger-mugger at the back.

Many had travelled from across the nation to sit at her feet and acknowledge the curtain coming down on an illustrious career. But as she stood and looked at them, Professor Burbage couldn't help recalling it hadn't always been that way.

◄o►

Margaret Alice Burbage had studied English literature at Radcliffe before sailing across the ocean to spend a couple of years at the other Cambridge, where she completed a PhD on Shakespeare's early sonnets.

Dr Burbage was offered the chance to remain in Cambridge as a teaching fellow at Girton, but declined as she wished to return to her native land, and like a disciple spreading the Gospel, preach about the Bard of Stratford-upon-Avon to her fellow countrymen.

Although vast areas of America had become emancipated, there still remained a small group of universities who were not quite ready to believe a woman could teach a man – anything. Among the worst examples of these heathens were Yale and Princeton, who did not allow women to darken their doors until 1969.

In 1970, when Dr Burbage applied for the position of assistant professor at Yale, she told her mother after being interviewed by the all-male panel that she had no hope of being offered the post, and indeed, she expected to return to Amersham, where she would happily teach English at the local girls' school where she had been educated. But to everyone's surprise, other than that of the interviewing panel, she was offered the position, albeit at two-thirds of the salary of her male colleagues.

Questions were whispered in the cloisters as to where she would go to the lavatory, who would cover for her when she was having her period, and even who would sit next to her in the dining room.

Several former alumni made their feelings clear to the president of Yale, and some even moved their offspring to other universities lest they be contaminated, while another more active group were already plotting her downfall.

When Dr Burbage had entered the same theatre some forty-two years before to deliver her first lecture, the troops were lined up and ready for battle. As she walked onto that same stage, she was greeted by an eerie silence. She looked up at the 109 students, who were ranged in the amphitheatre around her like lions who'd spotted a stray Christian.

Dr Burbage opened her notebook and began her lecture.

'Gentlemen,' she said, as there weren't any other ladies in the room, 'my name is Margaret Burbage, and I shall be giving twelve lectures this term, covering the canon of William Shakespeare.'

'But did he even write the plays?' said a voice who didn't attempt to make himself known.

She looked around the tiered benches, but wasn't able to identify which of the students had addressed her.

'There's no conclusive proof that anyone else wrote the plays,' she said, abandoning her prepared notes, 'and indeed—'

'What about Marlowe?' another voice demanded.

'Christopher Marlowe was unquestionably one of the leading playwrights of the day, but in 1593 he was killed in a bar-room brawl, so—'

'What does that prove?' Yet another voice.

'That he couldn't have written *Richard II*, *Romeo and Juliet*, *Hamlet* or *Twelfth Night*, all of which were penned after Marlowe's death.'

'Some say Marlowe wasn't killed, but to escape the law, went to live in France, where he wrote the plays, sent them back to England, and allowed his friend Shakespeare to take the credit.'

'For those who indulge in conspiracy theories, that

rates alongside believing the moon landings were set up in a TV studio somewhere in Nebraska.'

'The same doesn't apply to the Earl of Oxford.' Another voice.

'Edward de Vere, the seventeenth Earl of Oxford, was unquestionably a well-educated and accomplished scholar, but unfortunately he died in 1604, so he couldn't have written *Othello*, *Macbeth*, *Coriolanus* or *King Lear*, arguably Shakespeare's greatest work.'

'Unless Oxford wrote them before his death.' The same voice.

'There can't be many playwrights who, having written nine masterpieces, then leave them to languish in their bottom drawer and forget to mention them to anyone, including the producers and theatre owners of the day, one of whom, Edward Parsons, we know paid Shakespeare six pounds for *Hamlet*, because the British Museum has the receipt to prove it.'

'Henry James, Mark Twain and Sigmund Freud wouldn't agree with you.' Another voice.

'Neither would Orson Welles, Charlie Chaplin or Marilyn Monroe,' said Dr Burbage, 'and perhaps more interesting, they were unable to agree with one another.'

One young man had the grace to laugh.

'Can Francis Bacon be dismissed quite so easily? After all, he was born before Shakespeare, and died after him, so at least the dates fit.'

'Which is about the only thing that does,' said Dr Burbage. 'However, I acknowledge without question that Bacon was a true Renaissance man. What we would today call a polymath. A talented writer, an able lawyer, and a brilliant philosopher, who ended up as Lord Chancellor of England during the reign of King James I. But the one thing Bacon doesn't seem to have managed during his busy career was to write a play, let alone thirty-seven.'

'Then how do you explain that Shakespeare left school at fourteen, was not well versed in Latin, and somehow managed to write *Hamlet* without visiting Denmark, not to mention half a dozen plays set in Italy, having never set foot outside of England?'

'Only five of Shakespeare's plays are set in Italy,' she said, landing her first blow. 'And scholars also accept that neither Marlowe nor Oxford, or even Bacon, ever visited Denmark.' Which seemed to send her recalcitrant pupils into retreat, allowing her to add, 'However, the distinguished satirist, Jonathan Swift, who was born a mere fifty years after Shakespeare's death, put it so much better than I could:

'When a true genius appears in the world, you may know him by this sign, that the dunces are all in confederacy against him.'

As that seemed to silence them, Dr Burbage felt she had won the first skirmish, but suspected the battalions were reforming before they launched an all-out attack.

'How important is it to have a good knowledge of the text?' asked someone who at least had the courtesy to raise a hand so she could identify him.

'Most important,' said Dr Burbage, 'but not as important as being able to interpret the meaning of the words, so you have a better understanding of the text.'

Assuming the battle was over, she returned to her

lecture notes. 'During this semester, I shall require you all to read one of the history plays, a comedy and a tragedy, and at least ten sonnets. Although you may make your own selection, I shall expect you, by the end of term, to be able to quote at length from the plays and sonnets you have chosen.'

'If we were to, between us, select every play and every sonnet, could you also quote at length from the entire canon?' The first voice again.

Dr Burbage looked down at the names on the seating plan in front of her and identified Mr Robert Lowell, whose grandfather had been a former president of Yale.

'I consider myself familiar with most of Shakespeare's work, but like you, Mr Lowell, I am still learning,' she said, hoping this would keep him in his place.

Lowell immediately stood, clearly the leader of the rebels. 'Then perhaps you would allow me to test that claim, Dr Burbage.' And before she could tell the young man to sit down and stop showing off, he added, 'Shall we begin with something easy?

> *Our revels now are ended. These our actors,*
> *As I foretold you, were all spirits and*
> *Are melted into air, into thin air.*
> *And, like the baseless fabric of this vision,*
> *The cloud-capp'd towers, the gorgeous palaces,*
> *The solemn temples, the great globe itself—'*

Dr Burbage was impressed that he didn't once look down at the text, so she obliged him and took up where he had left off.

'Yea, all which it inherit, shall dissolve,
And, like this insubstantial pageant faded,
Leave not a rack behind. We are such stuff
As dreams are made on, and our little life
Is rounded with a sleep.'

One or two of the students nodded when she added, *'The Tempest*, act four, scene one.' But Lowell was right, he'd begun with something easy. Their leader sat down to allow a lieutenant to take his place, who looked equally well prepared.

'Give every man thy ear, but few thy voice;
Take each man's censure, but reserve thy judgement.
Costly thy habit as thy purse can buy,
But not express'd in fancy; rich, not gaudy;
For the apparel oft proclaims the man,'

the lieutenant recited, his eyes never leaving her, but she didn't flinch.

'And they in France of the best rank and station
Are most select and generous, chief in that.
Neither a borrower nor a lender be;
For loan oft loses both itself and friend,
And borrowing dulls the edge of husbandry.
This above all: to thine own self be true,
And it must follow, as the night the day,
Thou canst not then be false to any man.

Hamlet, act one, scene three.'

It was now clear to her that several among their dwindling ranks were not only following the text word for word in open books, but then turning a few pages clearly aware where the next volley would come from, and although another foot soldier had been shot down, someone quite happily rose to take his place. But this one looked as if he'd have been more at home on a football field, and read directly from the text.

'There shall be in England seven halfpenny loaves
sold for a penny: the three-hooped pot shall have ten
hoops and I will make it felony to drink small beer.
All the realm shall be in common; and in Cheapside
shall my palfrey go to grass.'

Dr Burbage had to concentrate as it had been some time since she'd read *Henry VI*. She hesitated for a moment while everyone's eyes remained fixed on her. A flicker of triumph appeared on Mr Lowell's face.

'And when I am king, as king I will be, there shall be
no money: all shall eat and drink on my score; and
I will apparel them all in one livery, that they may
agree like brothers, and worship me their lord.

Henry VI, Part Two—' She couldn't remember the act or scene, so to cover herself immediately said, 'But can you tell me the next line?'

A blank look appeared on the young man's face, and he clearly wanted to sit down.

'"*The first thing we do*",' said Dr Burbage, '"*let's kill all the lawyers.*"'

This was greeted with laughter and a smattering of applause, as the questioner sank back in his place. But they hadn't given up yet, because another foot soldier quickly took his place.

> *'Now is the winter of our discontent—'*

'Too easy, move on,' she said, as another soldier bit the dust to allow the next brave soul to advance over his fallen comrades. But one look at this particular young man, and Dr Burbage knew she was in trouble. He was clearly at home on the battlefield, his bayonet fixed, and ready for the charge. He spoke softly, without once referring to the text.

> *'Take but degree away, untune that sting,*
> *And, hark, what discord follows! Each thing meets . . .'*

She couldn't remember the play the lines were from, and she certainly wasn't able to complete the verse, but he'd made a mistake which just might rescue her.

'Wrong word,' she said firmly. 'Not sting, but string. Next?' she added, confident that no one would doubt she could have delivered the next four lines. She would have to look up the scene once she was back in the safety of her room.

Dr Burbage stared defiantly down at a broken army in retreat, but still their commanding officer refused to surrender. Lowell stood among the fallen, undaunted, unbowed, but she suspected he only had one bullet left in his barrel.

> *'The painful warrior famoused for fight,*
> *After a thousand victories once foil'd—'*

She smiled, and said:

83

'—Is from the book of honour razed quite,
And all the rest forgot for which he toil'd.

Can you tell me the number of the sonnet, Mr Lowell?'

Lowell just stood there, like a man facing the firing squad, as his fallen comrades looked on in despair. But in her moment of triumph, Margaret Alice Burbage allowed her pride to get the better of her.

'*"I would challenge you to a battle of wits*," Mr Lowell, *"but I see you are unarmed."*'

The students burst out laughing, and she felt ashamed.

—◦—

Professor Burbage looked down at her class.

'If I may be allowed to leave you with a single thought,' she said. 'It has been my life's mission to introduce fertile and receptive minds to the greatest poet and playwright that ever lived in the tide of times. However, I have come to realize in old age that Will was also the greatest story-teller of them all, and in this, my final lecture, I shall attempt to make my case.

'If we had all been visiting London in 1595, when I would have been a whore or a lady-in-waiting – often the same thing . . .' Professor Burbage had to wait for the laughter to die down before she could continue, 'I would have taken you to the Globe Theatre on Cheapside to see the Lord Chamberlain's Men, and for a penny, we could have stood among a thousand groundlings to watch my great ancestor Richard Burbage give you his Romeo. Of course we would have marvelled at the poetry, been entranced by the verse, but I would suggest that it would have been the tale that would have had you on the edge of your seats as we all waited to find out what was going to happen to our hero and his Juliet. What modern playwright would dare to poison the heroine, only to bring her back to life to find her lover, thinking she was dead, has taken his own life, and she, no longer wanting to live, stabs herself? Of course, we are all familiar with the story of Romeo and Juliet, but if there are those among you who have not read all thirty-seven plays, or seen them performed, you now have a unique opportunity to find out if I'm right. However, I wouldn't bother with *The Two Noble Kinsmen*, as I'm not altogether convinced Shakespeare wrote it.'

She looked at her enthralled audience, and waited only for a moment before she broke the spell.

'On a higher note, I would also suggest that if Shakespeare were alive today, Hollywood would insist on a happy ending to *Romeo and Juliet*, with the two star-crossed lovers standing on the prow of Drake's *Golden Hind* staring out into the sunset.'

It was some time before the laughter and applause died down, and she was able to continue.

'And as for the politically correct, what would the *New York Times* have made of a fourteen-year-old boy having sex with a thirteen-year-old girl on Broadway?'

While the professor waited for the applause to die down, she turned the last page of her notes.

'And so, ladies and gentlemen, despite this being my final lecture, you will not escape without attempting the Burbage witch test to discover who among you is a genuine scholar.' An exaggerated groan went up around the room, which she ignored. 'I shall now read a couplet from one of Shakespeare's plays, in the hope that one of the brighter ones among you will give me the next three lines.' She looked up and smiled at her audience, to be met with apprehensive looks.

> *'For time is like a fashionable host*
> *That slightly shakes his parting guest by the hand.'*

A silence followed, and Professor Burbage allowed herself a moment to enjoy the thought that she had defeated young and old alike in her final lecture, until a tall, distinguished-looking gentleman rose slowly from his place near the back of the auditorium. Although she hadn't seen him for over forty years, Margaret knew exactly who he was. Now gaunt of face, with grey hair, and a severed arm from war to remind her that he wasn't someone who retreated in the face of the enemy.

> *'And with his arms outstretch'd, as he would fly,*
> *Grasps in the comer: the welcome ever smiles,*
> *And farewell goes out sighing,'*

he offered in a voice she could never forget.

'Which play?' she demanded.

'*Troilus and Cressida*,' he said confidently.

'Correct. But for your bonus, which act and which scene?'

He hesitated for a moment before saying, 'Act three, scene two.'

It was the right act but the wrong scene, but Professor Burbage simply smiled and said, 'You're quite right, Mr Lowell.'

ALL'S FAIR IN LOVE
AND WAR

RALPH – PRONOUNCED Raif – Dudley Dawson became squire of the village of Nethercote when his father died. After all, his father and grandfather had always been addressed as 'squire' by the locals, and as he'd inherited Nethercote Hall, with its thousand acres of farmland and ten thousand sheep, he rather assumed he'd be treated with the same deference. So convinced was Ralph of his birthright, he refused to open letters that weren't addressed to Ralph Dudley Dawson Esq.

Any friends Ralph had, of whom there were few, were either richer than he was or listed in *Debrett's*, and, like the Royal Family, he considered it nothing less than his duty to marry someone from his own class, or preferably even higher. After all, Ralph was a good catch.

The only problem for Ralph was that he didn't come across too many young women living in the depths of Cornwall who fitted the bill. The lord lieutenant of the county, Sir Miles Seymour, had three daughters: Arabella, who was beautiful, Charlotte, who was charming, and Clare, who was neither, but inexplicably all three turned him down. The vicar's daughter, Maud, was a nice enough girl, but frankly he didn't want to go into the garden with her, and in any case she was about to disappear off to Lady Margaret Hall, which Ralph assumed was a nunnery.

Once Ralph had attained his fortieth year, he accepted that he might have to look further afield if he was to find anyone worthy of him, or at least that was until his eyes settled on Beth Trevelyan.

Ralph, as the village squire, had been invited to present the prizes at a local swimming gala, and when Beth pulled herself out of the water, he couldn't take his eyes off her. He continued to stare at the apparition as she took off her swimming cap and shook out a mass of golden curls that fell to her shoulders, completing a picture that had all the young men, and several of the older ones, looking in her direction.

Ralph was determined to add Beth to his many conquests, but as she passed by the judges' table, she didn't give him a second look. Perhaps the three-piece tweed suit, brown suede brogues, and half-hunter watch made him look a lot older than he was. He hung around outside the swimming pool hoping to speak to the goddess, but when Beth finally appeared, dressed in a simple yellow frock with a bow in her hair, she was on the arm of a fair-haired, good-looking young man who Ralph thought he recognized, but couldn't place. It didn't take Ralph long to discover that Jamie Carrigan was a tenant farmer who rented forty acres of his land and lived in one of the cottages on his estate, and that Beth was the daughter of a local publican who managed the Nethercote Arms, something else Ralph owned, but had never frequented.

What Ralph didn't know until he had made some enquiries was that the young sheep farmer had already approached Beth's father and asked for his daughter's hand in marriage. Mr Trevelyan had not only agreed to the match, but offered to hold the reception in his pub.

Despite these setbacks, Ralph assumed that once Beth knew of his interest, she wouldn't be able to resist his charms, as had been the case with several of the village girls. Not Beth, however, because when he invited her to tea at Nethercote Hall, she failed to reply. The young woman clearly didn't know her place.

As the weeks passed and several more invitations to tea, drinks and even a trip to London were refused, Ralph was at a loss to understand her attitude, not least because he wasn't in the habit of being rejected. In desperation, he resorted to suggesting a weekend in Paris, only to be turned down once again. The weeks turned into months, and nothing he came up with seemed to interest her, which only caused Ralph to become more and more obsessed with the Cornish beauty, until he could bear it no longer. He finally turned up at the Nethercote Arms unannounced and asked the publican for his daughter's hand in marriage. Mr Trevelyan was left speechless, until Ralph added a sweetener he felt confident would seal the bargain. Of course, Ralph had no intention of marrying the girl, but was determined to discover what it would be like to remove her seven veils. However, Beth was not Salome, and in any case, she already knew the man she was going to spend the rest of her life with, and it certainly wasn't Ralph Dudley Dawson Esq.

Although her father had given Jamie his blessing, neither of them had taken into consideration Beth's mother, who, like any self-respecting barmaid, knew an opportunity when she saw one. On hearing the news of the squire's interest, Mrs Trevelyan didn't waste a moment, attempting to persuade, cajole, and even bully her daughter into accepting his proposal. However, Beth continued to resist her mother's blandishments, until she discovered she was pregnant.

When Beth informed her parents who the father was, her mother was quick to point out that Jamie Carrigan was a penniless shepherd who rented forty acres of land and lived in a small cottage on the estate of a wealthy gentleman who wanted to marry her. However, Beth remained resolute in her determination to marry her lover, until the squire failed to renew the five-year lease on Jamie's forty acres, and also threatened to replace Mr Trevelyan as landlord of the Nethercote Arms, if his daughter didn't accept his proposal.

The hastily arranged marriage – Ralph couldn't wait – took place in a register office in Truro, and the reception was not held at Nethercote Hall for those in high places but at the Nethercote Arms for a select few, as Ralph didn't want his friends to realize he'd married below his station.

◄○►

Mr and Mrs Dudley Dawson spent their honeymoon on the island of Rhodes, where there was little chance of them bumping into anyone they knew. When Ralph watched his wife undress for the first time, he was entranced by Beth's Botticelli figure, even more voluptuous than he'd imagined. But when they finally made love, he was disappointed by her lack of enthusiasm, and assumed it was simply because she was a shy virgin, and that given time Beth would come to enjoy his particular sexual fantasies.

Not long after the newly-weds had returned to Nethercote, Beth announced she was pregnant. Ralph wasn't surprised, after all they hadn't stopped making love during their honeymoon. Five times a night, Ralph boasted to his friends, unaware that Beth was doing no more than carrying out her mother's instructions.

Seven months later, Rupert Dudley Dawson entered the world, or at least that was the name that appeared on the birth certificate. Ralph showed no surprise at the premature birth, but did admit he was disappointed that young Rupert hadn't inherited the Dudley Dawsons' distinctive red hair and prominent nose. All in good time, he assured his friends, because like the Royal Family, Ralph would require an heir and a spare. Indeed, this mundane tale might not have advanced beyond the fate of a sad, unrequited woman and an overbearing, arrogant man, had Germany not marched into Poland on 1 September 1939.

―◇―

Young Jamie Carrigan was among the first to report to the nearest recruiting office and sign up to serve his king and country with the Duke of Cornwall's Light Infantry. But then, he had lost his one true love and sought an honourable death.

Ralph, on the other hand, had no intention of joining up, and as he was over forty – just – was exempt from conscription. So while Jamie went off to fight the king's enemies, Ralph took advantage of the government's voracious appetite for more food to feed the troops, which only made him grow richer, while his marriage became impoverished.

Within a year of his betrothal, the squire's eye began to wander, and with so many of his countrymen serving on the front line his choice became even wider. He told his chums that despite Beth's unquestionable beauty, a chap needed variety. Caviar was all very well, he'd declared, but a fellow also needed the occasional dish of fish and chips.

It wasn't long before Ralph began to ignore his wife, and the only joy left in Beth's life was young Rupert, who she feared was looking more like Jamie with each passing day. Every night she would fall on her knees and pray that her former lover would survive the war and return home safely, but the only news she heard of him came from those soldiers home on leave who, whenever Jamie's name was mentioned, repeated the words brave, fearless and foolhardy.

Beth began to fear she might never see him again, but then, like so many of his comrades, he was wounded on the battlefield and sent home to recover. When she first saw Jamie limping through the village on crutches, she immediately realized what a terrible mistake she'd made, and it wasn't long before their dormant affair was rekindled.

It would be wrong to describe what took place during the next six weeks as an affair, because they fell even more deeply in love the second time around. But when Beth once again became pregnant, she realized she would have to tell her husband the truth, not least because he would know that this time it couldn't be his child.

Beth planned to tell him as soon as the doctor had

confirmed she was with child, and would have done so when she returned home that afternoon, had the parlour-maid not informed her that the squire had driven into Truro for an unscheduled meeting with his solicitor.

Beth was relieved that Ralph must have somehow found out that she was pregnant, and was well prepared to face the consequences whatever wrath might be brought down on her. She sat alone in the drawing room waiting for her husband to return so she could tell him the truth. If he refused to give her a divorce, Beth had already decided she would move out of the manor house and go and live with Jamie in his little cottage. But when Ralph returned several hours later, he marched into the house, slammed the front door, and disappeared into his study without a word passing between them.

Beth sat alone for hour upon hour until she could bear it no longer, and finally summoned up the courage to face him. She left the drawing room, walked slowly across the hall and knocked quietly on his study door.

'Come,' said a terse voice. She entered the room shaking, and without even turning to face her, Ralph handed her what looked like a legal document. She read the letter twice, before she realized what had made him so angry. It was a directive from the War Office requiring him to report to his local recruitment office. The summons pointed out that the call-up age had been extended from forty-one to fifty-one, and he was therefore now eligible to join the armed forces. The only choice they gave him was the army, the navy or the air force. Beth decided this wasn't the time to let her husband know that she was pregnant.

The following day, Ralph lost his temper with the family doctor when the damn man refused to sign a certificate citing his flat feet as a reason he should be exempt from war service. But Ralph didn't give in quite that easily. He immediately wrote to the Ministry of Agriculture, pointing out the vital role he was playing in the war effort. However, an under-secretary made it clear, by return of post, that being a landowner didn't qualify him for exemption.

Undaunted, Ralph continued to search for any string he could pull to avoid being sent to the front line. He filled in applications for the Intelligence Corps – unqualified; the NAAFI – over-staffed; and the Home Guard – too young. After a month of fruitless delays, he finally accepted that he had no choice but to report to officer-training school in Berkshire. Three months later he passed out of Mons as Second Lieutenant Ralph Dudley Dawson Esq., and was told to report back to his regimental headquarters in Truro, where he would receive his marching orders.

Beth would have enjoyed Ralph's three months' absence if Jamie hadn't fully recovered – for which she felt partly to blame – and been ordered to return to his regiment. The difference was, this time he wanted to live.

Before Jamie left, Beth wrote to her husband and told him that she would be seeking a divorce as soon as the war was over. He didn't reply.

-◆-

On returning to Truro, the newly gazetted subaltern suggested to his commanding officer that his particular skills might be put to better use serving on the home front.

However, as the colonel was unable to identify any such skills, Second Lieutenant Dudley Dawson was ordered to join the fifth battalion of the Duke of Cornwall's Light Infantry at Caen. That was when Ralph had his first stroke of luck. He was seconded to Command Headquarters behind Allied lines, where he quickly made himself invaluable, as he didn't intend to come face to face with the enemy if he could possibly avoid it.

During her husband's absence, Beth wrote him a second letter, fearing he might not have received the first, but once again Ralph didn't reply. He assumed the affair would quickly fizzle out, and she would surely fall in line. After all, think what she would be giving up.

Less than a mile away, serving on the front line, was Corporal Jamie Carrigan, who had just been promoted, and put in charge of his own section. As the regiment continued its advance towards the German border, Jamie was becoming more and more confident that the war was coming to an end, and it wouldn't be too long before he would return to Nethercote, marry the woman he loved and continue to farm his modest leasehold while Beth raised their children.

Unfortunately Ralph was also considering what he would do once the war was over and he had been demobbed. He'd already decided not to extend the lease on Carrigan's forty acres when it came up for its annual renewal. He would give the man thirty days' notice and tell him to vacate the cottage and seek employment elsewhere. He also intended to renege on his agreement with Mr Trevelyan to waive any future rent on the Nethercote Arms. After all, there was nothing in writing. Ralph assumed such threats would surely bring his wife to her senses, but even if she didn't fall in line, he had no intention of divorcing her.

◄○►

It was after the colonel's morning meeting with his staff officers that he asked Captain Dudley Dawson to stay behind.

'Ralph,' said the commanding officer once they were alone, 'a problem has arisen that I need you to deal with discreetly. We've lost radio contact with the other battalion, and I need to urgently get a message to their commanding officer and let him know that I intend to advance at first light. Otherwise I'll be stuck here until communications are restored.'

'Understood, sir,' said Dudley Dawson.

'I can't pretend the assignment isn't risky, and wonder if you can think of anyone who might be relied on to carry out such a dangerous mission.'

'I know just the man,' said Dudley Dawson, without hesitation.

'Good, then I'll leave all the details to you. Report back to me the moment your man returns—' he hesitated, 'or doesn't.'

Captain Dudley Dawson left the colonel's tent, jumped into his jeep and asked to be taken to the front line, which took his driver by surprise as he'd never been there before. On arrival, he immediately briefed Carrigan's section commander on the proposed mission. The young lieutenant was surprised by the colonel's choice of runner, remembering that the regiment's cross-country champion was also in his platoon, but he wasn't in the habit of questioning his commanding officer's orders.

Ralph watched from a distance as Lieutenant Jackson briefed Carrigan on the importance of the assignment. A few minutes later, the corporal climbed out of the trench, and without looking back set off across no-man's-land.

'How long do you think it will take him to reach the other battalion?' asked Ralph after Jackson reported back to him.

'If he makes it, sir, an hour at the most. But then he still has to get back.'

'Let's hope he does,' said Ralph in his most sincere voice.

Lieutenant Jackson nodded and said, 'God help the man.'

Ralph didn't believe in God, but decided he would hang around for a couple of hours or so before he reported back to the colonel that sadly Carrigan had not returned, and therefore the mission would have to be aborted.

An hour passed and there was no sign of Carrigan. Another fifteen minutes, still no sign. But Ralph remained huddled in a corner of the trench for another half hour before he allowed himself the suggestion of a smile.

'Damned fine effort,' he said to Lieutenant Jackson, who was peering through a pair of binoculars across the wooded landscape. 'One couldn't have asked more of Carrigan,' continued Ralph as he checked his watch. 'Well, I'd better get back to HQ and let the colonel know that the advance will have to be delayed until we can make radio contact. Damn fine effort,' he repeated. 'I'll be recommending to the colonel that Carrigan is awarded the

Military Medal for service above and beyond the call of duty. It's the least he deserves,' he added before he began to crawl along the trench.

'Hang on, sir,' said Lieutenant Jackson. 'I think I can see someone in the distance.'

Ralph crawled back, fearing the worst. 'He's about a hundred yards away,' added Jackson, 'and heading straight for us.'

'Where?' said Ralph, leaping up and staring across the barren terrain.

'Get down, sir,' shouted the lieutenant, but he was too late, because the bullet hit Captain Ralph Dudley Dawson Esq. in the forehead, and he sank back down into the mud just as Carrigan dived into the trench.

—◦—

The Duke of Cornwall's Light Infantry continued their advance towards Berlin at first light, while a coffin containing the body of Captain Dudley Dawson was shipped back to England, along with a letter of condolence from his commanding officer. The colonel was able to assure the grieving widow that her husband had sacrificed his life while serving his country on the front line.

The fifth battalion of the Duke of Cornwall's Light Infantry won a great battle that day, and a year later at a service held in Truro Cathedral, the name of Normandy was added to the regimental colours.

Among those seated in the congregation was Corporal Jamie Carrigan MM, along with his wife and two children, Rupert and Susie. Unfortunately, Ralph Dudley Dawson Esq. hadn't considered the possibility of mortality, and died intestate. His wife, being the next of kin, inherited a thousand-acre estate, ten thousand sheep, Nethercote Hall and all his other worldly goods.

Jamie Carrigan never thought of himself as the local squire, just a farm manager who'd been lucky enough to marry the only woman he'd ever loved.

THE CAR PARK ATTENDANT

It would never have happened if his uncle Bert hadn't taken him to the zoo.

Joe Simpson wanted to play football for Manchester United, and when he was selected to captain Barnsford Secondary Modern, he was confident it could only be a matter of time before United's chief scout would be standing on the touchline demanding to know his name. But by the time Joe walked onto the pitch for the last match of the season, not even the Barnsford Rovers coach had bothered to come and watch him, so with only one GCE (maths), he was at a bit of a loss to know what he was going to do for the rest of his life.

'You could always join Dad as a council car park attendant,' suggested his mum. 'At least the pay's steady.'

'You must be joking,' said Joe.

It only took a month and seven job interviews for Joe to discover it was the council car park, or stacking shelves at the local supermarket. Joe was just about to sign on the dole and join what his dad called 'the great unwashed' when he was offered a job at the Co-op.

Joe lasted ten days as a shelf stacker before he was shown the door, and he had to admit to his mum that perhaps it hadn't helped when he put two hundred cans of Whiskas next to the prime cuts of beef.

'A vacancy's come up at Lakeside Drive car park,' his father told him, 'and if you want, lad, I could have a word with boss.'

'I'll do it for a couple of weeks,' said Joe, 'while I look for a real job.'

Joe wouldn't admit to his father that he rather enjoyed being a car park attendant. He was out in the open air, meeting people and chatting to customers while working out how much to charge them once they'd told him how long they wanted to park; something his dad had never got the hang of, but then he hadn't got a GCE in maths.

Joe quickly got to know several of the regulars, and the cars they drove. His favourite was Mr Mason, who turned up in a different vehicle every day, which puzzled Joe, until his dad told him he was a second-hand car dealer, and he probably liked to know what he was selling.

'Your dad's right,' Mr Mason told him. 'But it's even more important to know what you're buying. Why don't you come over to the showroom sometime, and I'll show you what I mean?'

The next time Joe had a day off, he decided to take up Mr Mason's offer and visit the car showroom. It was love at first sight when he saw the Jaguar XK120 in racing green, and second sight when he saw the boss's book-keeper in dashing red, but neither was available for a council car park attendant. Not least because Molly Stokes had seven GCEs and had also taken a bookkeeping course at Barnsford Polytechnic.

From that day on, Joe found any excuse to visit Mr

Mason, not to see the latest models, but to talk to the first girl he didn't think was soppy. Molly finally gave in and agreed to go to the cinema with him to see John Wayne in *The Quiet Man*, not Molly's first choice. The following week they went to see Spencer Tracy in *Pat and Mike*, her choice, and Joe accepted that was how it was going to be for the rest of their lives.

◄○►

A year later, Joe proposed to Molly on bended knee, and even bought an engagement ring from H. Samuel, which he'd spent two weeks' salary on. But she turned him down. Not because she didn't want to marry Joe, but she wouldn't consider marriage until they could afford a place of their own.

'But if we get married,' said Joe, 'we can put our name down for a council house, and not have to go on living with my parents.' Molly didn't want to live in a council house.

And then the worst thing that could happen, happened. Joe got the sack.

'It ain't that you're no good at the job, lad,' said the supervisor, 'but bosses at council want cutbacks, so it's last in, first out, and as you've only been with us for a couple of years, I'll have to let you go. Sorry about that.'

Just when Joe thought it couldn't get any worse, Molly announced she was pregnant.

They were married a month later, his dad having told him in no uncertain terms, 'There's never been a bastard in our family, and we won't be startin' now.'

Once the banns had been read, the wedding was held three weeks later at St Mary the Immaculate parish church, with a reception afterwards at the King's Arms across the road. No expense spared. The girls drank Babycham, while the lads downed pints of Barnsford bitter and cleared the pub out of crisps and pork pies. Everyone had a good time. But when the newly married couple woke up in Mr Simpson's spare room the following morning, Joe was still on the dole, and Molly was still pregnant, and they didn't have enough money for a honeymoon, even a weekend in Blackpool.

That was when their uncle Bert, without intending to, changed their whole lives.

Uncle Bert worked at Barnsford Zoo, where he cleaned out Big Boris's cage, the lion folks came to see from all over the county. It was at his wedding bash over a pint of bitter that Bert told Joe a job might be coming up at the zoo, and if he popped in on Monday, he'd introduce him to the manager, Mr Turner.

On Monday morning, Joe put on a clean shirt and a pair of neatly pressed trousers, and borrowed one of his father's two ties. He was on the top deck of a double-decker bus on his way to the zoo, when he first spotted the piece of land in the distance. He couldn't take his eyes off it. When he got off the bus, he didn't head straight for the nearest turnstile, but walked in the opposite direction.

Joe stood and stared at a large plot of waste land that must have had a hundred vehicles parked on it. He spent the day watching as cars, vans, even coaches came and went, filling any space that was available with no rhyme or reason, some of the drivers not even visiting the zoo. An idea was beginning to form in his mind, and by the end of the day, Joe's only thought was, could he get away with it?

'So did Mr Turner offer you the job?' asked Molly when Joe arrived back just in time for tea.

'I never saw Mr Turner,' Joe admitted. 'Something came up.'

'What came up?' demanded Molly.

Joe buttoned his lip when his dad strolled in, and it wasn't until they climbed into bed later that night that he told Molly how he'd spent his day, and then shared his big idea with her.

'You're daft as a pumpkin, Joe Simpson. That's council land, and you'd be done for trespassing, and what's more I'll prove it, then you won't have to waste any more time and can go and get that job at the zoo before someone else grabs it.'

Molly spent the following morning at Barnsford Town Hall, where she visited the estates department, and got chatting to a young man who, after checking several ordnance survey maps, couldn't be sure who did own the land, the council or the zoo. Molly still wasn't convinced. But at least she now considered it a risk worth taking.

Joe took the bus to the zoo every day for the next week, where he made notes of how many people parked on the land, and roughly how long they spent visiting the zoo. He waited until they closed for the night and the last car had departed, before he paced out the boundaries. He wrote in his little book: 226 paces by 172.

The following day, he returned to his old stomping ground on Lakeside Drive, explaining that he needed a word with his old man. But once he got there, he measured a council parking space, this time not in paces, but in feet with an old school ruler: 18ft by 9ft for cars and vans, 40ft by 11ft for coaches. His dad couldn't make head nor tail of what the lad was up to.

Joe spent the weekend trying to calculate how many cars could be parked on the zoo site. After he double-checked his figures, he decided there was enough room for 114 cars and five coaches. When Molly returned from work that night, he showed her his planned layout for the car park. She was impressed, but remained sceptical.

'You'll never get away with it!' she said.

'Maybe not, but as no one else is offering me a job, I've got nothing to lose.'

Molly raised an eyebrow. 'So what are you going to do next?'

'I'm going to learn how to paint a parking space in the dark.'

'Then you'll need a torch, and a pot of white emulsion,' said Molly, 'not to mention a brush, a bucket of water, and a broom to clear the space, as well as some string and nails to mark out a straight line even before you can start thinking about painting anything. And by the way, Joe, while you're at it, I'd recommend you start by trying to paint four straight lines in the light.'

'I thought you didn't believe in my plan?' said Joe.

'I don't, but if you're going to give it a go, at least do the job properly.'

Joe visited every paint merchant in the town, while Molly went off to work at Mason's. After a day of comparing prices, Joe came to the conclusion he could only afford to buy six tins of white paint if he was still going to have enough money left over to get all the other bits and pieces Molly had insisted on.

'I can get the string, nails, a hammer and a large broom from Mason's,' said Molly when she arrived home after work that evening. 'So you can cross them off your list.'

'But what about the bucket?'

'Well, borrow Mr Mason's fire bucket, and then you can fill it up in the public toilet outside the zoo.' Joe nodded. 'Next thing you'll have to do is a dry run,' said Molly.

'A dry run?'

'Yes, you'll need to find a derelict council site and practise painting one space, until you've got the hang of it.'

When Molly went to work the next day, Joe headed off to an old bomb site on the outskirts of town, and painted his first car parking space. Not as easy as he had thought it would be. However, by the end of the week, he could complete one in forty minutes that wasn't half bad. The only problem was that he ran out of paint, and although he had nearly perfected his technique, Molly had to sacrifice a week's wages so he could replenish his stocks. By early December, he was ready to move onto the site.

'Our next problem,' said Molly, 'is finding a time when you can paint the parking spots while no one else is around to see what you're up to.'

'I've already worked that one out,' said Joe. 'This year Christmas Day falls on a Friday, so no one will be visiting the site on the Friday, Saturday or Sunday, and even bank holiday Monday, when the zoo will still be closed. So I could probably paint a hundred spaces in that time.'

'I think a dozen would be quite enough to start with,' said Molly. 'Let's make sure your big idea works before we spend any more money than necessary. Don't forget that

Mr Mason started his business with six cars, and now he's got a showroom with over a hundred in the forecourt, as well as a Jaguar dealership.'

Joe reluctantly agreed, and began to prepare himself for the big day.

◄◦►

Joe couldn't get to sleep on Christmas Eve, and was up the following morning even before Molly had woken. He put on a T-shirt, a pair of jeans, a sweater, and his old school gym shoes. He crept downstairs and collected an ancient pram from the shed at the bottom of the garden, which Molly had filled the night before with everything he would need.

He pushed the pram all the way to the zoo, and spent the next few hours sweeping the ground and clearing it of leaves, dirt and dust. Once he was satisfied that the site had been properly prepared, he measured out his first parking space with the help of a tape measure borrowed from his mum's sewing basket. He then knocked nails into the four corners, to which he attached a length of string. He stood back and admired the canvas on which the artist was about to work.

It was just after ten by the time Joe had completed his first parking space, and he was exhausted. He hid the pram in a clump of trees, and somehow still found enough energy to run all the way home. He arrived back even before his father had got up, and only his mother asked how he got white paint on his jeans.

'My fault,' said Molly, without explanation.

After Christmas lunch, Joe waited for everyone to

settle in front of the television, or fall asleep, before he once again set off for the zoo. By the time the street lights came on at four o'clock, he'd completed two more spaces. On Boxing Day, another four, and by five o'clock on 27 December all twelve spaces were finished and ready for occupation. He hoped they'd all be dry by the time he returned the following morning.

◄○►

Barnsford Zoo opened its doors to the public at ten o'clock on Tuesday morning, but business was slow. Joe stood on the corner of the site and watched at a distance. Whenever a car appeared, it immediately drove into one of his neatly painted spaces, now dry, which at least gave him a degree of confidence. He carried out the same routine for the next three days, and discovered the pattern didn't vary. But then, the British are a nation who believe in queues, and behaving in an orderly fashion.

On 31 December and 1 and 2 January, Joe went back to work, and he and Molly celebrated the New Year having painted twenty parking spaces.

'Quite enough,' declared Molly, 'because you've still got to find out if the public will wear it.'

◄○►

Joe rose at six o'clock the next morning, put on his old council parking attendant's uniform, and collected one of his father's discarded ticket collecting machines from the shed.

He took a bus to the site, and was standing on the

parking lot long before the zoo opened for business. He patrolled his twenty spaces like a lion protecting its cubs, and when his first potential customer appeared, he walked tentatively over to a man who had parked in one of the spaces.

'Good morning, sir,' said Joe. 'That will be two shillings.' If the man had told him to bugger off, he would have done just that, but he meekly handed over a florin.

'Thank you, sir,' said Joe, issuing him with a ticket before touching his peaked cap. His first customer.

By the end of the day, he'd had fourteen customers, and collected one pound and eight shillings. By the end of the first week, he'd pocketed £31, and took Molly out for a drink at the pub, where they shared a Scotch egg.

Joe wanted to splash out and go to the Swan, where you could get a three-course meal and a half bottle of wine for £3, but Molly wouldn't hear of it, saying, 'It will only make folks suspicious, and give the game away.' She even introduced him to the words 'cash flow'.

On the Monday, when the zoo was closed, Joe could have taken a day off, but instead, he laboured away, painting another six spaces, and as each day passed, the rectangles increased along with his income, causing him to grow more and more confident. However, it was on the Tuesday of the third week that he saw Mr Turner, the zoo manager, heading towards him and assumed the game was up.

'Morning, Mr . . . ?'

'Joe,' he said.

'Could we have a private word, Joe?'

'Yes, of course, Mr Turner.'

'When I've parked here in the past,' said the zoo manager, 'I've never had to pay.'

'And you won't have to in the future, Mr Turner,' said Joe.

'But now the council's taken over the site, surely I'll be expected—'

'You won't be expected to pay a penny, Mr Turner. In fact I'm going to allocate you your own private space that no one else will be able to park in.'

'Won't the council kick up a fuss?'

'I won't say anything if you don't,' said Joe, touching his nose.

'That's good of you, Joe,' said Turner. 'Let me know if I can ever do anything for you.'

Joe selected the space directly opposite the entrance to the zoo and spent the rest of the day carefully painting the words ZOO MANAGER ONLY.

When Molly left her job at Mason's to have the baby, Joe suggested she handle the cash and keep the books.

Molly also opened a bank account with Barclays, and paid in just over £20 a week, the average wage for a council parking attendant, and placed the rest of the cash under a floorboard in their bedroom.

Although Molly kept the books in apple pie order, even she had to take some time off when Joe Junior was born. His birth only gave the proud father the incentive to paint even more spaces, and within a year, all 119 slots were in place, with a special area reserved for coaches.

When the time came for Molly to return to work, she

didn't go back to Mason's, but joined Joe officially as his bookkeeper and secretary. She paid herself £25 a week. However, it didn't help the cash flow problem, as they had to take up more and more floorboards, but she was already working on how to deal with that particular problem.

‐◦‐

It was Molly who suggested that the time had come for them to take a trip to Macclesfield.

'Macclesfield wouldn't be my first choice for a holiday,' said Joe.

'We're not going on holiday,' said Molly, 'just a day trip. If you look at your father's latest ticket machine, you'll see who the manufacturer is, and I think it's time we paid them a visit.'

As the zoo was always closed on a Monday, Molly borrowed a van from Mr Mason and the three of them set off for Macclesfield. The showroom turned out to be a treasure trove of uniforms, machines and all the other accessories any self-respecting car park attendant needed to do his job. Joe ended up acquiring two outfits (summer and winter) with ZOO printed on the shoulder, the latest collecting machine, a peaked cap, and a small enamel badge that announced SUPERVISOR, which he couldn't resist, although Molly wasn't at all sure about it. Her only acquisitions were a large bookkeeper's ledger and a filing cabinet.

It was on the way back to Barnsford that Molly dropped two bombshells. 'I'm pregnant again,' she said, 'but at least the council have finally offered us a house.'

'But I thought you didn't want to live in a council

house, and in any case we've got enough cash to put down a deposit on a bungalow on the Woolwich estate,' said Joe.

'Can't risk it,' said Molly. 'If we did that, folks might start gossiping and wonder how you earned that sort of money as a car park attendant, and don't forget, most people think I'm still out of work.'

'But what's the point of making all this money, if we can't enjoy it?' demanded Joe.

'Don't worry yourself. I have plans for that too.'

—◦—

Six months later, Mr and Mrs Simpson, Joe Jr and Janet moved into their council house on the Keir Hardie estate. While folks might have thought their new neighbours were living in a council house, if they'd ever been invited inside they would have discovered the Simpsons weren't doing their shopping at the Co-op, but then they never were invited inside.

And as well as tufted carpets, a space age kitchen, a large-screen TV, and a three-piece suite that wasn't bought on the never-never, they still had a cash flow problem. But Joe felt confident Molly would come up with a solution.

'We won't be going to Blackpool for our summer holiday this year,' she announced over breakfast one morning.

'Then where are we going, Mum?' demanded Joe Jr.

'Don't speak with your mouth full,' said Molly. 'We're going to Majorca.'

Joe wanted to ask 'Where's that?', but was rescued by Janet, who asked the same question.

'It's an island in the Mediterranean, which not many

people from Barnsford will have heard of, and are even more unlikely to visit,' which seemed to silence all three of them.

Joe and Molly always took their holiday in the zoo's quietest fortnight of the year, and as the day approached, the children became more and more excited, because it would be their first trip on a plane. Joe's and Molly's too, come to that, but they didn't mention it.

To do Joe justice, it was his idea to employ a bright university student, preferably an immigrant, to cover for him whenever he was away on holiday. He always paid the lad in cash, and although he didn't make much of a profit during that fortnight, the regulars were kept happy, and there were never any questions about why the car park wasn't manned.

'And if anyone asks where I am,' said Joe, 'just tell them I'm on holiday with the family in Blackpool.'

Once the family arrived in Majorca, Molly didn't waste any time. While Joe took the children to the beach, she visited every estate agent in Palma. When they got back on the plane a fortnight later, Joe had put on half a stone, the children were nut brown, and Molly had put down a deposit on a front-line plot in Puerto de Pollença, over-looking the sea.

The estate agent made no comment when she signed the contract and handed over the £5,000 deposit in cash. By the time they'd visited Majorca six times, the land belonged to them.

Molly then set about looking for a local architect. She chose a German, much to Joe's disapproval, who also didn't raise an eyebrow when his quarterly payments were made in cash.

A year later, a JCB rolled onto the site, and the builder licked his lips when rolls of twenty-pound notes changed hands on a regular basis, even if the project manager found Molly a bit of a handful.

So while Joe and Molly continued to live a frugal existence in Barnsford, with Joe's only extravagance a season ticket for Barnsford Rovers, who still languished in the bottom half of the third division, Molly did allow herself the occasional visit to The Smoke to see the latest musical and have an Indian curry at Veeraswamy. But they always travelled back to Barnsford second class in case anyone spotted them. However, during the summer holidays, the family could always be found residing in their luxury villa overlooking the sea in the Bay of Pollença.

-<o>-

When Joe's father retired at the age of sixty, Joe sent his mum and dad for a cruise on the *QE2*, explaining that they'd had a little win on the Premium Bonds. And two years later, when the zoo had an appeal for a new elephant house, the manager (Joe's fifth) was delighted when they received an anonymous donation of £10,000, but was just a little surprised that it arrived in a large brown paper bag.

Joe was particularly proud when Joe Jr was offered a place at Leeds University to study law, another first for the Simpson family, but Janet trumped her brother two years later when she won a scholarship to read English at Durham.

'What are we going to do when the time comes for us to retire?' asked Joe, aware that Molly would have already given the problem some considerable thought.

'We'll go and live in Majorca and, to quote the good Lord, enjoy the fruits of our labour.'

'But what about my car park?'

'You can leave someone else to worry about that.'

—◦—

Being a conventional sort of chap, Joe also retired on his sixtieth birthday, and after handing back the keys of their council house, he and Molly packed up everything they needed (very little), and headed for the airport with two one-way tickets.

It wasn't long before Joe became a vice president of Real Mallorca, who were at least in the top half of the second division, and deputy chairman of the local Rotary club, while Molly became honorary treasurer of the residents' association.

Joe Jr was now a practising barrister on the northern circuit, while Janet taught English at Roundhay grammar school. They both paid regular visits to their parents in Majorca, accompanied by Charlie, Rachel and Joe very Jr, who Joe and Molly adored.

—◦—

'Have you seen what they've done with my car park?' said Joe one evening, after reading his weekly copy of the *Yorkshire Post*. 'Daft pillocks,' he said as he continued to read the article.

On 2 January, the new manager of the zoo, a Mr

Braithwaite, called the estates department at Barnsford City Council, to ask when Joe Simpson's replacement would be reporting for work.

'Who's Joe Simpson?' the estates manager asked.

'He's the man who ran the car park opposite the zoo. Has done for the past forty years. We even gave him a farewell party.'

'I don't know what you're talking about,' said the estates manager, 'I always assumed you owned the land.'

'But we thought you did!' said Braithwaite.

'Daft pillocks,' repeated Joe as he put down his paper and joined Molly in the kitchen. 'If manager 'ad bin half awake, he'd 'ave kept his mouth shut, and only the zoo would have benefited,' he told his wife, 'which is what I'd always wanted. But no, he had to consult council chairman, Alderman Appleyard, who thought they should take legal advice, which has ended up with a lengthy court battle between Barnsford City Council and the zoo. Result? Both sides lost out, while weeds are sprouting up all over my car park.'

Three years later a judge finally ruled that the council should take charge of the car park, but any profits were to be divided equally between the two. A typical British compromise, where only the lawyers benefit, was Joe's opinion when he read the latest news coming out of Yorkshire.

'I'm only surprised,' said Molly, 'that they've not come after us.'

'No chance,' said Joe. 'I reckon that'd make council look like a bunch of wallies. No, least said, soonest mended. And you can be sure of one thing, no one will stand up and take responsibility. Don't forget, that lot will be coming up for re-election in May, so mum's the word.'

⭜o⭞

When I last had dinner with Joe and Molly in Pollença, I couldn't resist asking him how much he thought he'd made over the years, as a car park attendant.

'Supervisor,' he corrected me, not answering my question.

'Three million, four hundred and twenty-two thousand, three hundred and nineteen pounds,' replied Molly.

'That sounds 'bout right,' said Joe, 'but next time you're in Barnsford, Jeff lad, take a look at zoo's new aquarium. Summat the missus and I are right chuffed about!'

⭜o⭞

Joe and Molly Simpson are buried next to each other in the churchyard of St Mary the Immaculate in Barnsford. Something else Molly insisted on.

A WASTED HOUR

KELLEY ALWAYS thumbed a ride back to college, but never told her parents. She knew they wouldn't approve.

Her father would drive her to the station on the first day of term, when she would hang around on the platform until she was certain he was on his way back home. She would then walk the couple of miles to the freeway.

There were two good reasons why Kelley preferred to thumb a ride back to Stanford rather than take a bus or train. Twelve round trips a year meant she could save over a hundred dollars, which her father could ill afford after being laid off by the water company. In any case he and Ma had already made quite enough sacrifices to ensure she could attend college, without causing them any further expense.

But Kelley's second reason for preferring to thumb rides was that when she graduated she wanted to be a writer, and during the past three years she'd met some fascinating people on the short journey from Salinas to Palo Alto, who were often willing to share their experiences with a stranger they were unlikely to meet again.

One fellow had worked as a messenger on Wall Street during the Depression, while another had won the Silver

Star at Monte Cassino, but her favourite was the man who'd spent a day fishing with President Roosevelt.

Kelley also had golden rules about who she wouldn't accept a ride from. Truck drivers were top of the list as they only ever had one thing on their mind. The next were vehicles with two or three young men on board. In fact she avoided most drivers under the age of sixty, especially those behind the wheel of a sports car.

The first car to slow down had two young fellows in it, and if that wasn't warning enough, the empty beer cans on the back seat certainly were. They looked disappointed when she firmly shook her head, and after a few raucous catcalls continued on their way.

The next vehicle to pull over was a truck, but she didn't even look up at the driver, just continued walking. He eventually drove off, honking his horn in disgust.

The third was a pick-up truck, with a couple in the front who looked promising, until she saw a German shepherd lounging across the back seat that looked as if he hadn't been fed in a while. Kelley politely told them she was allergic to dogs – well, except for Daisy, her cocker spaniel back home, whom she adored.

And then she spotted a pre-war Studebaker slowly ambling along towards her. Kelley faced the oncoming car, smiled, and raised her thumb. The car slowed, and pulled off the road. She walked quickly up to the passenger door to see an elderly gentleman leaning across and winding down the window.

'Where are you headed, young lady?' he asked.

'Stanford, sir,' she replied.

'I'll be driving past the front gates, so jump in.'

Kelley didn't hesitate, because he met all of her most stringent requirements: over sixty, wearing a wedding ring, well-spoken and polite. When she got in, Kelley sank back into the leather seat, her only worry being whether either the car or the old man would make it.

While he looked to his left and concentrated on getting back onto the road, she took a closer look at him. He had mousy grey hair, a sallow, lined complexion, like well-worn leather, and the only thing she didn't like was the cigarette dangling from the corner of his mouth. He wore an open-neck checked shirt, and a corduroy jacket with leather patches on the elbows.

Her supervisor had told her on numerous occasions that if she wanted to be a writer she would have to get some experience of life, especially other people's lives, and although her driver didn't look an obvious candidate to expand her horizons, there was only one way she was going to find out.

'Thanks for stopping,' she said. 'My name's Kelley.'

'John,' he replied, taking one hand off the wheel to shake hands with her. The rough hands of a farm labourer, was her first thought. 'What are you majoring in, Kelley?' he asked.

'Modern American literature.'

'There hasn't been much of that lately,' he suggested. 'But then times are a changin'. When I was at Stanford, there were no women on the campus, even at night.'

Kelley was surprised that John had been to Stanford. 'What degree did you take, sir?'

'John,' he insisted. 'It's bad enough being old, without being reminded of the fact by a young woman.' She laughed. 'I studied English literature, like you. Mark Twain, Herman Melville, James Thurber, Longfellow, but I'm afraid I flunked out. Never took my degree, which I still bitterly regret.'

Kelley gave him another look and wondered if the car would ever move out of third gear. She was just about to ask why he flunked out, when he said, 'And who are now considered to be the modern giants of American literature, dare I ask?'

'Hemingway, Steinbeck, Bellow and Faulkner,' she replied.

'Do you have a favourite?' he asked, his eyes never leaving the road ahead.

'Yes I do. I read *The Grapes of Wrath* when I was twelve years old, and I consider it to be one of the great novels of the twentieth century. *"And the little screaming fact that sounds through all history: repression works only to strengthen and knit the repressed."*'

'I'm impressed,' he said. 'Although my favourite will always be *Of Mice and Men*.'

'*"Guy don't need no sense to be a nice fella,"*' said Kelley. '*"Seems to me sometimes it jus' works the other way around. Take a real smart guy and he ain't hardly ever a nice fella."*'

'I don't think you'll be flunking your exams,' said John with a chuckle, which gave Kelley the opportunity to begin her interrogation.

'So what did you do after you left Stanford?'

'My father wanted me to work on his farm back in Monterey, which I managed for a couple of years, but it just wasn't me, so I rebelled and got a job as a tour guide at Lake Tahoe.'

'That must have been fun.'

'Sure was. Lots of dames, but the pay was lousy. So my friend Ed and I decided to travel up and down the California coast collecting biological specimens, but that didn't turn out to be very lucrative either.'

'Did you try and look for something more permanent after that?' asked Kelley.

'No, can't pretend I did. Well, at least not until war broke out, when I got a job as a war correspondent on the *Herald Tribune*.'

'Wow, that must have been exciting,' said Kelley. 'Right there among the action, and then reporting everything you'd seen to the folks back home.'

'That was the problem. I got too close to the action and ended up with a whole barrel of shotgun up my backside, and had to be shipped back to the States. So I lost my job at the *Trib*, along with my first wife.'

'Your first wife?'

'Did I forget to mention Carol?' he said. 'She lasted thirteen years before she was replaced by Gwyn, who only managed five. But to do her justice, which is quite difficult, she gave me two great sons.'

'So what happened once you'd fully recovered from your wounds?'

'I began working with some of the immigrants who were flooding into California after the war. I'm from German stock myself, so I knew what they were going through, and felt a lot of sympathy for them.'

'Is that what you've been doing ever since?'

'No, no. When Johnson decided to invade Vietnam, the *Trib* offered me my old job back. Seems they couldn't find too many people who considered being shipped off to 'Nam a good career move.'

Kelley laughed. 'But at least this time you survived.'

'Well, I would have done if the CIA hadn't asked me to work for them at the same time.'

'Am I allowed to ask what you did for them?' she said, looking more closely at the old man.

'Wrote one version of what was going on in 'Nam for the *Trib*, while letting the CIA know what was really happening. But then I had an advantage over my colleagues that only the CIA knew about.'

Kelley would have asked how come, but John answered her question before she could speak.

'Both my sons, John Jr and Thomas, were serving in the front line, so I was getting information my fellow hacks weren't.'

'The *Trib* must have loved that.'

'I'm afraid not,' said John. 'The editor sacked me the minute he found out I was workin' for the CIA. Said I'd forfeited my journalistic integrity and gone native, not to mention the fact I was being paid by two masters.'

Kelley was spellbound.

'And to be fair,' he continued, 'I couldn't disagree with them. And in any case, I was gettin' more and more disillusioned by what was happening in 'Nam, and even began to question whether we still occupied the moral high ground.'

'So what did you do when you got back home this time?' asked Kelley, who was beginning to consider the trip was every bit as exciting as the journey she'd experienced with the fellow who'd spent a day fishing with President Roosevelt.

'When I got home,' John continued, 'I discovered my second wife had shacked up with some other fella. Can't say I blame her. Not that I was single for too long, because soon after I married Elaine. I can only tell you one thing I know for sure, Kelley, three wives is more than enough for any man.'

'So what did you do next?' asked Kelley, aware it wouldn't be too long before they reached the university campus.

'Elaine and I went down South, where I wrote about the Civil Rights movement for any rag that was willing to print my views. But unfortunately I got myself into trouble again when I locked horns with J. Edgar Hoover and refused to cooperate with the FBI, and tell them what I'd found out following my meetings with Martin Luther King Jr and Ralph Abernathy. In fact Hoover got so angry, he tried to label me a communist. But this time he couldn't make it stick, so he amused himself by having the IRS audit me every year.'

'You met Martin Luther King Jr and Ralph Abernathy?'

'Sure did. And John Kennedy come to that, God rest his soul.'

On hearing that he'd actually met JFK, Kelley suddenly had so many more questions she wanted to ask, but she could now see the university's Hoover Tower becoming larger by the minute.

'What an amazing life you've led,' said Kelley, who was disappointed the journey was coming to an end.

'I fear I may have made it sound more exciting than it really was,' said John. 'But then an old man's reminiscences cannot always be relied on. So, Kelley, what are you going to do with your life?'

'I want to be a writer,' she told him. 'My dream is that in fifty years' time, students studying modern American literature at Stanford will include the name of Kelley Ragland.'

'Nothing wrong with that,' said John. 'But if you'll allow an old man to give you a piece of advice, don't be in too much of a hurry to write the Great American Novel. Get as much experience of the world and people as you can before you sit down and put pen to paper,' he added as he brought the car to a stuttering halt outside the college gates. 'I can promise you, Kelley, you won't regret it.'

'Thank you for the lift, John,' said Kelley, as she got out of the car. She walked quickly round to the driver's side to say goodbye to the old man as he wound down the window. 'It's been fascinating to hear all about your life.'

'I enjoyed talking to you too,' said John, 'and can only hope I live long enough to read your first novel, especially as you were kind enough to say how much you'd enjoyed my work, which, if I remember, you first read when you were only twelve years old.'

THE ROAD TO DAMASCUS

DO YOU, like me, sometimes wonder what happened to your school contemporaries when they left and went out into the real world, particularly those in the year above you, whose names you could never forget? While those who followed in the forms below, you would rarely remember.

Take Nick Atkins, for example, who was captain of cricket. I assumed he would captain Yorkshire and England, but in fact after a couple of outings for the county Second XI, he ended up as a regional manager for the Halifax Building Society. And then there was Stuart Baggaley, who told everyone he was going to be the Member of Parliament for Leeds Central, and twenty years later reached the dizzy heights of chairman of Ways and Means on the Huddersfield District Council. And last, and certainly least, was Derek Mott, who trained to be an actuary, and when I last heard, was running an amusement arcade in Blackpool.

However, it was clear to me even then that one boy was certain to fulfil his ambition, not least because his destiny had been decided while he was still in the womb. After all, Mark Bairstow was the son of Sir Ernest Bairstow, the chairman of Bairstow & Son, the biggest iron foundry in Yorkshire, and therefore in the world.

I never got to know Bairstow while we were at school: not only because he was in the year above me, but because he was literally in a different class. While most boys walked, cycled or took the bus to school, Bairstow arrived each morning in a chauffeur-driven limousine. His father couldn't spare the time to drive his son to school, it was explained, because he was already at the foundry, and his mother couldn't drive.

I really didn't mind the fact that his school uniform was so much smarter than mine, and that his shoes were handmade escaped me altogether. However, I was aware that he was taller and better-looking than me, and clearly brighter, because he was offered a place at Gonville and Caius College, Cambridge (pronounced Keys – something else I didn't know at the time), to read modern languages.

I actually spoke to Bairstow for the first time when I entered the lower sixth, and he had been appointed school captain, but then only because I was a library monitor and had to report to him once a month. And indeed, if we hadn't gone on holiday together – well, I shouldn't exaggerate . . .

Fred Costello, the senior history master, was organizing one of his annual school excursions to the Continent, as it was known before it became the Common Market, or the EEC, and as I was studying history and hoping to go to university, my parents thought it might be wise for me to sign up for the trip to Germany.

When we all clambered on board the train at Leeds

Central to set out on the journey, I was surprised to see Mark Bairstow was among our party. Well not quite, because he sat in a first-class carriage with Clive Danger-field, who was also going up to Cambridge, so we didn't see them again until we all pitched up at our little hotel in Berlin. I shared a room with my best friend Ben Levy, while Bairstow and Dangerfield occupied a suite on the top floor.

There were fifteen of us in the party, and I spent most of my time with Ben who, like me, supported Leeds United, Yorkshire and England, in that order. It was our first trip abroad and therefore one we weren't likely to forget.

Mr Costello was an enlightened schoolmaster who had served as a lieutenant in the Second World War and seen action at El Alamein, but believed passionately that Brit-ain should join the Common Market, if for no other reason than it would ensure there wouldn't be a third world war.

My abiding memory of Berlin was not the Opera House, or even the Brandenburg Gate, but a concrete monstrosity that stretched like a poisonous snake across the centre of a once united city.

'I want you to imagine,' said Mr Costello, as we stared up at the Wall, 'a twelve-foot barrier being built from the Mersey to the Humber, and you never being able to visit any of your family or friends who live on the other side.'

The thought had never crossed my mind.

After a few days in Berlin, we boarded a charabanc for Dresden, but never once left the coach as we stared out of the windows in disbelief to see what was left of that once historic city. It made me feel that perhaps at times the British had also behaved like barbarians. I was pleased when the coach turned round and headed back to Berlin.

The following day was a schoolboy's dream. After driving to Regensburg, we spent the morning on a coal barge trudging sedately up the Danube, billowing black smoke as we made our way to Passau. After lunch, we took a train to Munich, where we spent three days in a youth hostel with young women actually sleeping in dorms on the floor below us. The next morning we explored the capital of Bavaria, and there wasn't much sign that this had once been the birthplace of the Nazi party. I much admired the Residenz, the vast palace of the Wittelsbachs, where Mark Bairstow looked so relaxed he might have been visiting an old friend at home.

In the evening, we went to the Cuvilliés-Theater to see *La Bohème*, my first introduction to opera, which was to become a lifelong passion. It would be years before I appreciated how much I owed to Mr Costello, a teacher whose lessons stretched far beyond the classroom.

The following day, we visited the Alte Pinakothek, and I can't pretend I was able to fully appreciate Dürer or Cranach, as I couldn't take my eyes off a group of girls who were being shown around the gallery by the same guide. One in particular caught my attention.

My extra-curricular activities in Bavaria included my first experience of beer, frankfurters, attending the opera, and being kissed goodnight by a girl, although I don't think she was overwhelmed. I just wished we'd had another week as she was clearly in the class above me.

On our final day, Mr Costello brought us all back down

to earth when we boarded a bus that didn't announce its destination on the front. We must have travelled some fourteen miles north of Munich before we reached a small town called Dachau. Of course, I knew my closest friend was Jewish, but I only thought of him as a class-mate, and we never quarrelled about anything except who should open the batting for Yorkshire. And when Ben once told me that his grandmother kept a packed suitcase by the front door, I had no idea what he was talking about.

When the bus came to a halt outside the entrance of the concentration camp, we all got off in an uneasy silence and stared up at the uninviting rusty gates. I didn't want to go in, but as everyone else trooped after Mr Costello, I meekly followed. Our first stop was at a vast black wall, where a thousand names had been chiselled into the marble to remind us who had been there only a few years before, and not during a holiday excursion with a tour guide. I saw Ben weeping quietly as he stared at the thirty-seven Levys, three of whom hadn't lived as long as he had. I looked across to see Mark Bairstow looking thoughtful, but apparently unmoved, while the rest of the group remained unusually silent.

The young German guide then took us through the huts that had remained untouched since their occupants were liberated by the Americans. Row upon row of four-tiered bunks, with inch-thick mattresses and no pillows. At one end of the hut, a half-filled bucket of water that had been the lavatory for the fifty-six occupants, emptied once a day. But worse was to come, because Mr Costello had no intention of sparing us.

We climbed back on the bus and took the journey to

Hartheim, where our young guide led us into a large soul-less building, where we entered a cold eerie room where time had stood still. He pointed to the holes in the ceiling where, he explained, the gas was released into the chamber, but only after the prisoners had been stripped and the doors locked. I felt sick, and didn't have the courage to enter the final room to view the vast ovens that our guard told us had been built in 1933 soon after Hitler had come into power, and where the bodies of his innocent victims were finally turned into dust.

When Ben eventually emerged, he fell to his knees and was violently sick. I thought of his grandmother, and for the first time understood the 'packed suitcase'. I rushed across to join my friend, surprised to find Mark Bairstow already kneeling beside him with an arm around his shoulders, trying to comfort a boy he'd never spoken to before.

‑‑◁◦▷‑‑

I was delighted to follow Mark Bairstow as school captain, even if I couldn't hope to emulate his style and panache. I worked diligently during my final year and, with the conscientious help of Mr Costello, was offered a place at Manchester University to read history. I accepted the offer, even though for a Yorkshireman to cross the Pennines into Lancashire in order to further his education was tantamount to high treason.

By the time I graduated, I didn't need Mr Costello to tell me the profession I was best suited for. And if this tale had been about a schoolmaster, and the years of fulfilment he gained from being a teacher . . . but it isn't.

‑‑◁◦▷‑‑

I was teaching at a grammar school in Norfolk when my wife became pregnant, and I had to explain to her why she would have to travel up to Yorkshire to give birth to our son otherwise the lad couldn't play for the county. Not that she had any interest in the game of cricket. It turned out to be a girl, so the subject was never mentioned again. However, I took advantage of being back in Leeds to look up my old friend Ben Levy, now a local solicitor, to suggest we spend a day at Headingley and watch the Roses Match.

Being Yorkshiremen, we were in our seats long before the first ball was bowled, and by the morning break the county were at 77 for two. 'A spot of lunch?' I suggested as I rose from my place in the Hutton stand and glanced up at the President's box to see a face I could have sworn I recognized, despite the passing of time. But he was wearing a dog collar and purple shirt, which threw me for a moment.

I touched Ben on the elbow and, pointing to the box, said, 'Is that who I think it is?'

'Yes, it's Mark Bairstow, the new Bishop of Ripon. Still loves his cricket.'

'But I always assumed he was destined to be the next chairman of Bairstow's, the finest iron forgers in the county.'

'And therefore the world,' laughed Ben. 'But when he went up to Cambridge, he changed courses in his first term and read theology. So no one was surprised he ended up as a bishop.'

Like Mr Costello, I too organized an annual trip to Europe, and after excursions to Rome, Paris and Madrid, I felt the time had come to return to Berlin and see how much the German capital had changed, since the Wall had finally come down.

I found the city was transformed. Only one small graffiti-covered section of the Wall still stood firmly in place, an ugly monument to remind the next generation what their parents and grandparents had endured, which they were now studying as history.

Dresden turned out to be a modern city of steel and glass, and you would have had to search Munich to believe the Germans had ever been involved in a war. And when we visited the Cuvilliés-Theater, two of the boys showed the same excitement that I had felt when I saw my first opera.

When the final day came, I considered, like Mr Costello, it was my duty to visit Dachau, as anti-Semitism was once again rearing its ugly head in my country. I was just as apprehensive as I had been the first time, although I tried not to let the boys and girls know how I felt. When the bus came to a halt outside the main entrance, I silently led the children through the even rustier gates and into the camp, and as far as I could see nothing had changed. My young wards spent some time staring at the names on the memorial wall, and when I saw the thirty-seven Levys, I thought of Ben. The huts remained untouched, and I could see the look of disbelief in the children's eyes when they saw the water bucket at the end of the room. They would never complain again about their cramped dormitories.

Our guide then took us into the museum, where we studied the photographs of prisoners whose black-and-white striped pyjamas hung on their skeletal frames, and of the bodies of lifeless men and women being dragged from the gas chambers to the ovens. There was even a photograph of Himmler to remind us who had carried out Hitler's orders.

I felt sorry for our German guide, not much older than myself, whose sad eyes suggested that the Nazi era couldn't be that easily cast aside, although like myself, he would have been born after the war.

And then the final stage of the tour, which I had been dreading. I still felt sick when I entered the gas chamber, but at least this time I had the courage to follow my wards into the building where the ovens were situated. I stared at the temperature gauges and switches on the wall and bowed my head. When I raised it again, my eyes settled on the large oven door, and I understood for the first time the journey one young man had taken before he became the Bishop of Ripon.

BAIRSTOW & SON

IRON FORGERS

FOUNDED 1866

THE CUCKOLD

ADAM WESTON and Gareth Blakemore always met on a Sunday evening to share a bottle of wine and put the world to rights.

The venue never changed, only the wine, which was always vintage and selected by Adam. But then he was the proprietor of the Swan Inn, a popular gastropub on the outskirts of Evesham.

Gareth was Adam's oldest friend, a successful lawyer by profession, with chambers in Lincoln's Inn. He'd recently been appointed a QC, and he and his wife Angela lived in a Victorian pile at the the other end of the village. Gareth would usually drop into the Swan around seven, before travelling on to London. Tonight, he was late, very late, and Adam knew why.

Gareth walked in just after nine, looking tired and depressed. He gave his friend a weak smile, before seating himself on a stool at the far end of the bar. Adam uncorked a bottle of wine, poured two glasses and joined his friend.

'What is it?' asked Gareth after taking a sip.

'An underrated Cabernet Sauvignon from Napa Valley that's proving rather popular with my regulars.'

'I can see why,' said Gareth, taking another sip.

'How's your week been?' asked Adam, aware there was no time to waste.

'You don't want to know. Tell me your news, because it's got to be better than mine.'

'We had a good week,' said Adam. 'Greene King have offered me the opportunity to buy the pub, but at the moment I just don't have that sort of money.'

'How much are they asking?'

'Two million. It's a fair price, and the only stipulation they're insisting on is that I continue to sell their beer for the next ten years.'

'That seems fair enough,' said Gareth, 'assuming you made a decent return last year.'

'Turnover was almost a million, and after rent, rates and taxes, I showed a profit of around ninety thousand, not including my salary.'

'Sounds like a worthwhile investment to me.'

'And I have plans to add another dozen or so covers in the restaurant. I've also got my eye on a chef who's working at the Savoy. Tells me he's sick of commuting up and down to London every day.'

'That all seems rather promising, but what's the bank's attitude?'

'They'd loan me a million at four per cent, but would expect to have a lock on all my assets, including the pub. So I still need to raise another million from other sources, and wondered if you'd consider coming in as my partner?'

'I'd love to,' said Gareth, 'but you couldn't have chosen a worse time.'

'But I keep reading in the press that you're one of the most successful barristers in the royal courts.'

'Yes, but not for much longer.'

'How come?'

'Angela's filed for divorce. I have a preliminary meeting with her lawyers tomorrow morning. They're the
meanest in the business, and I should know – I recommended them.'

'How come?'

'Angela told me she was asking on behalf of a friend,
and the friend turned out to be her.'

'I'm really sorry,' said Adam. 'I had no idea,' he added
as he looked across the bar at his old classmate.

'I have to admit that it hasn't been a bundle of laughs
lately,' Gareth said, after taking another sip of his drink,
'and I'm mostly to blame. If you spend the week in London
and can't always get back at the weekends, it doesn't help.'

'But divorce or no divorce, you must still have a worthwhile income from the bar.'

'And I'm going to need every penny of it,' said Gareth.
'Angela's lawyers are driving a hard bargain. They're
demanding the manor house as well as the villa in the
south of France, and that's just for starters.'

'But you've still got the Chelsea flat, which must be
worth a bob or two,' said Adam.

'True, but I'll need to hold on to it if I'm going to
survive,' said Gareth. 'Fortunately she thinks it's rented
and I told her it's coming up for renewal next year.'

'Then perhaps it might be wise to settle with her
before she finds out how much it's really worth.'

'I'd agree with you in normal circumstances,' said
Gareth, lowering his voice, 'if I hadn't just found out she's

having an affair. And if I could only discover who the bastard is, I'd be in a stronger position.'

'What makes you so sure she's having an affair?'

'I found a cufflink under the bed, and it certainly wasn't mine.'

—◦—

'Gareth found a cufflink under the bed and told me it wasn't his.'

Angela calmly lit a cigarette. She inhaled deeply before saying, 'Then we'll have to be more careful in the future. If Gareth were to find out we're having an affair, there would be no chance of me getting my hands on the two million my lawyers are demanding. Which would also mean I wouldn't be able to invest in the pub.'

'But you still want to be my partner?' said Adam nervously.

'In every sense of the word, my darling,' Angela replied, blowing out a cloud of smoke. 'But if I don't get hold of that money, I could end up serving behind the bar.'

'That wasn't part of my overall plan,' said Adam. 'Although the moment I can move in with you, I'm going to convert the top floor of the pub into bedrooms, which would bring in some much needed extra income. But I'll need your help when it comes to the interior design.'

'Only too happy to play my part,' said Angela as she stubbed out her cigarette. 'But I still think it would be wise for us to cool it for the time being.' Adam couldn't hide his disappointment.

She leant across and kissed him gently on the lips. 'But

once he's signed the divorce papers,' she added, breaking away, 'I'll not only be free to become your partner, but your wife.'

'I can think of another way that would convince him to settle quickly.' Angela raised an eyebrow. 'Demand to see the details of the lease on his flat in Chelsea.'

'No. It's much better he still believes that's his trump card, and in any case, it would only hold up your deal with Greene King.' She lay back on her pillow and pulled the sheet over her. 'How's that going, by the way?'

'I had a meeting with a brewery representative last week, and we agreed terms. They told me as soon as I'm ready to put down a deposit, they'll draw up a contract.'

'Then all you'll need to do on Sunday is convince Gareth that he should come up with the two million, and the pub will be yours.'

'Ours,' said Adam, as he placed a hand on the inside of her leg and slipped back down under the sheet.

—◦—

'It's a burgundy,' said Gareth.

'You'd have known that,' said Adam, 'by just looking at the shape of the bottle.'

Gareth frowned and took another sip. 'I must admit it's quite superb. My bet is a Clos de Tart?'

Adam half nodded. 'Close, try again.'

Gareth took another sip, and looked up at the ceiling as if seeking inspiration. 'Got it. Chambolle-Musigny.'

'Bravo, quite right.'

'In which case, it's about the only thing I've got right this week,' said Gareth, draining his glass.

'That bad?'

'Worse. Angela's upped the ante, and is now demanding two million.'

'Then perhaps it might be wise to settle before she demands more.'

'You may well be right, but if I could only find out who lover boy is, Angela might suddenly become more reasonable.'

'But if she found out about the flat, you could end up having to pay even more, and surely that's not a risk worth taking.'

'Possibly, but I think I'll still give it another week before I finally decide.'

Adam was about to pour him a second glass when Gareth raised a hand. 'Not for me, old chum. I have to be off. I've got a breaking and entering at ten tomorrow morning, and I still haven't read the brief. See you next Sunday.'

'And let's hope it's settled by then,' said Adam, 'one way or the other.'

'It would be if I could only find out who the other cufflink belongs to,' said Gareth, as he jumped off his stool and quickly left the pub.

Adam refilled his own glass, but left it untouched until he saw Gareth's car drive onto the London road. He then took the rest of the bottle through to his office. He picked up the phone and dialled a number he called every Sunday evening.

'He's seriously thinking about coming up with the two million,' said Adam once he'd heard the familiar voice.

'And I warned him of the consequences if you were to find out the real value of the apartment.'

'That sounds encouraging,' said Angela.

'Except that he's going to give it another week in the hope he'll find out who your lover is.'

'So we certainly can't risk seeing each other this week,' said Angela.

'But it's been almost a month,' said Adam plaintively, 'and I can't wait to see you again.'

'I know how you feel, my darling, but it won't be much longer before we can spend the rest of our lives together.'

'Let's hope so.'

'Stop being so pessimistic, Adam. I'll call you the moment I have any news.'

◄○►

'Can you talk?'

'Yes,' whispered Adam.

'He's agreed to the two million.' Adam wanted to scream out loud, but not while the pub was so crowded. 'My lawyers are drawing up a contract,' continued Angela, 'that he's promised to sign on Monday morning, and as you'll be seeing him on Sunday evening, all you have to do is make sure he doesn't change his mind.'

'Not a chance of that,' said Adam. 'I've even selected his favourite bottle of wine for the occasion.'

'Why don't you put a bottle of champagne on ice at the same time, and if he does sign on Monday, you could join me for dinner and we can celebrate by spending our first night together in your new home?'

◄○►

Adam had been standing impatiently by the phone for some time before it eventually rang. He grabbed the receiver.

'He's just left the house so should be with you in a few minutes.'

'Why's he so late?' asked Adam edgily. 'I was beginning to think he might have found out about us and driven straight up to London.'

'You're over-reacting again, my darling,' said Angela. 'He just had rather a lot of packing to do before he finally left.'

'That's a relief, because I can't stall the brewery for much longer.'

'I'm sure they can wait until Monday.'

'And if you can call me the moment he's signed, I'll put down the deposit of two hundred thousand they're demanding, though I confess it will clear me out.'

'No need to worry yourself about that, my darling. Once he's signed I'll immediately transfer a million to your account and the pub will be yours.'

'Ours,' Adam reminded her, as he watched Gareth's Jaguar driving into the car park. 'He's just arrived,' he whispered.

'Good. Just make sure he doesn't change his mind.'

'No fear of that,' said Adam before putting down the phone. He bent down and extracted a dusty bottle of 1987 Pouilly-Fumé from under the counter. He'd uncorked it by the time Gareth marched in, looking happy for the first time in months.

'No need for you to guess this week,' said Adam,

placing two glasses on the bar in front of him. 'Because I've chosen one of your favourites.'

'What are we celebrating?'

'Your freedom, of course.'

'How could you possibly know about that?' said Gareth.

'I could tell from the expression on your face,' said Adam, a little too quickly. 'So it will be just like old times,' he added, raising his glass.

'Not quite. I still have to sign the document tomorrow morning.'

'But surely you're not having second thoughts?'

'I was, but decided on balance to take your advice and try to move on.'

'Even though it's going to cost you two million?'

'Along with the family home and our villa in the south of France.'

'Well, at least you still have the Chelsea flat.'

'And a cufflink,' said Gareth.

'A cufflink?'

'Don't you remember, the proof that Angela's having an affair?'

'Ah, yes,' said Adam. 'I remember.'

'And what's more, I'm fairly certain I now know who owns the other one.'

Adam could feel his cheeks going red. He quickly took a gulp of wine. 'Anyone we know?'

'No.'

'Then, how do—'

'Because I found two BA tickets for a flight to Nice in her handbag.'

Adam didn't speak as Gareth put a hand in his trouser pocket, took out a cufflink and placed it on the bar. Adam stared at a blue and silver crested cufflink.

'I suspect that lover boy will be joining her at Heathrow tomorrow morning, before they go on to our – her – villa in the south of France.'

Adam continued to stare at a cufflink he'd never seen before.

THE HOLIDAY OF
A LIFETIME

'STOP NAGGING, WOMAN,' said Dennis, but not loudly enough for his wife to hear.

Dennis Pascoe would have got divorced years ago, but couldn't afford to. He'd been married to Joyce for thirty-four years, and assumed it must now, unfortunately, be till death do us part.

She hadn't been his first choice, but then he suspected he hadn't been hers. Dennis used to tell himself they'd stayed together because of the children, but that was no longer convincing, as both Joanna and Ken now lived abroad, so the truth was they remained together because of inertia.

Dennis had recently retired as the deputy station master at Audley End, a branch line for Saffron Walden. It hadn't exactly been an earth-shattering career. He'd left school at fourteen, with no qualifications, and failed several interviews for other jobs before he signed on as an apprentice with British Rail. He told his mother Audley End was no more than a stepping stone for something bigger. The problem was, Dennis had no idea what that something bigger might be, and never found out.

Dennis progressed from apprentice, to ticket collector, to booking clerk, finally ending up as deputy station master in charge of a team of five. Only three of them on duty at any one time. In reality, 'deputy' meant he couldn't afford to join the local golf club, and was unlikely to be invited to become a Rotarian.

However, the real problem came when Great Eastern took over the franchise from BR and Dennis opted for early retirement on a full pension at the age of fifty-five, convinced he was still young enough to find another job to supplement his meagre income. Wrong again, because there weren't many jobs in the private sector for retired deputy station masters, other than as a night watchman or a lollipop man, both of which Joyce wouldn't allow him to consider.

Within days of retirement, Dennis also discovered that marriage may well have been ordained for better or worse, but not for seven days a week. Joyce, who had never done a day's work in her life – other than to keep the house clean, do the shopping, feed him, handle all the household bills and bring up the children – didn't appreciate Dennis getting under her feet while she was trying to do the house-work. Housewives don't retire, she often reminded him.

The other problem Dennis had to face was that his pension didn't allow him to indulge in many luxuries and, with inflation, that was only likely to get worse as he approached old age. He had a season ticket for Norwich Football Club at the wrong end of the ground, which he could just about afford, and their fortunes were not much better than his. They were either trying to survive in the first division or attempting to reach the play-offs in the second. And then there was the love of his life, not Joyce, but his stamp collection – a hobby that had begun at the age of seven, when his grandfather had given him a packet of 'Commonwealth Specials' to celebrate the Queen's coronation. Dennis now had over a thousand examples of stamps from all over the world, proudly mounted in five separate albums.

His only other extravagance was to subscribe to Stanley Gibbons' monthly newsletter and catalogue, which he then spent hours perusing, aware that he would never be able to afford the rare examples he would have most liked to add to his collection.

Dennis tried to fill his day with long walks, not always possible when it was raining, and a visit to the local pub, where he sat in the corner drinking a half pint of bitter slowly, while reading the *Sun*. He made sure he was back in time for lunch, after which he migrated to the sofa only to fall asleep while watching afternoon television or turning the pages of his stamp albums.

It was while Dennis was reading the *Sun* and Joyce was vacuuming the front room that he spotted the advertisement for a package holiday on the Costa del Sol, which sounded a lot more exciting than their annual visit to Skegness. Dennis studied the advertisement more carefully, while Joyce attempted to vacuum around him. They were offering bed and full board, flights included, for £200. Too good to be true, thought Dennis, but would Joyce even consider the prospect? During his morning walk, he thought about how to convince her the time had come to be a little more adventurous.

Dennis waited until the end of lunch before he said, 'Damn good sausage and mash, luv.' Joyce looked suspicious, as praise didn't often flow from that side of the table, so she could only wonder what he was after. She didn't have to wait long to find out. 'I was thinking you might like a change from Skeggie this year,' he suggested.

'What did you have in mind, Dennis, a fortnight in Venice perhaps? A leisurely drive along the Corniche? Possibly a trip down the Nile before stopping off in Cairo to see the treasures of Tutankhamun?'

Dennis ignored the sarcasm and pushed his newspaper across the table to show her the photograph of a villa on the Costa del Sol. Before Joyce could offer an opinion, Dennis added, 'And don't forget, even the train journey to Heathrow will be free.' A deputy station master's perk, he reminded her.

Joyce actually thought it was one of his brighter ideas, just a pity she would have to spend the fortnight with Dennis, but nevertheless she agreed he could look into it.

—◦—

Mr and Mrs Pascoe set out from Audley End for their summer vacation with mixed emotions, so were pleasantly surprised when it turned out to be, as stated boldly in the advertisement, the holiday of a lifetime. They both enjoyed joining the jet set, even if it was only Ryanair, and landing in a country where the sun only left the sky at night; something you couldn't always guarantee in Skeggness, even in the summer.

Their room couldn't have been described as luxurious, but it was clean and comfortable, and the three meals a day never once included sausage and mash. Joyce may have been past her bikini days and her husband had bulges in all the wrong places, but at least the beach was not littered with empty beer bottles, while stepping into the sea was like taking a warm bath, and, an added bonus, they made lots of new friends. Whenever Joyce was asked what her husband did, she told them he was a retired station master.

Two weeks later, Mr and Mrs Pascoe returned to England tanned, relaxed and already looking forward to repeating the experience in a year's time; possibly, Joyce suggested, they might even consider going further afield.

The perfect holiday might have been ruined at the last moment when they had to hang around in the baggage hall at Stansted waiting for Dennis's suitcase to appear on the carousel. It didn't. But all was not lost, because when Joyce read the small print on the holiday brochure later that evening, it claimed all losses under £50 were covered by insurance, and as the suitcase had belonged to her mother, and contained little of any real value, she could not have been more delighted when a cheque for thirty-four pounds and fifty-five pence dropped on the mat three weeks later.

Joyce, being a frugal housewife, waited for the January sales before she bought a new suitcase and a handbag she wouldn't have considered in normal circumstances, and even felt a little guilty about. That was until she discovered Dennis had purchased a set of Prince of Wales commemoration stamps without telling her.

--o--

All would have been well in the Pascoe household, if the missing suitcase had not been found in lost luggage and later returned to Railway Cuttings. Dennis immediately wrote to inform the insurance company, who replied with a standard letter addressed to 'Dear Sir or Madam', above which were stamped the words 'CASE CLOSED'.

Joyce was relieved that they wouldn't have to return the £34 that she'd already spent, but it did make her wonder . . .

Dennis spent the following month writing to all the leading travel companies, and the next six studying the different brochures they all sent by return of post. He took the task seriously, as if he was preparing for an examination, Joyce being the examiner. But it was still some time before he was ready to suggest to his wife where they should spend their next summer holiday.

Joyce also sent away for several brochures, and studied them just as intently, so that by the time Dennis was ready to present his findings on when and where they should go that year, she was equally prepared to tell him what she'd been up to for the past six months.

After a long discussion they settled on Lanzarote, and that was when Joyce shared with her husband a refinement that she felt would make the holiday even more rewarding. Dennis listened in disbelief to what his wife had in mind, and immediately dismissed the idea out of hand. After all, he said, it's dishonest. However, a week later, after several long walks and too many lingering half pints in the local pub, he asked Joyce to talk him through the idea once again. But it wasn't until he'd studied the latest Stanley Gibbons catalogue and spotted a Penny Black he coveted, that he agreed to go along with her suggestion.

Joyce had clearly given the matter a great deal of

thought, and took Dennis carefully through what they would have to do, minute by minute, while allowing her husband to ask questions and point out any weaknesses in her plan. Dennis could only come up with one problem he considered was insurmountable, but was surprised to find that his wife had even thought of a way around that. Dennis was impressed, and even though he still had his doubts, he allowed her to go ahead and fill in all the necessary forms.

—◦—

When Mr and Mrs Pascoe stepped onto the train for Heathrow they were both looking forward to the second 'holiday of a lifetime', and indeed, the break might have gone even better if Dennis had stopped fretting about the consequences of something going wrong with Joyce's plan. But by the time they returned home a fortnight later, they both agreed Lanzarote had turned out to be even more enjoyable than the Costa del Sol. And whenever the subject had arisen, Dennis didn't deny he'd recently retired as a director of Great Eastern, which sounded quite convincing in Lanzarote.

After everyone on their flight had collected their luggage from the carousel, Joyce burst into tears and Dennis did everything he could to console her. She then explained to a sympathetic young baggage handler that one of her suitcases had not appeared on the carousel. An extensive search was carried out, but no one seemed able to find the missing bag. Joyce continued to sob.

Once they were back in Saffron Walden, Joyce waited for a couple of days before she posted two claims for a lost suitcase to two different insurance companies, listing the contents as three dresses, several items of underwear, two pairs of shoes, a bottle of perfume, a washbag and even a lucky charm bracelet (photo attached).

Two cheques, one for £84.20 and a second for £110, arrived within days of each other. The cheques were deposited in two different banks in two different names.

During the Christmas sales, Joyce purchased half a dozen new suitcases of varying sizes from several different department stores in central London, while Dennis acquired an unperforated set of Penny Reds, which he proudly added to his collection.

—◦—

Cunard couldn't have been more apologetic about mislaying one of Mr and Mrs Pascoe's large suitcases – green and clearly labelled Joyce Pascoe, she insisted – while it was being taken off the ship after their third voyage. The purser assured Mrs Pascoe that everything would be done to find it.

A few weeks later, the first of several cheques arrived to cover the loss, while further payments for the same suitcase began to appear at regular intervals over the next six months, as did rarer and rarer, mint and franked, stamps from Stanley Gibbons.

'We mustn't get too greedy,' said Joyce after returning from a winter break in the Caribbean, a holiday that yielded nine further cheques.

So successful were their 'holidays of a lifetime' that after five years, they had accumulated more than enough to make it possible for them to move out of their rented semi-detached in Saffron Walden and buy a small thatched cottage, which they named The Sidings, in Steeple Bumpstead, where Joyce felt they were more likely to come across the sort of people they met on vacation.

—<o>—

When the Pascoes sat down to plan their next summer holiday, Joyce warned her husband she was beginning to run out of insurance companies, as she couldn't afford to make a claim to the same one twice. Dennis was disappointed by this news, because he'd recently joined the local golf club, acquired a season ticket for Norwich City FC, quite near the centre line, and been invited to become a vice president of Rotary. He'd also begun to stick rarer and rarer stamps into his eighth album. Dennis would have been the first to accept that none of this would have been possible had it not been for his new-found wealth. He realized that he'd climbed onto a bandwagon that he didn't want to get off.

—<o>—

Joyce woke her husband in the middle of the night when she came up with her latest idea. Dennis listened intently and couldn't get back to sleep. If they pulled it off, he might even consider standing for the parish council.

'It will have to be our last job,' she warned her husband, 'because there are only three major insurers left.' She didn't add, whom we haven't robbed.

Joyce wrote out a list of jobs Dennis had to do before they embarked on their summer holiday, including taking out any spare cash they had in their bank accounts. She checked the small print of the three insurance companies where they hadn't made a claim, while Dennis told his friends at the golf club and Rotary that he and Joyce were planning a trip down the Nile to celebrate their fortieth wedding anniversary, because his wife had always wanted to see the Pyramids and visit Tutankhamun's tomb.

Once Joyce had filled in all the forms, and the letters and cheques had been dispatched, everything was in place by the time they set off for Southampton.

On 17 July 2001, Dennis and Joyce boarded the SS *Balmoral*, which was setting out on a voyage to Salalah, Port Said, and through the Suez Canal, before returning to Southampton via Istanbul.

AUTHOR'S NOTE

At this point in the story I came up with three different endings, and because I couldn't choose between them, decided to write all three and leave you to pick which one you prefer.

A

When the ship docked in Istanbul, several passengers leant over the railings and watched with interest as two police officers climbed aboard the luxury liner, and asked the purser for the number of Mr and Mrs Pascoe's cabin.

Joyce burst into tears when she and Dennis were escorted off the ship and driven to the nearest airport. She didn't stop weeping on the flight to Heathrow, or when a black limousine drove them back to Steeple Bumpstead.

When the Barrington courtesy car pulled up outside the front gate of The Sidings, Joyce burst into tears once again. Dennis climbed out of the car and said nothing as he stared at the smouldering remains of what was left of their little home.

The local fire chief, a fellow Rotarian, hurried across to join them.

'I'm so sorry, Dennis,' he said. 'My men got here as quickly as they could, but once the flames touched the thatched roof, there was little they could do about it.'

'I'm sure you did everything you possibly could, Alan,' said Dennis, trying to look suitably distressed.

'But we've lost everything,' Joyce told a reporter from the local paper, 'and no amount of money will compensate for that.' A quote that was reported on the front page next to a photo of a tearful Joyce, who felt confident the insurance companies wouldn't have missed it. Well, not everything, thought Dennis, because he'd hidden the stamp collection in his locker at the golf club.

Joyce and Dennis booked into the Bumpstead Arms (covered by one of the three insurance policies) and then spent the next month looking for a new home. The company that had insured their contents settled fairly quickly, while the buildings claim took a little longer.

Once Mr and Mrs Pascoe had purchased a similar cottage on the other side of the village, not thatched – too risky, Dennis told his friends at the golf club – and furnished it, there was more than enough left over to live a very comfortable existence, as well as enjoy the occasional off-peak-season holiday while no longer having to mislay any of their luggage.

However, a problem arose that neither of them had anticipated. Boredom set in, and they quickly began to get on each other's nerves again.

It was Joyce who came up with a solution to which Dennis happily agreed. They would change their name, move to the West Country, and once again start looking for 'the holiday of a lifetime'.

B

The first port of call on their trip to the Middle East was Salalah, where they hired a taxi to take them to the souk. They took their time strolling around the crowded bazaar, with its hundreds of colourful market stalls, displaying thousands of different-quality carpets. But Joyce was far more interested in finding the right dealer than the right carpet. Once they'd selected a man who wouldn't have been invited to give a talk at the Rotary club, they joined him for a cup of Turkish coffee before the bargaining could begin for an exquisite, thousand-thread silk carpet that the dealer claimed was unique.

An hour later Joyce agreed on a sum, which Dennis paid in cash. The dealer then supplied them with a receipt for four times the amount they had paid for the rare silk carpet.

In Port Said, they visited several emporiums, and selected only the finest pieces of jewellery, including a gold brooch of Nefertiti, a string of pearls worthy of Cleopatra, and a diamond-studded bracelet that Joyce felt confident would be the envy of her fellow lady Rotarians. The proprietors were equally obliging when it came to the receipts. Replacement value for insurance purposes, Joyce explained.

In Istanbul, they purchased an oil painting of a fishing boat on the Bosphorus that Joyce felt would look perfect above the mantelpiece in their front room, and although the price was exorbitant, triple the amount was entered on the receipt.

By the time the *Balmoral* docked in Southampton, the Pascoes had spent all their spare cash, but they now possessed some extremely valuable merchandise, and Joyce had the receipts to prove it.

Joyce took her time packing everything they'd bought on the trip into a large green suitcase before a porter arrived to pick up their trunk and two other smaller suitcases. When the Pascoes arrived in the baggage hall, Joyce gave a farewell performance worthy of Elizabeth Taylor.

'One large green suitcase, you say, madam?'

'Yes,' said Joyce, 'full of all the beautiful things we bought on the trip.' Dennis appeared to be making every effort to comfort his wife, something he was getting rather good at.

After the promise of a reward, several members of the ship's crew set out in search of a large green suitcase, but an hour later, no one was able to claim the reward.

The Pascoes were among the last to leave the baggage hall, but not before they were convinced there was no longer any hope of finding their missing treasures. A porter placed their trunk and the two other suitcases on a trolley and began pushing it towards the exit.

Dennis and Joyce trudged mournfully after him, and as if to add insult to injury, a recently promoted Customs officer pulled them to one side and asked them to place their luggage on the counter. The porter obeyed without hesitation.

'May I ask if you purchased anything of value while you were abroad, madam?'

'No,' Joyce said, 'just a few souvenirs. Nothing of any real value.'

She happily opened the two suitcases to reveal Dennis's dirty laundry and washbag in one, and her neatly folded clothes in the other.

'Thank you,' he said. 'And the trunk?' The porter once again heaved it up onto the counter.

'Would you open it, please, sir,' said the Customs officer, as Dennis turned to look at his wife.

Once again Joyce burst into tears, but this time she wasn't greeted with the same sympathetic look.

'Would you please open the trunk, sir,' the young officer repeated a little more firmly.

After what seemed an eternity, Dennis reluctantly stepped forward, unlocked the trunk and pushed up the lid to reveal a large green suitcase that almost took up the entire space.

'Would you now open the suitcase,' said the young man, as a more senior officer walked across to join them.

Dennis unzipped the suitcase and slowly lifted the lid to reveal all the carefully selected purchases they had made during the past fortnight. The junior officer started to take them out and unwrap them one by one, while the senior officer began to make a note of each item. He spoke for the first time.

'Have you kept any receipts for these souvenirs?' he asked.

'Yes,' said Dennis.

'No,' said Joyce, which caused the senior officer to ask the woman to hand over her bag, where he quickly found an envelope stuffed with forty-two receipts.

He took his time checking each item before transferring the amounts onto a large calculator. It was some time before he declared, 'You may wish to check my figures, madam, but I think you'll find the overall amount comes to twenty-seven thousand, seven hundred and sixteen pounds. Now, I am sure you are both aware there is a forty per cent import tax levied on any goods purchased while abroad, above the cost of fifty pounds.' He returned to his calculator. 'Which means you are liable to pay Her Majesty's Customs and Excise eleven thousand and eighty-six pounds and forty pence. Should you be unable to do so, all the goods will be confiscated until you have covered the full amount.'

C

During the train journey back to Audley End, Dennis and Joyce agreed it was the best holiday they'd ever been on, and were already planning where they should go next year.

Joyce felt it might be wise to take a taxi back to Steeple Bumpstead rather than drag all the suitcases on and off the bus. Dennis agreed, although he was down to his last ten pounds.

When the taxi pulled up outside the front gate of The Sidings, Joyce collapsed in tears.

Dennis climbed out of the taxi, and said nothing as he stared at the smouldering remains of what was left of their little cottage.

The local fire chief, a fellow Rotarian, hurried across to join them.

'I'm so sorry, Dennis,' he said. 'My men got here as quickly as they could, but once the flames touched the thatched roof, there was little they could do about it.'

'I'm sure you did everything you possibly could, Alan,' said Dennis, trying to look suitably distressed.

Joyce didn't stop crying, and Dennis wondered if she wasn't overdoing it. 'Look on the bright side,' he whispered, placing an arm around his wife's shoulder, 'No doubt you took out several policies on the house.'

'But I didn't insure the house,' said Joyce with feeling. 'Never could see much point.'

DOUBLE OR QUITS

'I THINK WE'VE got a problem on table number three,' said the manager, staring intently at the screen on his desk.

'Which punter?' asked the head of security, as he joined his boss and looked over his shoulder.

'Young guy, with an attractive woman standing behind him. What do you think, André?'

'Zoom in,' said the security chief, 'and let's take a closer look.' The manager touched a button and waited until the young man's face filled the screen. 'I agree,' said André, 'he's a double or quits merchant. I think from the sweat on his forehead, he's probably got a lot riding on it.'

'And the girl?' said the manager, as he switched the camera to a young woman, whose right hand rested on the gambler's shoulder.

'All I can tell you is she's not a one-night stand.'

'How can you be sure?'

'They're both wearing wedding rings.'

'Get Duval up here.'

André quickly left the room as the manager of the casino watched the young man place another thousand francs on 13.

'Idiot,' said the manager, as he glanced at the front page of *Le Figaro*, which was on the desk by his side. He didn't need to read the article a third time. The headline was bad enough.

ELEVENTH SUICIDE REPORTED IN MONTE CARLO FOLLOWING HEAVY GAMBLING LOSSES

He looked back at the screen to see the young punter place a further thousand francs on 13. 'Idiot,' he repeated. 'Haven't I got enough problems without you?'

Claude Richelieu, the owner of the casino, had been on the phone from Paris earlier in the week, concerned about the latest government directive. The French interior minister was pressing the Monte Carlo gaming council to close the recently opened casino. Too many stories in the press about suicides, broken marriages and bankruptcies caused by gambling, which was illegal in France, and precisely the reason why they were making so much money in Monte Carlo. The manager had cursed when Richelieu added, 'We don't need any more suicides.'

'But what am I supposed to do,' he asked, 'if someone loses badly and then decides to kill themselves?'

'Fix the wheel,' said Richelieu. 'Make sure he wins.'

'And if that fails?'

The owner told his manager exactly what he should do if fixing the wheel wasn't enough.

There was a knock on the door, and the head of security returned, accompanied by one of the few members of staff who wasn't wearing a dinner jacket that evening. In fact, if you had passed Philippe Duval in the street, you might have thought the short, balding middle-aged man was a schoolmaster, or perhaps an accountant. But he had other talents that were far more valuable to the casino. Mr Duval could lip-read in five different languages.

'Which one?' he asked, as he stared down at the screen.

'The young guy,' said the manager, once again zooming in on him. 'What can you tell me about him?'

Duval watched carefully, but it was some time before he offered an opinion, during which the young man had lost another thousand francs on 13. 'He's French,' Duval eventually said, 'a Parisian, and the lady standing behind him is his wife, Maxine, unless they're both married to someone else.'

'Tell me what they're saying,' said Marcel.

Duval leant forward and watched carefully.

'Him, "My luck's got to change soon."'

'Her, "I'd rather you stopped, Jacques. Let's go back to the hotel while we've still got enough money to pay the bill."'

'Him, "It's not the hotel bill I'm worried about, as you well know, Maxine. It's that loan shark who'll be waiting for me the moment I show my face in Paris."'

The young man placed another thousand francs on 13. The ball landed on 26.

'Him, "Next time."'

'Is Tony on tonight?' the manager asked.

'Yes, boss,' replied the head of security. 'Table nine.'

'Switch him with the guy on table three, and tell him to make sure the ball lands in 13.'

'He's still only got a one in five chance,' said the head of security.

'That's better than thirty-seven to one,' said the manager. 'Get on with it.'

'On my way, boss,' said the head of security. He hurried out of the room and headed down to the casino floor, but not before the young man had lost another thousand francs.

'Pull the camera back,' said Duval. The manager zoomed out. 'I want to take a closer look at that man leaning against the pillar in the far corner.' The camera moved onto a middle-aged man who was also staring intently at the table. 'He's that journalist from *Le Figaro*.'

'Are you sure?' the manager barked.

'Look at the photo next to his byline on the front page,' he said, tapping the newspaper on the desk.

'François Colbert,' said the manager. 'I could kill him.'

'I think that's what he has in mind for you,' said Duval, as the camera returned to the roulette table, where two of the croupiers were swapping stations.

'Make it land in 13, Tony,' said the manager as the new croupier began to spin the wheel. While everyone's eyes were on the ball, the croupier's right hand slipped under the table.

Jacques placed another thousand francs on 13, as the croupier sent the little white ball on its way. The young man, the manager, the head of security and Duval all followed the progress of the ball, which ended up in 27, one slot to the left of 13.

'He'll get it right next time,' said the manager.

'He'd better,' said Duval, 'because the mark's only got two chips left.'

The young man put them both on 13. Once again, the

croupier sent the ball spinning, and once again his index finger felt for the hidden lever under the table, as six people with a vested interest watched to see where the ball would land. 36.

'Now Tony's managed both sides of thirteen,' said the manager, 'surely he'll get it right a third time.'

'But I think our guy's run out of money,' said Duval, as the young man swung round to face his wife.

'What's he saying?' demanded the manager.

'I can't tell you while he's got his back to me. But zoom in on the woman. She's saying, "But it's all I've got left, Jacques, and if I let you have it, we'll be cleaned out."'

The croupier once again spun the wheel and released the ball before flicking the lever of the trip pin a third time, when the ball finally landed in 13, but the gambler hadn't had time to place a bet. As the young man turned back, a gasp went up from those standing around the table, and he said in despair, 'If only you'd believed in me, Maxine, I could have won the three hundred thousand I needed to clear my debt.'

The young woman quickly unclasped her bag and handed over a wad of notes to the croupier. He counted them slowly.

'Ten thousand francs, sir?' he said impassively, before dropping the money into a plastic box by his side.

'Keep your eye on the journalist,' said Duval. The manager glanced across at François Colbert, who was writing down every word Jacques and his wife were saying.

'*Merde!*' he said, and turned his attention back to the croupier.

'Put it all on 13,' said the young man.

The croupier glanced across at the deputy manager, who nodded. He spun the wheel and released the ball, feeling for the lever once more. It landed in 13, but only for a moment before it popped back out and settled in 27. The young man let out a piercing scream, and as he stood up and left the table, yelled at the woman, 'You've left me with no choice.'

Maxine collapsed into the nearest chair and burst into tears, as her husband ran out of the back of the casino and onto the terrace. The manager left his desk and walked quickly out onto the balcony. He watched as the young man ran out onto the beach, and continued running towards the sea. The manager looked more closely, and could have sworn he was holding a gun in his right hand.

He quickly returned to his desk and was trying to get his security chief on the phone, when he heard a single shot ring out.

'Get back up here,' said the manager when André came on the line. 'And quickly.'

The manager walked over to a large safe embedded in the wall. He entered an eight-digit code and pulled open the heavy door. 'How much did he say would solve his problems?'

'Three hundred thousand francs,' said Duval, as André burst into the room.

'Take this money,' said the manager, handing over an armful of cash, 'and carry out the boss's orders.'

The security chief slipped out of the room, walked down the back stairs and out of a rear entrance onto the beach. He quickly identified a set of fresh prints in the moonlight, and followed them until he came to a body lying in the sand, blood pouring out of his mouth, a pistol by his side. The head of security looked up to check no one was watching him, before he began to stuff wads of cash into the dead man's jacket pockets, and then his trouser pockets, finally leaving a few francs scattered in the sand by his side.

André double-checked to make sure no one had seen what he'd done, before he got off his knees and made his way back towards the casino. Once inside, he ran up the back stairs and into the manager's office.

'Job done,' was all he said.

'Good. Now no one will be able to suggest he committed suicide because he lost heavily at the tables.'

―◦―

Maxine waited until the head of security had disappeared back into the casino, before she made her way out onto the beach. She kept glancing back to be sure no one was watching her.

When she found the body, she knelt down on the sand, and began to extract the francs from his pockets, before placing the bundles of cash in a large empty handbag. She even picked up the few stray ones that were lying by his side.

Maxine knelt down and kissed her husband gently on the forehead. 'The coast is clear, my darling,' she whispered, glancing back up towards the casino.

Jacques opened his eyes and smiled. 'I'll see you and François back in Paris,' he said as his wife picked up the bag and slipped quickly away.

THE SENIOR
VICE PRESIDENT

1

ARTHUR DUNBAR studied Mr S. Macpherson's account with some considerable satisfaction, bordering on pride. His eyes returned to the bottom line: $8,681,762. He checked it against last year's figure, $8,189,614. An increase of 6 per cent, and one mustn't forget that during the past year his client had spent $281,601 on personal expenditure, which included all his household bills, and a quarterly payment to a Mr and Mrs Laidlaw, who, Arthur assumed, must be his long-serving staff.

Arthur leant back in his chair, and not for the first time thought about the man who hailed from Ambrose in the Highlands of Scotland. When Arthur had first been given the responsibility of handling the account, some eighteen years ago, all his predecessor had told him was that a man, not much older than Arthur was at the time, had turned up at the bank and, having made a fortune on the railroad, deposited $871,000 in cash, and announced he was going home to Scotland.

It made Arthur smile to think that anyone who turned up with $10,000 in cash today would be subject to an investigation by their recently formed money-laundering team, and if they didn't tick all the boxes, their file would be handed over to the Toronto police's special investigation squad.

Arthur had long ago stopped trying to fathom why Mr Macpherson still did business with the National Bank of Toronto, when there were so many Scottish banks that were just as competent and considerably more convenient. But as he had conducted his affairs in an exemplary fashion for the past twenty-five years, the subject no longer arose, and in any case, NBT wouldn't have wanted to lose one of their most important customers.

Although Arthur knew very little about his client other than that they both shared the same heritage, one thing he had learnt over the years was that he was unquestionably a shrewd, intelligent businessman. After all, he had multiplied his original investment tenfold, while at the same time withdrawing enough money to live an extremely comfortable lifestyle. In fact, only once in the past eighteen years had he failed to show a profit, despite stock market collapses, changes of governments and countless skirmishes around the globe. He appeared to have no vices, and his only extravagance was purchasing the occasional painting from Munro's, a fine art dealer in Edinburgh – and then only if it was by a Scottish artist.

Arthur had long ago accepted he didn't have Mr Macpherson's flair for finance, but he was quite happy to sit at the feet of the master and when any new instructions came, he would invest a portion of his own money in the same shares at a level no one would have noticed. So when the bank's senior vice president checked his own account at the end of the quarter, it stood at $243,519. How he would have liked to thank Mr Macpherson in person, because retirement was fast approaching for Arthur, and with his little nest egg and a full pension, he looked forward to ending his days in a degree of comfort he felt he had earned.

If there was a Mrs Macpherson there were no clues to suggest it, so Arthur rather assumed that, like him, his client was a bachelor. But like so many mysteries surrounding the man, he didn't know for sure, and assumed he never would.

However, something had been worrying Arthur about the account for some weeks, though he couldn't put a finger on it. He opened the file again and noted the figure, $8,681,762, before checking every entry meticulously. But all seemed to be in order.

He then studied each cheque that the different individuals and companies had presented during the past month, before checking them against the entries in the ledger. Every one tallied. All the usual household expenses and utility bills, food, wine, gas, electricity, even Hudsons, the local newsagent. But he still felt something wasn't quite right. And then, in the middle of the night, it hit him like a thunderbolt. Less, not more.

On arrival at the bank the following morning, the first thing Arthur did was to take Mr Macpherson's ledger out of the bottom drawer. He turned the pages back to the previous quarter, and was able to confirm the most recent bills were considerably less than those for any other quarter. Had they been considerably more, Arthur would have spotted it immediately, and become suspicious. The fact that they were less, aroused his interest. The only entry that remained consistent was the monthly banker's order for his long-serving retainers, Mr and Mrs Laidlaw.

He leant back in his chair and wondered if he should inform the manager of this break in routine, but decided against it for two reasons. It was coming up to quarter day, when he would receive his new instructions from Mr Macpherson, and with it no doubt a simple explanation as to why the bills had fallen, and second, he didn't care much for the new manager of the bank.

There had been a time, not so very long ago, when Arthur had considered the possibility of being appointed manager himself, but his hopes were dashed when that position was filled by a Mr Stratton from their Montreal branch, who was half his age, but a graduate of McGill and the Wharton Business School. Arthur on the other hand had, to quote his late father – a former sergeant in the Seaforth Highlanders – risen through the ranks, and quite recently acquired the title of senior vice president. However, everyone in banking circles knew there were several vice presidents, and you only became the senior VP because everyone else had retired and you were next in line. 'Buggins' turn', as his father would have described it.

Arthur had applied to be the manager of one of the bank's smaller branches a couple of times, but hadn't even made the shortlist. On one occasion he'd overheard a member of the panel say, 'Dunbar's a good enough chap but simply isn't officer material.'

He had also considered leaving NBT to join one of their rivals, but quickly discovered he wouldn't be starting at the same salary, and he certainly couldn't hope to be offered the same pension plan as he was entitled to after so many years of loyal and devoted service. After all, in eighteen months' time he would have been with the bank for thirty years, which meant he could retire on two-thirds of his current salary; less than thirty years, and it would only be half. So he only had to cling on for another eighteen months.

Arthur turned his attention back to the pile of cheques on his desk, and was about to go over them once again, when the phone rang. He picked it up and immediately recognized the cheerful voice of Barbara, Mr Stratton's secretary.

'Mr Stratton wondered if you could pop round and see him when it's convenient – ' code for as soon as possible – 'as there's something he'd like to discuss with you fairly urgently – ' code for now.

'Of course,' said Arthur. 'I'll be with you in a moment.'

He disliked being summoned to the manager's office because it was rarely, if ever, good news. Last time Stratton had called for him was when he needed a volunteer to organize the Christmas party, and the responsibility had ended up taking hours of his spare time without any remuneration, and gone were the days when he could hope that one of the girls from the typing pool would go home with him later that evening.

The happiest of these occasions was when Barbara had joined the bank, and they had what might be described as a fling. He found they had so much in common, even enjoying the same passion for classical music, although he still couldn't understand why she preferred Brahms to Beethoven. And the biggest regret in Arthur's life was that he didn't ask her to marry him. When she married Reg Caldercroft in accounts, he ended up as best man.

He closed the Macpherson file and placed it in the top drawer of his desk, which he locked. He left his room and walked slowly down the corridor, knocked on the manager's door and received a curt 'Come' in response. Something else he didn't like about Mr Stratton.

Arthur opened the door and entered a large, well-furnished office, and waited to be told he could sit down. Stratton smiled up at him and pointed to the chair on the other side of his desk. Arthur returned the smile, equally insincere, wondering what voluntary chore was about to be thrust upon him.

'Good morning, Arthur,' said the young man.

'Good morning, Mr Stratton,' replied Arthur, who had once addressed him as Gerald when he first took over as manager, only to be told, 'not during working hours'. And as they never met socially, it was also the last time he had addressed the manager by his Christian name.

'Arthur,' he said, the same smile. 'I've had a letter from head office that I felt I ought to share with you, remembering that you are the bank's senior vice president and our longest-serving member of staff.'

What's he after? was Arthur's first thought.

'I have been instructed to make cutbacks on staff. The figure they are insisting on,' Stratton said, looking down at a letter on his desk, 'is ten per cent. And the board are recommending we start by offering senior staff the opportunity to take early retirement.'

To make way for younger people who they will only

have to pay half the salary, Arthur wanted to say, but kept his counsel.

'And of course, I thought you might consider this an ideal opportunity, after your little scare last year.'

'It wasn't a scare,' said Arthur, 'and I was off work for four days. The only four days in nearly thirty years with the bank,' he reminded Stratton.

'Indeed, most commendable,' said Stratton. 'But don't you think these things are sometimes a warning?'

'No, I do not,' said Arthur. 'I've never felt fitter, and as you well know, I only need to serve another eighteen months to qualify for a full pension.'

'I realize that,' said Stratton, 'and please don't think I'm not sympathetic. But my hands are tied.' He looked down at the letter, clearly trying to place the blame on someone else. 'I'm sure you'll appreciate the problem I'm facing . . .'

'It's me who's facing the problem, not you,' said Arthur, bolder than he'd ever been in the past.

'And the board asked me to say,' said Stratton, 'how much they appreciate the long and dedicated service you have given the bank. And I feel sure you'll be pleased to know they have agreed that a farewell party should be thrown in your honour, along with an appropriate gift to mark your remarkable service to the National Bank of Toronto.'

'A cocktail party with crisps, peanuts, a glass of *vin ordinaire*, and a gold-plated watch. Thanks very much. But I'd rather have the full pension I'm entitled to.'

'And I want you to know, Arthur,' said Stratton, ignoring the outburst, 'how hard I fought your corner, but the board . . . well, I feel sure you know what they're like.'

Actually Arthur didn't have any idea what they were like. In fact if a member of the board had passed him in the street, he doubted if they would recognize him.

'But I did manage one small coup on your behalf,' continued Stratton, the same insincere smile returning to his face. 'I got you a stay of execution.' And from the look on the manager's face, he clearly regretted the words the moment he'd uttered them, but it didn't stop him charging on. 'While everyone else will have to leave by the end of the next quarter, six months at the most, you can retain your position as the senior VP for another year.'

'Just six months before I would have scraped over the line,' said Arthur with considerable feeling.

'I did the best I could given the circumstances,' insisted Stratton. 'And will be writing to you in the next few days, setting out the finer details.' The manager hesitated for a moment before adding, 'I was rather hoping, Arthur, I might rely on you to brief other senior colleagues of the board's decision. You're so good at that sort of thing.'

Arthur rose from his place with as much dignity as he could muster, and said calmly, 'Go to hell, Gerald. You can do your own dirty work for a change.' He gave the manager the same ingratiating smile, and left without another word.

Once Arthur was back in his office, he swore out loud, something he hadn't done since the Toronto Maple Leafs lost to the Montreal Canadiens during the last minute of extra time in the Stanley Cup.

He paced aimlessly around his little office for some time before he finally sat down and began to write a letter to Mr Macpherson explaining why someone else would be handling his account in the future.

◄◦►

A fortnight passed, but there was no reply from Ambrose Hall. This surprised Arthur, because if there was one thing he knew about his most esteemed customer, it was that he was never less than courteous and unfailingly punctilious.

The bank's senior VP continued to double-check his mail every morning, but there was still no response to his letter. Even more out of character, when quarter day appeared on the calendar, the usual long typewritten letter detailing Mr Macpherson's investment instructions and any other requirements he expected the bank to carry out during the next three months did not appear.

It was while Arthur was trying to get to sleep that the only other possibility for Mr Macpherson's uncharacteristic behaviour crossed Arthur's mind. He sat bolt upright and didn't sleep that night.

Nevertheless, it was still another fortnight before Arthur would accept that the 'only other possibility' had become a probability. But it wasn't until he'd opened a letter from Mr Stratton confirming the day of his retirement and his pension details, that the first dishonest thought crossed Arthur Dunbar's mind in twenty-eight years of service to the National Bank of Toronto.

However, Arthur was, by nature, a cautious man, so he allowed the dishonest thought to mature for a while before he even considered a provisional plan – and then only in his mind.

During the following month, he continued to clear

every cheque that was presented in his client's name, as well as Mr and Mrs Laidlaw's monthly banker's order deposited to their joint account at the Bank of Scotland in Ambrose. However, when a new chequebook arrived from the printers, Arthur did not send it on to Mr Macpherson, but locked it in the top drawer of his desk.

He felt confident that would elicit an immediate response if . . .

Arthur kept rereading the letter that had landed on his desk. It was hand delivered by Mr Stratton's secretary, and was short and to the point.

It is with much regret . . .

Nowhere in the letter were the words 'sacked' or 'made redundant', because they had been replaced with wishing him a happy retirement, and how much he was looking forward to continuing working with him for the next ten months. Arthur swore for the second time that year.

The rest of the month passed without incident, although no letter was forthcoming from Mr Macpherson. The staff party was considered a great success by everyone except Arthur, who was the last to leave, and spent Christmas alone.

-◆-

Arthur checked his calendar: 7 January, and he still hadn't received any further communication from Mr Macpherson, although he was aware any payments would soon come to an end, because he hadn't issued a new chequebook for the past quarter. But then Arthur was in no hurry, because he still had another nine months to work on his exit strategy, as befitted a banker who believed in the long game.

When no instructions came from Mr Macpherson by the end of the following quarter, Arthur decided he must either be too ill to communicate, or he was dead. He considered his next move most carefully. He thought about writing to Mr Macpherson concerning a recent dividend he'd received from the Shell Oil Company, asking if he wanted to accept payment, or to take up their offer of new shares. After considerable thought, he didn't send the letter, as he feared it might alert Mr and Mrs Laidlaw to the fact that someone at the bank was becoming suspicious.

Arthur decided he would wait for the cheques to run out before he made his next move, and every time a new chequebook arrived from the printers, he placed it in his top drawer along with the others.

Patience paid off, because the Laidlaws finally gave themselves away. When the last four cheques were sent to be cleared, Arthur noted that the sums were becoming larger and larger, and he made a bold decision that, despite the account still having over eight million dollars in cash, stocks and bonds, he would 'bounce' the final cheque made out to Cooks Travel for a package holiday for two in Ibiza. He waited for an irate letter from Mr Macpherson demanding an explanation, but none was forthcoming, which gave Arthur the confidence to put the second part of his plan into action.

2

WHENEVER ANYONE at the bank asked Arthur where he was going for his summer holiday, and not many people did, he always replied, 'I will be visiting my sister in Vancouver.' However, by the time it came for him to leave for his summer vacation, he not only had a sister, but a whole family in place: Eileen and Mike, who worked in local government, and a niece and nephew, Sue and Mike Jr. Not very imaginative, but when you haven't lied for twenty-nine years, your friends and colleagues have a tendency to accept everything you tell them.

During the next month, Arthur continued to invest Mr Macpherson's fortune in an orderly, if somewhat conservative fashion, keeping to a well-trodden path. At the same time, he withdrew small amounts of cash each week from his personal account, until he had a little over three thousand dollars locked away in his top drawer, not unlike a bridegroom preparing for his wedding.

On the Monday morning a week before he was due to go on holiday, Arthur placed the cash in his lunch box and headed off for his favourite bench in the park. However, on the way he dropped into the Royal Bank of Canada, where he waited in line at the currency counter, before changing his dollars into pounds.

During the Tuesday lunchbreak, he made a further detour, to a local travel agent, where he purchased a return flight to Vancouver. He paid by cheque, and when he arrived back at the bank, left the ticket on the corner of his desk for all to see, and if anyone mentioned it, he once again told them all about his sister Eileen and her family in Vancouver.

On the Wednesday, Arthur applied for a new credit card on Mr Macpherson's behalf, and issued an order to cease any trading on the old one. A bright, shiny black card appeared on his desk forty-eight hours later. Arthur was ready to carry out stage two of his plan.

He had carefully chosen the dates he would be away from the office, selecting the two weeks before Mr Stratton was due to take his annual leave.

Arthur left the bank just after six on Friday evening, and took the usual bus back to his small apartment in Forest Hill. He spent a sleepless night wondering if he'd made the right decision. However, by the time the sun eventually rose on Saturday morning, he was resolved to go ahead with his plan and, as his father would have said, 'let the devil take the hindmost'.

After a leisurely breakfast, he packed a suitcase and left the flat just before midday. Arthur hailed a cab, an expense he normally wouldn't have considered, but then for the next few days everything he did would be out of character.

When the cab dropped him off at the domestic terminal, Arthur went straight to the Air Canada desk and traded in his return flight to Vancouver for a one-way window seat at the back of a plane destined for London.

He paid the difference in cash. Arthur then took the shuttle bus across to the international terminal, where he was among the first to check in. While he waited to board the aircraft, he sat behind a large pillar and, head down, remained hidden behind the *Toronto Star*. He intended to be among the first on, and the last off the plane, as he hoped it would cut down the chances of anyone recognizing him.

Once he'd fastened his seat belt, he made no attempt to strike up a conversation with the young couple seated next to him. During the seven-hour flight, he watched two films, which he wouldn't have bothered with back at home, and in between pretended to be asleep.

When the plane touched down at Heathrow the following morning, he waited patiently in line at Immigration, and by the time his passport had been stamped, his one suitcase was already circling around on the baggage carousel. Once he'd cleared Customs, he took another shuttle bus to terminal five, where he purchased a ticket to Edinburgh, which he also paid for in cash. On his arrival in the Scottish capital, another taxi took him to the Caledonian, a hotel recommended by the cabbie.

'How long will you be staying with us, sir?' asked the receptionist.

'Just the night,' replied Arthur, as she handed him his room key.

Arthur feared he'd have another restless night, but in fact fell asleep within moments of putting his head on the pillow.

-◇-

The following morning, he ordered breakfast in bed, another first. But the moment he heard nine chiming on a nearby clock, he picked up the phone on his bedside table and dialled a number he did not have to look up.

'Royal Bank of Scotland, how can I help you?'

'I'd like to speak to the senior accounts manager,' said Arthur.

'Buchan,' said the next voice that came on the line. 'How can I help you?'

'I'm thinking of moving my account to your bank,' said Arthur, 'and wondered if I could make an appointment to see you as soon as possible.'

'Of course,' said the voice, suddenly sounding more obliging. 'Would eleven o'clock this morning suit you, Mr . . . ?'

'Macpherson,' said Arthur. 'Yes, that would be just fine.'

Arthur left the hotel just after ten thirty and, following the doorman's instructions, made his way down Princes Street, occasionally stopping to window shop, as he didn't want to be early for his appointment.

He entered the bank at 10.55 a.m., and a receptionist accompanied him to Mr Buchan's office. The senior accounts manager rose from behind his desk and the two men shook hands.

'How can I help you, Mr Macpherson?' Buchan asked once his potential new client had sat down.

'I'll be moving back to Scotland in a few months' time,' said Arthur, 'and your bank was recommended to me by the senior vice president at NBT.'

'Our partner bank in Toronto,' said Buchan, as he opened a drawer in his desk and extracted some forms.

For the next twenty minutes, Arthur answered a series of questions that he was in the habit of asking. Once the last box had been filled in, and Arthur had signed S. *Macpherson* on the dotted line, Buchan asked if he had any form of identity with him, such as a passport.

'I'm so sorry,' said Arthur, 'I left my passport at the Caledonian. But I do have my credit card.'

The production of a platinum credit card seemed to be more than enough to satisfy the account manager.

'Thank you,' said Buchan, as he handed back the card. 'And may I ask when you expect the transfer to take place?'

'Sometime in the next few weeks,' replied Arthur, 'but I will ask Mr Dunbar, the bank's senior vice president, who has handled my account for the past twenty years, to give you a call.'

'Thank you,' said Buchan, making a note of the name. 'I look forward to hearing from him.'

Arthur walked slowly back to his hotel feeling the meeting couldn't have gone much better. He collected his case from his room, and returned to reception.

'I hope you enjoyed your stay with us, Mr Macpherson,' said the receptionist, 'and it won't be too long before we see you again.'

'In the not too distant future, I hope,' said Arthur, who settled his bill in cash, left the hotel, and asked the doorman to hail a taxi.

When he was dropped off at the station, Arthur joined another queue, and purchased a first-class return ticket to

Ambrose. He sat alone in a comfortable carriage watching the countryside race by as the train travelled deeper and deeper into the Highlands, skirting several lochs and pine forests, which he might have enjoyed had he not been going over the most crucial part of his plan.

To date, everything had run smoothly, but Arthur had long ago accepted the real hurdle that still needed to be crossed would be when he came face to face with Mr and Mrs Laidlaw for the first time.

On arrival in Ambrose, Arthur climbed into the back of another taxi, and asked the driver to take him to the best hotel in town. This was greeted with a chuckle, followed by, 'You've obviously never visited these parts before. You have two choices, the Bell Inn or the Bell Inn.'

Arthur laughed. 'Well then, that's settled. And can I also book you for ten o'clock tomorrow morning?'

'Yes, sir,' said the driver cheerfully. 'Would you prefer this car, or I also have a limousine?'

'The limousine,' said Arthur, without hesitation. He needed the Laidlaws to realize who they were dealing with.

'And where will we be going?' the driver asked, as they drew up outside the Bell Inn.

'Ambrose Hall.'

The driver turned and gave his passenger a second look, but said nothing.

Arthur walked into the pub, where the bar doubled as the reception desk. He booked a room for the night, and told the landlord he couldn't be certain how long he would be staying, not adding, because if the front door of

Ambrose Hall was opened by Mr Macpherson, he'd be on the next flight back to Toronto.

Once Arthur had unpacked, taken a bath and changed his clothes, he made his way back downstairs to the bar. The few locals stared at him disapprovingly, assuming he was an Englishman, until he opened his mouth, when their smiles returned.

He ordered cock-a-leekie soup and a Scotch egg, delighted to find that although the regulars continued to view him with suspicion, the landlord seemed quite happy to chat, especially if it was accompanied by the offer of a wee dram.

During the next hour and after nearly emptying a bottle of wee drams, Arthur discovered that no one in the town had ever met Mr Macpherson, although, the landlord added, 'the shopkeepers have no complaints, because the man always pays his bills on time and supports several local charities' – which Arthur could have listed. He noted the words 'pays' and 'supports', so certainly the landlord thought Macpherson was still alive.

'Came over from Canada in my father's day,' continued the barman. 'Said to have made a fortune on the railroad, but who knows the truth?'

Arthur knew the truth.

'Must be lonely up there in the winter,' said Arthur, still fishing.

'And the ice rarely melts on those hills before March,' said the barman. 'Still the old man's got the Laidlaws to take care of him, and she's a damned fine cook, even if he's not the most sociable of people, especially if you stray onto his land uninvited.'

'I think I'll turn in,' said Arthur.

'Care for a nightcap?' asked the landlord, holding up an unopened bottle of whisky.

'No, thank you,' said Arthur.

The landlord looked disappointed, but bade his guest goodnight.

Arthur didn't sleep well, and it wasn't just jet lag: after the barman's remarks he feared Macpherson might still be alive, in which case the whole trip would have been a complete waste of time and money. And worse, if Stratton got to hear about it . . .

—◆—

When the sun rose the following morning, which Arthur noted was quite late in this part of the world, he took a bath, got dressed and went downstairs to enjoy a breakfast that would have been appreciated in a New York deli: porridge with brown sugar, kippers, toast, marmalade and steaming hot coffee. He then returned to his room and packed his small suitcase, still not certain where he would be spending the night.

He came back downstairs and, on being handed his bill, discovered just how many wee drams the landlord had enjoyed. But this was not somewhere to hand over a credit card in the name of Mr S. Macpherson. That remained in his wallet. For now, its only purpose had been to prove his identity to Mr Buchan. Arthur settled the bill with cash, which brought an even bigger smile to the landlord's face.

When Arthur stepped out of the hotel just before ten

o'clock, he was greeted with the sight of a gleaming black Daimler.

'Good morning,' he said, as he climbed into the back seat and sank down into the comfortable leather upholstery.

'Good morning, sir,' said the driver. 'Hope the car's to your liking.'

'Couldn't be better,' replied Arthur.

'Usually only comes out for weddings or funerals,' admitted the driver.

Arthur still wasn't sure which this was going to be.

The driver set off on the journey to Ambrose Hall, and it quickly became clear he hadn't visited the house for some time, and like everyone else in the town, had never set eyes on Mr Macpherson, but he added with a chuckle, 'They'll have to call for Jock when the old man dies.'

Once again Arthur feared his client must still be alive.

The hall turned out to be a journey of about fourteen miles, during which the roads became lanes, and the lanes, paths, until he finally saw a turreted castle standing four-square on a hill in the distance. Arthur had one speech prepared, should Mr Macpherson answer the door, and another if he was met by the Laidlaws.

The car proceeded slowly up the driveway, and they must have been about a hundred yards from the front door when Arthur first saw him. A massive giant of a man wearing a tartan kilt, with a cocked shotgun under his right arm, looking as if he hoped a stag might stray across his path.

'That's Hamish Laidlaw,' whispered Jock, 'and if you don't mind, I think I'll stay in the car.'

When Arthur got out, he heard the car doors lock. He began walking slowly towards his prey.

'What di ye want?' demanded Laidlaw, his gun rising a couple of inches.

'I've come to see Mr Macpherson,' said Arthur, as if he was expected.

'Mr Macpherson doesn't welcome strangers, especially those who dinnae have an appointment,' he said, the gun rising a couple more inches.

'He'll want to see me,' said Arthur, who took out his wallet, extracted a card, and handed it to the giant. Arthur suspected this might be one of those rare occasions when senior vice president embossed in gold below National Bank of Toronto might just have the desired effect.

While Laidlaw studied the card, Arthur watched as a moment of apprehension crossed his face, a look he'd experienced many times when a customer was asking for an overdraft, and didn't have the necessary security to back it up. The balance of power had shifted, and Arthur knew it.

'He's not here at the moment,' said Laidlaw, as the gun dropped.

'I know he isn't,' said Arthur, taking a risk, 'but if you don't want the whole town to know why I've come to visit you,' he added, looking back at Jock, 'I suggest we go inside.' He began walking slowly towards the front door.

Laidlaw got there just in time to open it, and led the intruder into the drawing room, where all the furniture was covered in dust sheets. Arthur pulled one off and let it fall to the floor. He sat down in a comfortable leather chair, looked up at Laidlaw and said firmly, 'Fetch Mrs Laidlaw. I need to speak to both of you.'

'She wasn't involved,' said Laidlaw, fear replacing bluster.

Involved in what? thought Arthur, but repeated, 'Fetch your wife. And while you're at it, Laidlaw, put that gun away, unless you want to add murder to your other crimes.'

Laidlaw scurried away, leaving Arthur to enjoy the magnificent paintings by Mackintosh, Farquharson and Peploe that hung on every wall. Laidlaw reappeared a few minutes later with a middle-aged woman in tow. She was wearing an apron, and didn't raise her head. It wasn't until she stopped half a pace behind her husband that Arthur realized just how much she was shaking.

'I know exactly what you two have been up to,' said Arthur, hoping they would believe him, 'and if you tell me the truth, and I mean the whole truth, there's just a chance I might still be able to save you. If you don't, my next visit will be to the local police station. I'll start with you, Mrs Laidlaw.'

'We didnae mean to do it,' she said, 'but he didn't leave us with a lot of choice.'

'Hold your tongue, woman,' said Laidlaw. 'I'll speak for both of us.'

'You'll do nothing of the sort,' said Arthur. He looked back at Mrs Laidlaw and played what he hoped was his trump card. 'The first thing I want to know is when Mr Macpherson died?'

'Just a few months back,' said Mrs Laidlaw. 'I found

him in bed, white as a sheet he was, so he must have passed away during the night.'

'Then why didn't you call for a doctor, the police, even Jock?'

'Because we didn't think straight,' she said. 'We thought we'd lose our jobs and be turfed out of the lodge. So we waited to see what would happen if we did nothing, and as the monthly cheque kept arriving from the bank, we assumed no one could be any the wiser.'

'What did you do with the body?'

'We buried him. On the other side of the copse,' chipped in Mr Laidlaw, 'where no one would find him.'

'We didn't mean any harm,' she said, 'but we'd served the laird for over twenty years, and not so much as a pension.'

I know the feeling, thought Arthur, but didn't interrupt.

'We didn't steal nothing,' said Laidlaw.

'But you signed cheques in his name, and also went on receiving your monthly pay packet.'

'Only enough to keep us alive, and not allow the house to go to rack and ruin.'

'I told him we had to keep the expenses low,' said Mrs Laidlaw, 'so they wouldn't become suspicious.'

'That's what gave you away,' said Arthur.

'Will we go to jail?' asked Mrs Laidlaw.

'Not if you carry out my instructions to the letter,' said Arthur as he stood up. 'Is that understood?'

'I don't care about going to jail,' said Laidlaw, 'but not Morag. It wasn't her fault.'

'I'm afraid you're both in this together,' said Arthur.

Mrs Laidlaw began to shake again. 'Now I want to see Mr Macpherson's study.'

The Laidlaws both looked surprised by the request, but quickly led Arthur out of the drawing room and up a wide sweeping staircase to a large comfortable room on the first floor that had been converted to an office.

Arthur walked across to a desk that overlooked the hills of Arbroath. He was surprised to find not a speck of dust on the furniture, only perpetuating the myth that their master was still alive. The Laidlaws stood a few paces back, as their unwelcome visitor sat down at the desk. A flicker of a smile crossed Arthur's lips when he spotted the Remington Imperial typewriter on which Mr Macpherson had written so many letters to him over the years.

'Would you like a cup of tea, sir?' asked Mrs Laidlaw, as if she were addressing the master of the house.

'That would be nice, Morag,' said Arthur. 'Milk and one sugar, please.'

She disappeared, leaving her husband almost standing to attention. Arthur opened the top drawer of the desk to find a stack of used chequebooks, the stubs filled in with Macpherson's familiar neat hand. He closed the drawer and took out a piece of Ambrose Hall headed notepaper, and slipped it into the typewriter.

Arthur began to write a letter to himself, and after he'd typed 'Yours sincerely', he pulled the page out and read it, before turning to Laidlaw. 'I want you to read this letter carefully and then sign it.'

Laidlaw couldn't hide his surprise long before he finished reading the letter. But he took the quill pen from its holder, dipped it in the inkwell and slowly wrote 'S. Macpherson'. Arthur was impressed, and wondered how long it had taken Laidlaw to perfect the forgery, because he'd never spotted it. He took an envelope from the letter rack, placed it in the machine and typed:

> *Mr A. Dunbar*
> *Senior Vice President*
> *The National Bank of Toronto*

He placed the letter in the envelope and sealed it, as Mrs Laidlaw returned carrying a tray of tea and shortbread biscuits. Arthur took a sip. Just perfect. He placed the cup back on its saucer and set about writing a second letter. When he had finished, he asked Laidlaw to once again add the false signature, but this time he didn't allow him to read the contents.

'Post one today,' said Arthur. 'And this one a week later,' he added, before passing both envelopes across to Laidlaw. 'If the second letter arrives on my desk within a fortnight, I shall return in a few weeks' time. If it doesn't your next visitor will be a police officer.'

'But how will we survive while you're away?' asked Laidlaw.

Arthur opened his briefcase and took out three chequebooks. 'Use them sparingly,' he said, 'because if I consider you have overstepped the mark, the cheque will not be cleared. Is that understood?' They both nodded. 'And you'll also need to order some more writing paper and envelopes,' continued Arthur, as he opened the drawer. 'And stamps.'

Arthur was just about to close the drawer when he

spotted some documents tucked away in a corner. He pulled out Mr Macpherson's old passport, his birth certificate, and a will, and could feel his heart hammering in his chest. The three finds supplied him with a wealth of information that might prove useful in the future, and he finally discovered what the S. stood for. Macpherson's passport also revealed that he was sixteen years older than Arthur, but given the blurriness of the old photograph he felt he could get away with it. But he would still need to order a replacement before he returned to Toronto. He placed the passport, birth certificate and the will in his briefcase and locked it. He stood up and began to walk towards the door. The Laidlaws followed obediently in his wake.

'Mrs Laidlaw, I want all the dust sheets removed, and the house returned to the state it was in when Mr Macpherson was still in residence. Spare no expense, just be certain to send me every bill, so I can double-check it,' he added, as they walked downstairs together.

'By the time you return, Mr Dunbar, everything will be just as you would expect it,' she promised.

'As Mr Macpherson would expect it,' Arthur corrected her.

'Mr Macpherson,' she said. 'I'll prepare the master bedroom so it will be just like old times.'

'Is there anything else you'd like me to do, sir?' asked Laidlaw when Arthur reached the bottom of the staircase.

'Just be sure to post those two letters, and carry on as if Mr Macpherson was still alive, because he is,' said Arthur, as Laidlaw opened the front door.

When Jock saw them coming out of the house with

Hamish Laidlaw clutching on to his hat, and no longer holding a gun, he jumped out of the car, ran around and opened the back door so his fare could climb in.

'Where to, sir?' said Jock.

'The station,' Arthur said, as he looked out of the window to acknowledge the Laidlaws waving, as if he were already the master of Ambrose Hall.

◄○►

During the flight back to Heathrow, Arthur studied Mr Macpherson's last will and testament line by line. He had left generous legacies to the Laidlaws, while no other individual was mentioned. The bulk of the estate was to be divided between several local organizations and charities, the two largest amounts being allocated to the Scottish Widows and Orphans Fund, and the Rehabilitation of Young Offenders Trust. Did those simple bequests, Arthur wondered, explain why the young Scot had set sail for Canada, and ended his days as a recluse in a remote part of his homeland?

Arthur knew the passport and birth certificate could prove useful if he was to go ahead with the deception, but had already decided that when he died, the executors would find the will exactly where Mr Macpherson had left it.

On arrival back at Heathrow, Arthur took a train to Paddington and a taxi on to Petty France. Once he'd entered the building, he spent some considerable time filling in a long form, something he was rather good at.

After double-checking every box, he joined a slow-moving queue, and when he eventually reached the front he handed the document to a young lady seated behind the counter. She studied the application carefully, before asking to see Mr Macpherson's old passport, which Arthur handed over immediately. He'd made only one subtle change, 1950 had become 1966, while his own photograph had replaced the original one. She was clearly surprised not to have to make any corrections on his application form, or ask for further information. She smiled up at Arthur and stamped APPROVED.

'If you come back tomorrow afternoon, Mr Macpherson,' she said, 'you'll be able to pick up your new passport.'

Arthur thought about making a fuss as he had a flight booked for Toronto that night, but simply said, 'Thank you,' as he didn't want to be remembered.

Arthur checked into a nearby hotel, where he spotted a poster advertising a performance of Schubert's Fifth, to be given at the Festival Hall by the Berlin Philharmonic under their conductor, Simon Rattle.

He was beginning to think the trip couldn't have gone much better.

3

ARTHUR PICKED UP the phone on his desk and pressed a button that would put him through to the manager's office.

'Barbara, it's Arthur Dunbar.'

'Welcome back, Arthur. Did you have a nice time in Vancouver?'

'Couldn't have been better. In fact I'm considering moving out there when I retire.'

'We'll all miss you,' said Barbara. 'I'm not sure how the place will survive without you.'

'I'm sure it will,' said Arthur, 'but when are you expecting Mr Stratton back?'

'He and his wife flew to Miami on Friday. He'll be away for three weeks, so there couldn't be a better time for us to rob the bank.'

'And run away together,' laughed Arthur. 'Toronto's answer to Bonnie and Clyde! Still, while I'm the senior officer, could you keep me briefed if anything important arises?'

'Of course,' said Barbara. 'But as you well know, not a lot happens in August while so many customers are away on holiday. But I'll give you a buzz if anything comes up.'

Arthur checked his post every morning, but it wasn't until the sixth day that the first of the two letters landed on his desk. Arthur didn't rest on the seventh day, now he felt confident that the Laidlaws were keeping their side of the bargain. He picked up the phone and pressed another button.

'Standing orders,' said a voice he recognized.

'Steve, it's Arthur Dunbar. I've just received a letter from Mr Macpherson, and he's instructed the bank to raise Mr and Mrs Laidlaw's monthly allowance.'

'I wish someone would do that for me,' said Steve.

'I'll send down a copy of the letter for your files,' said Arthur, ignoring the comment. 'And can you make sure that everything is in place for the September payment.'

'Of course, Mr Dunbar.'

The second letter took a little longer to arrive, and Arthur even wondered if the Laidlaws had changed their mind, until the post boy delivered an envelope post-marked Ambrose on Monday morning, leaving him only five working days to complete the next part of his plan. But like a good Boy Scout, Arthur was well prepared.

He checked his watch. Buchan would still be at his desk for at least another couple of hours, but he needed to make an internal call before he contacted Edinburgh. He picked up the phone, pressed another button and waited until the head of accounts came on the line.

'Have you seen a copy of the Macpherson letter, Reg, that I sent down to your office earlier this morning?'

'Yes I have,' replied Caldercroft, 'and I'm sorry, Arthur, because you must be disappointed after all these years.'

'It was bound to happen at some time,' said Arthur.

'But sad that it's just when you're leaving. Will you get in touch with Mr Macpherson and try to persuade him to change his mind?'

'Not much point,' said Arthur. 'He hasn't done so for the past twenty years, so why would he now?'

'I'm sure you're right,' said Caldercroft. 'But shouldn't we wait until Stratton gets back, and see how he wants to play it?'

'I'm afraid the new banking laws don't allow us that luxury,' said Arthur. 'If a client requests to move his account, we must carry out their wishes within fourteen days, and as you can see, the letter is dated the eleventh.'

'Perhaps we should call Mr Stratton in Miami, and alert him to the situation?'

'You call him if you want to, Reg . . .'

'No, no,' said Caldercroft. 'You're in charge during the manager's absence, so what do you want me to do next?'

'Gather up all Mr Macpherson's bonds, stocks and any other financial instruments, and courier them to a Mr Buchan at RBS in Edinburgh, who appears to be the person he's appointed to take over the account. I'm just about to phone Buchan and find out when it will be con-venient to complete the transfer. I'll keep you briefed.' He put the phone down.

Arthur took a deep breath and checked over his script one more time before he picked up the phone again and asked the switchboard operator to get him a number in Edinburgh. He waited to be put through.

'Good morning, Mr Buchan, my name is Arthur Dun-bar, and I'm the senior VP at the National Bank of Toronto.'

'Good morning, Mr Dunbar,' said his opposite number.

'I've been expecting your call. I had a visit from a Mr Macpherson a couple of weeks ago, and he said you'd be in touch.'

'Indeed,' said Arthur, 'although we will be sorry to lose Mr Macpherson, a most valued client, but pleased he'll be moving to our partner bank in Edinburgh. And to that end,' said Arthur, trying to sound pompous, 'I have already given instructions to send all the necessary paperwork to you by courier, which I anticipate should be dealt with by the end of the week.'

'Thank you,' said Buchan, 'and when will it be convenient for you to transfer Mr Macpherson's current account?'

'Would Thursday morning suit you? Around this time.'

'That should be fine. I'll make sure everything is in place to receive the funds on Thursday afternoon, and may I ask roughly how much we should be looking out for?'

'I can't be certain of the exact figure,' said Arthur, 'because I won't know the dollar–sterling exchange rate until that morning. But it will certainly be in excess of four million pounds.'

There was no response, and Arthur even wondered if they'd been cut off. 'Are you still there, Mr Buchan?'

'Yes, I am, Mr Dunbar,' Buchan eventually managed. 'And I look forward to hearing from you again on Thursday.'

◄०►

Mr Stratton returned from his holiday the following Monday, and had only been in his office for a few minutes before he called for the senior vice president.

'Why didn't you try and contact me in Miami?' were his first words as Arthur entered the room.

'As you can see,' said Arthur, placing his own typewritten letter on the desk, 'Mr Macpherson's instructions couldn't have been clearer, and as I have no way of contacting him other than by post, there wasn't a lot I could do.'

'You could have held things up, even flown to Scotland to see if you could get him to change his mind, which I would have approved.'

'That would have been pointless,' said Arthur, 'as he had already visited RBS in Edinburgh and instructed a Mr Buchan to carry out the transfer as expeditiously as possible.'

'Which I see you did last Thursday.'

'Yes,' said Arthur. 'We just managed to complete the transaction within the time stipulated by the new government regulations.' Stratton pursed his lips. 'However, a little coup I thought you would appreciate,' continued Arthur, enjoying himself, 'the Toronto end handled the exchange from dollars into pounds sterling, earning the bank some seventy-three thousand, one hundred and forty-one dollars.'

'A small compensation,' said Stratton begrudgingly.

'How kind of you to say so, Gerald.'

―◦―

Arthur spent his last month making sure everything was in apple pie order, no more than his mother would have expected, so by the time Reg Caldercroft moved into his office and took over as the new senior vice president,

Arthur had only one responsibility left: preparing a farewell speech for his retirement party.

'I think I can safely say,' said Mr Stratton, 'that few people have served this bank more conscientiously, and certainly none longer, than Arthur Dunbar. Twenty-nine years, in fact.'

'Twenty-nine years and seven months,' said Arthur with some feeling, and several of the longer-serving staff stifled a laugh.

'We're all going to miss you, Arthur.' The insincere smile returning to the manager's lips. 'And we wish you a long and happy retirement when you leave us to join your family in Vancouver.'

Loud 'Hear, hears' followed this statement.

'And on behalf of the bank,' continued Stratton, 'it's my pleasure to present you with a Rolex Oyster watch, and I hope whenever you look at it, you will be reminded of your time at the bank. Let's all raise a glass to our senior vice president, Arthur Dunbar.'

'To Arthur,' said over a hundred voices, as they raised their glasses in the air, which was quickly followed by cries of 'speech, speech!' from the guests. They all fell silent when Arthur walked up to the front and took Stratton's place.

'I'd like to begin,' said Arthur, 'by thanking those people, and in particular Barbara, for organizing such a splendid party, and to all of you for this magnificent gift. And to you, Gerald,' he said, turning to face the manager, 'I must say it will be quite hard to forget who gave me the watch, when engraved on the back is the inscription, "To Arthur, from all his colleagues at NBT".' Everyone laughed and applauded as Arthur strapped the watch on his wrist. 'And if any of you should ever find yourself at a loose end in Vancouver, do please look me up.' He didn't add, but should you do so, you won't find me.

Arthur was touched by how warm the applause was when he rejoined the guests.

'We'll all miss you,' said Barbara.

Arthur smiled at the bank's biggest gem. 'And I'll miss you,' he admitted.

4

ARTHUR LEFT the bank at six o'clock on quarter day. He took the bus back to his small apartment and packed up all his belongings before spending his last night in Toronto.

The following morning, after handing over the keys to his apartment to the janitor, he took a cab to the airport. He only made one stop on the journey, when he donated four packed suitcases of his past to a grateful volunteer worker at the local Red Cross shop.

After checking in at the domestic terminal, Arthur boarded the midday flight for Vancouver. On arrival on the west coast, he collected his only suitcase from the carousel, and took a shuttle bus across to the international terminal. He waited in line before purchasing a business-class ticket to London, which he paid for with the last of his Canadian dollars. By the time Arthur boarded the plane he was so exhausted he slept for almost the entire flight.

When he landed at Heathrow and had passed through Customs, he once again transferred to terminal five and purchased a ticket to Edinburgh, also with cash. Arthur checked the departure board, and although he had an hour to spare, he made his way slowly across to gate 43. He stopped at every lavatory en route, locked himself into a cubicle, ripped out one page of his Canadian passport, tore it into little pieces and flushed it down the toilet.

By the time Arthur reached the check-in desk, all he had left of his old passport was the cover. Mr Dunbar dropped it into the bottom of a waste bin outside McDonald's.

'Will all passengers . . .'

Mr Macpherson stepped onto the plane.

On arrival in Edinburgh, Arthur took a taxi to the Caledonian Hotel and checked in.

'Welcome back,' said the desk clerk, as he checked his credit card against the customer's reservation. He handed him a room key and said, 'You've been upgraded, Mr Macpherson.'

'Thank you,' said Arthur, who was shown up to a small suite on the sixth floor, to be greeted with a bottle of champagne in an ice bucket, and a handwritten note of welcome from the manager. He gave the bellboy a handsome tip.

Once he'd unpacked, he called Mr Buchan and made an appointment to see him later that afternoon. Following a light lunch in the brasserie, Arthur took a stroll along Princes Street and arrived outside the bank with a few minutes to spare.

'How nice to see you again, Mr Macpherson,' said Buchan, leaping up from behind his desk when Arthur entered the account manager's office.

'It's nice to see you too,' said Arthur, as the two men shook hands.

'Can I offer you a tea or coffee?' asked Buchan once his client was seated.

'No, thank you. I only wanted to check that my bank in Toronto had carried out the transfer, and there hadn't been any problems.'

'None that I'm aware of,' said Buchan. 'In fact, the transfer couldn't have gone more smoothly, thanks to Mr Dunbar, and I'm looking forward to representing you in the future. So can I ask, Mr Macpherson, is there anything you require at the moment?'

'A new credit card and some chequebooks.'

'Can I suggest our gold club card,' said Buchan, 'which has a daily credit limit of one thousand pounds, with no security checks, and I've already put in an order for some new chequebooks, which should be with us by Monday. Would you like me to forward them on to Ambrose Hall?'

'That won't be necessary,' said Arthur, 'as I intend to spend a few days in Edinburgh before I return to Ambrose. So perhaps I can drop in on Monday and pick them up.'

'Then I'll put a foot on the pedal and make sure they're ready for you to collect by then.'

'And my old NBT card?' asked Arthur.

'We'll cancel that when we hand over the new one on Monday. Do you have enough cash to see you through the weekend?'

'More than enough,' said Arthur.

⸺◦⸺

Arthur left the bank and began walking back down Princes Street. What he hadn't told Buchan was that he intended to do some shopping before he headed for Ambrose, and even take in a concert or recital. In fact he dropped into four shops on his way back to the hotel, and purchased three suits, six silk shirts, two pairs of Church's shoes and an overcoat in the sale. Arthur had done more shopping in three hours than he'd previously managed in three years. As he continued down Princes Street, Arthur stopped to look at the painting in the window of Munro's, a Peploe of a bowl of fruit that he much admired. But he already had half a dozen of his own. In any case, he decided it might not be wise to enter the gallery where Mr Macpherson had purchased so many pictures in the past, so he continued on his way back to the hotel.

After a cold shower and a change of clothes, Arthur made his way down to the hotel dining room, where he enjoyed an Aberdeen Angus steak with all the trimmings, and a bottle of red wine he had read about in one of the colour supplements.

By the time he'd signed the bill – he nearly forgot his name – he was ready for a good night's sleep. He was passing Scott's Bar on his way to the lifts when he turned and saw her image in the mirror. She was sitting on a stool at the far end of the bar sipping a glass of champagne. Arthur continued on towards the lifts, and when one opened, he hesitated, turned around and began walking slowly back towards the bar. Could she really have been that attractive? There was only one way he was going to find out. In any case, someone had probably joined her by now.

A second look, and he was even more captivated. She must have been about forty, and the elegant green dress that rested just above her knees only convinced Arthur she couldn't possibly be alone. He strolled up to the bar and took a seat on a stool two places away from her. He ordered a drink, but he didn't have the nerve to even glance in her direction, and certainly wouldn't have considered striking up a conversation.

'Are you here for the conference?' she asked.

Arthur swung round and stared into those green eyes before murmuring, 'What conference?'

'The garden centres annual conference.'

'No,' said Arthur. 'I'm on holiday. But is that why you're here?'

'Yes, I run a small garden centre in Durham. Are you a gardener by any chance?'

Arthur thought about his flat in Toronto where he'd had a window box, and Ambrose Hall, that couldn't have been less than a thousand acres.

'No,' he managed. 'Always lived in a city,' he added, as she drained her champagne. 'Can I get you another?'

'Thank you,' she said, allowing the barman to refill her glass. 'My name's Marianne.'

'I'm Sandy,' he said.

'And what do you do, Sandy?'

'I dabble in stocks and shares,' he replied, taking on the persona of Macpherson. 'And when you said "run", does that mean you're the boss?'

'I wish,' she said, and by the time Marianne's glass had been refilled three times, he'd discovered she was divorced, her husband had run away with a woman half his age, no children, and she had planned to go to the Schubert concert at the Usher Hall that night only to find it was sold out. After another drink, he even found out she didn't consider Brahms to be in the same class as

Beethoven. He was already wondering how far the journey was from Edinburgh to Durham.

'Would you like another drink?' he asked.

'No, thank you,' she replied. 'I ought to be getting to bed if I'm still hoping to make the opening session tomorrow morning.'

'Why don't we go up to my suite? I have a bottle of champagne, and no one to share it with.' Arthur couldn't believe what he'd just said, and assumed she'd get up and leave without another word, and might even slap his face. He was just about to apologize, when Marianne said, 'That sounds fun.' She slipped off her stool, took his hand and said, 'Which floor are you on, Sandy?'

In the past, Arthur had only dreamed of such a night, or read about it in novels by Harold Robbins. After they'd made love a third time, she said, 'I ought to be getting back to my room, Sandy, if I'm not going to fall asleep during the president's address.'

'When does the conference end?' asked Arthur, as he sat up and watched her getting dressed.

'Usually around four.'

'Why don't I try to get a couple of tickets for the Schubert concert, and then we could have dinner afterwards.'

'What a lovely idea,' said Marianne. 'Shall we meet in reception at seven tomorrow evening?' She giggled. 'This evening,' she added, as she bent down and kissed him.

'See you then,' he said, and by the time the door had closed, Arthur had fallen into a deep contented sleep.

-◆-

When Arthur woke the following morning, he couldn't stop thinking about Marianne, and decided to buy her a present and give it to her at dinner that evening. But first he must get two tickets, the best in the house for a show that was obviously sold out, and then ask the desk clerk which he considered was the finest restaurant in Edinburgh.

Arthur had a long shower, and found himself humming the aria from Mendelssohn's *Midsummer Night's Dream*. He continued to hum as he put on a new shirt, new suit and began to think about what sort of present Marianne would appreciate. Mustn't be over the top, but shouldn't leave her in any doubt he considered last night so much more than a one-night stand.

He went to his bedside table to pick up his wallet and watch, but they weren't there. He opened the drawer, and stared at a copy of Gideon's Bible. He quickly checked the table on the other side of the bed, and then the bathroom, and finally his new suit that was strewn on the floor. He sat on the end of the bed for some time, unwilling to accept the truth. He didn't want to believe such a divine creature could be a common thief.

He reluctantly picked up the phone by the side of the bed and dialled Mr Buchan's private number at the Royal Bank of Scotland. He sat there in a daze until he heard a voice he recognized on the other end of the line.

'I'm sorry to bother you,' said Arthur, 'but I've lost my credit card.'

'That's not a problem,' said Buchan. 'Happens all the time. I'll cancel it immediately and your new one will be ready for collection on Monday morning. If you need some cash in the meantime, just pop in and I'll arrange it.'

'No, I've got enough to get me through until Monday,' said Arthur, not wanting to admit that his money had also been stolen.

Arthur went downstairs for breakfast, and wasn't surprised to discover that there was no garden centres conference, and no one called Marianne registered at the hotel. When he left the Caledonian to go for a walk after breakfast, it was back to window shopping and he even spotted the ideal present for Marianne. It didn't help. And when he passed the Usher Hall on the way back, there was already a queue for returns. At least that was true.

It was a long weekend of walks around the ancient city, hotel food and watching B movies in his room that he'd already seen. When he walked past Scott's Bar on Saturday night and saw an attractive young blonde sitting alone, he just kept on walking.

By Monday he'd exhausted the hotel menu as well as the films of the week and just wanted to return to Ambrose Hall and begin his new life. The only surprise was that he still couldn't get Marianne out of his mind.

5

BY THE TIME Arthur had packed his bags on Monday morning, he'd decided the loss of a couple of hundred pounds and a watch he'd never cared for, was a fair exchange for the best night he'd ever had in his life.

He checked his watch. It wasn't there. Arthur smiled for the first time in days. Once he'd seen Buchan, he would take the first train to Ambrose and try to forget the whole incident, but he knew he wouldn't be able to. He was feeling a little better by the time he left the hotel to keep his appointment with Mr Buchan, and when he walked into the bank, his secretary was standing in the hall waiting to greet him. A gesture, he realized, that was only extended to the most important customers.

'I hope you had an enjoyable weekend, Mr Macpherson?' she said, as she accompanied Arthur through to Mr Buchan's office.

'Yes, thank you,' he replied politely, as she opened the door and stepped aside to allow him to enter.

Arthur froze on the spot when he saw Mr Stratton seated on the right of Mr Buchan, with a large burly man he didn't recognize seated on his left.

'Sit down, Dunbar,' said Stratton, as the door closed behind him.

Arthur obeyed the manager's order as if they were back in Toronto, but said nothing.

'It wasn't difficult for me to work out what you've been up to for the past year,' said Stratton, 'and at least we caught up with you before you could do any real damage. We have Chief Inspector Mullins of the Edinburgh city police to thank for that,' he added, revealing who the third person was.

Arthur still didn't speak, although he would have liked to ask the policeman how long his sentence was likely to be, but satisfied himself with, 'How did you find out?'

'The watch,' said Chief Inspector Mullins matter-of-factly. '"To Arthur, from all his colleagues at NBT". Once we'd cracked NBT, the rest was easy. And after she'd described you as a nice gentleman with a mid-Atlantic accent, one call to the bank and Mr Stratton even told us he'd presented you with the Rolex Oyster.'

'And Marianne, how did you catch her?'

'She tried to buy a train ticket to Durham with your credit card, but fortunately Mr Buchan had already cancelled it.'

'And as far as I can tell,' said Stratton, taking over, 'you've only spent two thousand, seven hundred and eighty-two dollars of Mr Macpherson's money. However, that doesn't include the seventy-three thousand, one hundred and forty-one dollars the bank will have to return to Mr Macpherson's private account, following the abortive exchange rate deal.'

'And a further forty-nine thousand, one hundred and twenty-four pounds,' said Buchan, 'that will have to be charged to NBT after converting the four million pounds back into dollars.'

'Mr Buchan has already supplied me with all the share certificates, bonds and other financial instruments which I will be taking back to Toronto later today, and once I return, Mr Macpherson's account will be repaid in full. So with a bit of luck, he will never find out what happened. However,' Stratton continued, 'you have cost the National Bank of Toronto one hundred and twenty-three thousand, four hundred and sixty-eight dollars, not to mention the irreparable damage you might have caused to the bank's reputation had this story ever got out. But, thanks to the cooperation of the Edinburgh police, to whom we will be eternally grateful,' continued Stratton, nodding in the chief inspector's direction, 'if you will agree to cover any costs, they will not press charges.'

'And if I don't?' said Arthur.

'As a senior banking officer, in a position of trust,' said Chief Inspector Mullins, 'you could be looking at six to eight years in a Scottish prison. I would'nae recommend it, laddie,' he paused, 'given the choice.'

Mr Stratton stood up and walked down from the other end of the table and handed over a cheque made out to the bank for $123,468. All it needed was a signature.

'But that would almost clean me out.'

'Perhaps you should have thought about that in the first place,' said Stratton, handing him a pen.

Arthur reluctantly signed the cheque, accepting that the alternative, as Mullins had so subtly pointed out, wasn't that attractive.

Stratton retrieved the cheque and placed it in his wallet. He then turned to the chief inspector and said, 'Like you, we will not be pressing charges.'

Mullins looked disappointed.

Typical Stratton, thought Arthur. Make sure you cover your own backside, and to hell with everyone else. Arthur even wondered if the board would ever be told what had really happened. But Stratton hadn't finished. He picked up a carrier bag from under his chair, and emptied a pile of Canadian dollars onto the table in front of Arthur.

'Your account has been closed,' he said, 'and the bank is no longer willing to do business with you in the future.'

Arthur slowly gathered up the neat cellophane packages, aware that he would even be paying for Stratton's first-class flight back to Toronto. He dropped the money into the carrier bag.

'And what about my watch, Chief Inspector?' said Arthur, turning to face Mullins.

'Mrs Dawson comes up in front of the magistrate at ten o'clock tomorrow morning, so you can collect it any time after that, but not until she's been sentenced.' He smiled at Arthur for the first time.

'I don't suppose you'd be willing to appear as a witness for the Crown?' he said, raising an eyebrow.

Arthur smiled back. 'You suppose correctly, Chief Inspector. I wouldn't, even if you'd made it a condition.'

Mullins frowned as Arthur rose from his place, and quietly left the room; no smiles, no handshakes, and certainly no one accompanied him to the front door. He left the bank in a daze and began to make his way slowly back to the hotel, not certain what to do next.

He'd only gone about a hundred yards along Princes Street, when he spotted a sign on a window in neat black letters, Henderson & Henderson, Attorneys at Law.

6

WHEN THE DEFENDANT took her place in the dock, she looked tired and vulnerable.

A court officer rose and read out the charges. 'Marianne Dawson, you come before the court on three charges. One: that you stole a credit card from a Mr Macpherson, and attempted to use it to purchase a rail ticket to Durham. How do you plead to this charge, guilty or not guilty?'

'Guilty,' said the defendant, almost in a whisper.

'The second charge,' continued the officer, 'is that you did steal a sum of around two hundred pounds from the said Mr Macpherson. How do you plead, guilty or not guilty?'

'Guilty,' she repeated.

'And the third count is that you did steal a Rolex Oyster watch also from the same gentleman. How do you plead, guilty or not guilty?'

Marianne looked up and facing the magistrate said quietly, 'Guilty.'

The chairman of the magistrates stared down into the well of the court and asked, 'Is the defendant represented?'

A tall, distinguished-looking man, dressed in a pinstriped suit, white shirt and black tie, rose from the bench and said, 'I have the privilege of representing Mrs Dawson.'

The Justice of the Peace was surprised to find one of Edinburgh's leading advocates appearing before him on such a minor case.

'Mr Henderson, as your client has pleaded guilty to all three charges, I presume you will be offering a plea in mitigation?'

'I most certainly will, sir,' he said, tugging the lapels of his jacket. 'I would like to start by bringing to the attention of the court that Mrs Dawson has recently experienced a most acrimonious divorce, and despite the family division awarding her maintenance payments, her husband has made no attempt to fulfil his responsibility, even after a court order was issued against him. Until recently,' continued Mr Henderson, 'Mrs Dawson held a senior management position at the Durham Garden Centre, until it was taken over by Scotsdales, and she was made redundant. I feel sure the Bench will also take into consideration that this is a first offence, other than a parking fine some four years ago. However, Mrs Dawson is not only extremely remorseful, but determined to pay Mr Macpherson back every penny she owes him, just as soon as she can find a job. I would finally like to point out that until today, Mrs Dawson enjoyed an unblemished reputation as an upright citizen, which I hope the Bench will take into consideration before passing sentence.'

'I am grateful to you, Mr Henderson,' said the justice. 'Please allow me a few moments to consult with my colleagues.'

Henderson bowed, as the chairman and his two colleagues discussed the case among themselves, before coming to an agreement.

The chairman turned back to face the defendant.

'Mrs Dawson,' he began, 'despite learned counsel's moving plea in mitigation, someone in your position must have been well aware they were breaking the law.' Marianne bowed her head. 'So I am left with no choice but to sentence you to six months in prison, which will be suspended for two years. However, should you appear before me again, I will not hesitate to issue you with a custodial sentence. But on this occasion, I shall order you to pay a fine of two hundred pounds.' He switched his attention back to Mr Henderson, and asked, 'Is the defendant able to pay this sum?'

Mr Henderson turned round and looked towards the back of the courtroom where his client was seated. Arthur nodded.

7

ARTHUR TOOK a piece of headed paper from the letter rack on his desk and placed it in the typewriter.

Dear Mr Stratton,

Thank you for your most recent letter, and the three new chequebooks that arrived this morning.

May I begin by placing on record how much I appreciate the years of dedicated service Mr Arthur Dunbar carried out on my behalf, and would you be kind enough to pass on my best wishes to him and the hope he will have a long and happy retirement.

I have checked my latest accounts which appear to be in order. However, I will be writing to you at the end of the quarter concerning some future investments I am presently considering.

I should also like you to know that I have recently married, so you may find a new pattern will emerge in some of my transactions. My wife and I intend to travel abroad occasionally, to visit the great concert halls and opera houses of Europe. While we're away, Mr and Mrs Laidlaw will continue to run Ambrose Hall, so you can expect the usual bills for household expenses in addition to their monthly salaries.

May I also add . . .

There was a knock at the door, and Arthur stopped typing. 'Come in.'

Morag popped her head round the door and said, 'I just wondered what you and Mrs Macpherson would like for lunch? I still have some of that game pie you're rather partial to.'

'Perfect,' said Arthur, 'but not too much. Mrs Macpherson has already chastised me for putting on weight.'

'And Mrs Macpherson also asked me to remind you that you're going into Edinburgh this evening for some concert.'

'Not some concert, Morag, Beethoven's Third at the Usher Hall.'

'Will there be anything else, sir?'

'Yes, I'm just finishing off a letter to Mr Stratton, so could you ask Hamish to come up? I'd like him to drive into the village and post it.'

'Of course, sir.'

Arthur returned to the letter.

May I also add how delighted I was to learn that you will personally be supervising my account in the future. It gives me succour to know that my affairs will be in such safe hands.

Yours sincerely

There was a knock on the door and Laidlaw walked in. 'You asked to see me, sir?'

'Yes, Hamish. Just a signature.'

A GOOD TOSS TO LOSE

MR GRUBER handed back the boys' essays before returning to his desk at the front of the class.

'Not a bad effort,' the young schoolmaster said, 'except for Jackson, who clearly doesn't believe Goethe is worthy of his attention. And as this is a voluntary class, I'm bound to ask, Jackson, why you bothered to enrol?'

'It was my father's idea,' admitted Jackson. 'He thought there might come a time when it would be useful to speak a little German.'

'How little did he have in mind?' asked the schoolmaster.

Jackson's friend Brooke, who was seated at the desk next to him, whispered loudly enough for everyone in the class to hear, 'Why don't you tell him the truth, Oliver?'

'The truth?' repeated Gruber.

'My father is convinced, sir, that it won't be too long before we are at war with Germany.'

'And why should he think that, may I ask? When Europe has never been at peace for such a long period of time.'

'I accept that, sir, but Pa works at the Foreign Office. Says the Kaiser is a warmonger, and given the slightest opportunity will invade Belgium.'

'But, remembering your treaty obligations,' said Gruber as he walked between the desks, 'that would also drag Britain and France into the conflict.' The schoolmaster paused for thought. 'So the real reason you want to learn German,' he continued, attempting to lighten the exchange, 'is so you can have a chat with the Kaiser when he comes marching down Whitehall.'

'No, I don't believe that's what Pa had in mind, sir. I think he felt that once the Kaiser had been sent packing, if I could speak a little German, I might be in line to be a regional governor.'

The whole class burst out laughing, and began to applaud.

'We must hope for the sake of your countrymen as well as mine, Jackson, that it's a very long line.'

'If Kaiser Bill were to wage war, sir,' said Brooke, sounding more serious, 'would you have to return to your country?'

'I pray that will never happen, Brooke,' said Gruber. 'I look upon England as my second home. Europe is at peace at the moment, so we must hope Jackson's father is wrong. Nothing would be gained from such a pointless act of folly other than to set the world back a hundred years. Let us be thankful that King George V and Kaiser Wilhelm are cousins.'

'I've never cared much for my cousin,' said Jackson.

-◦-

'Have you heard the news?' said Brooke, as he and Jackson strolled across to the refectory a few weeks later.

'What news?' said Jackson.

'Mr Gruber will be returning to Germany within a fortnight.'

'Why?' said Jackson.

'It seems the headmaster thought it wise given the circumstances.'

'I'm sorry to hear that,' said Jackson as they sat down on a wooden bench and waited to be served lunch.

'But I thought you didn't like having to study German,' said Brooke, as he attempted to spear a soggy carrot with his fork.

'And I still don't. But that doesn't mean I don't like Mr Gruber. In fact he's always struck me as a thoroughly decent fellow. Not at all the sort of chap one would want to go to war with.'

'We might even be at war with him in a few months' time,' said Brooke, 'and if you're still thinking of making the army your career, you could find yourself on the front line.'

'I don't think you'll be exempt from that privilege, Rupert,' said Oliver, swamping his food with gravy, 'just because you're going up to Cambridge to swan around writing poetry.'

'Which reminds me,' said Brooke. 'My mother wondered if you'd like to join us in Grantchester for a couple of weeks this summer. And I can promise you some rather interesting gals will be joining us.'

'Can't think of anything better, old chap. That's assuming Kaiser Bill hasn't got other plans for us.'

◄○►

Oliver Jackson did spend a couple of carefree weeks with his friend, Rupert Brooke, that summer, before they parted and went their separate ways. Brooke to read Classics at King's, while Jackson reported to the Royal Military Academy at Sandhurst, to accept the king's shilling and spend the next two years being trained as an officer in the British Army.

‑◄о►‑

In October 1913, Second Lieutenant Jackson of the Lancashire Fusiliers reported to his regiment's depot in Chester, where he quickly discovered that talk of war with Germany was no longer confined to the Foreign Office, but was now on everyone's lips. However, no one could be sure what would light the fuse.

When Kaiser Wilhelm's close friend and ally, the Archduke Franz Ferdinand of Austria, was assassinated in Sarajevo, the German emperor had at last found the excuse he needed for his troops to invade Belgium, giving him the chance to expand his empire.

The only good thing that had happened while Oliver was serving his tour of duty in Chester was that he fell in love with a Miss Rosemary Carter, the daughter of one of his father's colleagues at the Foreign Office. In the fathers' eyes, the marriage was no more than an *entente cordiale*, whereas both mothers quickly realized that this particular treaty had never required Foreign Office approval.

One of the many things Kaiser Bill did to irritate Oliver was to declare war while he and Rosemary were still on their honeymoon. Lieutenant Jackson received a telegram delivered to his Deauville hotel ordering him to report back to his regiment immediately.

‑◄о►‑

A few weeks later the Lancashire Fusiliers were among the first to be shipped out to France, where Oliver quickly discovered that it was possible to live in far worse conditions and force down even more disgusting grub than he'd been made to endure at Rugby.

He settled down in a trench where rats were his constant companions, three inches of muddy water his pillow, and slowly learnt to sleep despite the sound of gunfire.

'It will be over by Christmas,' was the optimistic cry being passed down the line.

'But which Christmas?' asked a bus driver from Romford as he forked a billycan of corned beef and baked beans, while refilling his mug with rainwater.

In fact the only present the young subaltern got that Christmas was a third pip to be sewn next to the other two already on his shoulder, and then only after he replaced a brother officer who had not made it into 1915.

Captain Jackson had already been over the top three times by the winter of 1916, and didn't need reminding that the average survival period for a soldier on the front line was nineteen days; he was now in his third year. But at least they were allowing him to return home for a three-week furlough. What old soldiers referred to as a 'stay of execution'.

Jackson returned to the Marne after spending an idyllic carefree break with Rosemary in their country cottage at Crathorne. He was grateful to find that even his father was beginning to believe the war couldn't last much longer. Oliver prayed that he was right.

On arriving back at the front, Jackson immediately reported to his commanding officer.

'We are expecting to mount another attack on Jerry in a few days' time,' said Colonel Harding. 'So be sure your men are prepared.'

Prepared for what?, thought Oliver. Almost certain death, and not quick like the hangman's noose, but probably prolonged, in desperate agony. But he didn't voice his opinion.

Once he was back in the trenches, Oliver quickly tried to get to know the young impressionable men who'd just arrived at the front line, and hadn't yet heard a shot fired in anger. He couldn't think of them as soldiers, just keen young lads who had responded to a poster of a moustachioed old man pointing a finger at them and declaring YOUR COUNTRY NEEDS YOU.

'Once you go over the top, you need only remember one thing,' Oliver instructed them. 'If you don't kill them, as sure as hell they'll kill you. Think of it like a football match against your most bitter rivals. You've got to score every time you shoot.'

'But whose side is the ref on?' demanded a young, frightened voice.

Oliver didn't reply, because he no longer believed God was the referee and that therefore they must surely win.

◄◦►

The colonel joined them just before the kick-off and blew a whistle to show the match could begin. Captain Jackson was first over the top, leading his company, who followed closely behind. On, on, on, he charged as his men fell like fairground soldiers beside him, the lucky ones dying quickly. He kept going, and was beginning to wonder if he was out there on his own, and then suddenly, without warning, he saw a lone figure running through the whirling smoke towards him. Like Oliver, the man had his bayonet fixed, ready for the kill. Oliver accepted that it would not be possible for both of them to survive, and probably neither would. He held his rifle steady, like a medieval jouster, determined to fell his opponent. He was prepared to thrust his bayonet, not this time into a horsehair bag while training, but into a petrified human being, but no more petrified than he was.

Don't strike until you see can the whites of his eyes, his training sergeant had drilled into him at Sandhurst. You can't be a moment too early, or a moment too late. Another oft-repeated maxim. But when he saw the whites of his eyes, he couldn't do it. He lowered his rifle, expecting to die, but to his surprise the German also dropped his rifle as they both came to a halt in the middle of no-man's-land.

For some time they just stared at each other in disbelief. But it was Oliver who burst out laughing, if only to release his pent-up tension.

'What are you doing here, Jackson?'

'I might ask you the same question, sir.'

'Carrying out someone else's orders,' said Gruber.

'Me too.'

'But you're a professional soldier.'

'Death doesn't discriminate in these matters,' said Oliver. 'I often recall your shrewd opinion of war, sir, and looking around the battlefield can only wonder how much talent has been squandered here.'

'On both sides,' said Gruber. 'But it gives me no pleasure to have been proved right.'

'So what shall we do now, sir? We can't just stand around philosophizing until peace is declared.'

'But equally, if we were to return meekly to our own side, we would probably be arrested, court-martialled and shot at dawn.'

'Then one of us will have to take the other prisoner,' said Jackson, 'and return in triumph.'

'Not a bad idea. But how shall we decide?' asked Gruber.

'The toss of a coin?'

'How very British,' declared Gruber. 'Just a pity the whole war couldn't have been decided that way,' added the schoolmaster as he took a Goldmark out of his pocket. 'You call, Jackson,' he said. 'After all, you're the visiting team.'

Oliver watched as the coin spun high into the air and cried, 'Tails,' only because he couldn't bear the thought of the Kaiser's image staring up at him in triumph.

Gruber groaned as he bent down to look at the eagle. Oliver quickly took off his tie, bound the prisoner's wrists behind his back, and then began to march his old schoolmaster slowly back towards his own front line.

'What happened to Brooke?' asked Gruber as they squelched through the mud while stepping over the bodies of fallen men.

'He was attached to the Royal Naval Division when he last wrote to me.'

'I read his poem about Grantchester. Even attempted to translate it.'

'"The Old Vicarage",' said Jackson.

'That's the one. Ironic that he wrote it while he was on a visit to Berlin. Such a rare talent. Let's hope he survives this dreadful war,' Gruber said as the sun dipped below the horizon.

'Are you married, sir?' asked Oliver.

'Yes. Renate. And we have a son and two daughters. And you?'

'Rosemary. Just got married when the balloon went up.'

'Bad luck, old chap,' said Gruber, before taking his former pupil by surprise. 'I don't suppose you'd consider being a godfather to my youngest, Hans? You see, I consider it no more than my duty once the war is over to make sure this madness can never happen again.'

'I agree with you, Ernst, and I'd be honoured. And perhaps in time . . .'

'May I suggest, Oliver, for both our sakes,' said Gruber as the British front line came into sight, 'that when you hand me over, you don't make it too obvious we're old friends.'

'Good thinking, Ernst,' said Oliver, and grabbed his prisoner roughly by the elbow.

The next voice they heard demanded, 'Who goes there?'

'Captain Jackson, Lancashire Fusiliers, with a German prisoner.'

'Advance and be recognized.' Oliver pushed his old schoolmaster forward. 'Bloody good show,' said the lookout sergeant. 'You can leave him to me, sir. And you can keep moving, you fucking Kraut.'

'Sergeant,' said Oliver sharply, 'try to remember he's an officer.'

◄o►

The war was over by Christmas. Christmas 1918.

Captain Ernst Gruber spent two years in a prisoner-of-war camp on Anglesey. He passed the mornings teaching his fellow prisoners the local tongue as there might come a time when it would prove useful to speak a little English, he suggested, echoing Jackson's words.

Oliver sent Gruber the collected works of Rupert Brooke, which he translated in the evenings while he waited for the war to end.

Ernst Gruber was shipped back to Frankfurt in November 1919, and within days he wrote to Oliver to ask if he was still willing to be a godfather to his son Hans. It was several weeks before he received a reply from Oliver's wife Rosemary, to say that her husband had been killed on the Western Front only days before the Armistice was signed. They also had a son, Arthur Oliver, and on her husband's last furlough he'd told her that he hoped Ernst would agree to be one of Arthur's godparents.

With the assistance of Oliver's father, Herr Gruber was allowed to visit England to fulfil his role in the christening ceremony. As Ernst stood by the font alongside Oliver's family, he couldn't help wondering what would have happened if he had won the toss.

POSTSCRIPT

19 September 1943
LIEUTENANT HANS OTTO GRUBER was blown up by
a landmine while serving on the Western Front. He died
three days later.

6 June 1944
CAPTAIN ARTHUR OLIVER JACKSON MC was killed
while leading his platoon on the beaches of Normandy.

15 November 1944
PROFESSOR ERNST HELMUT GRUBER was executed
by firing squad in Berlin for the role he played in the failed
attempt to assassinate Adolf Hitler at Wolf's Lair.

May They Rest in Peace

WHO KILLED THE MAYOR?

CORTOGLIA IS a delightfully picturesque town in the heart of Campania. It rests high on a hill, forty miles north of Naples, with commanding views towards Monte Taburno to the east, and Vesuvius to the south. It is described in *Fodor's Italy* quite simply as 'heaven on earth'.

The population of the town is 1,463, and hasn't varied greatly for over a century. The town's income is derived from three main sources: wine, olive oil and truffles. The Cortoglia White, aromatic with a vibrant acidity, is one of the most sought-after wines on earth and, because its production is limited, is sold out long before it's bottled. And as for the olive oil, the only reason you never see a bottle on the shelves of your local supermarket is because many of the leading Michelin-starred restaurants won't consider allowing any other brand on their premises.

The bonus, which allows the locals to enjoy a standard of living envied by their neighbours, is their truffles. Restaurateurs travel from all four corners of the globe in search of the Cortoglia truffle, which is then only offered to their most discerning customers.

It is true that some people have been known to leave Cortoglia and seek their fortunes further afield, but the more sensible among them return fairly quickly. But then, life expectancy in the medieval hill town is eighty-six years for men and ninety-one for women, eight years above the national average.

In the centre of the main square is a statue of Garibaldi, now more famous for biscuits than battles, and the town boasts only half a dozen shops and a restaurant. The council wouldn't sanction any more for fear it might attract tourists. There is no train service, and a bus appears in the town once a week for those foolish enough to wish to travel to Naples. A few of the residents own cars, but have little use for them.

The town is run by the Consiglio Comunale, made up of six elders. The most junior member, whose lineage only goes back three generations, is not considered by all to be a local. The mayor, Salvatore Farinelli, his son Lorenzo Farinelli, chairman (ex officio), Mario Pellegrino, the manager of the olive oil company, Paolo Carrafini, the owner of the winery, and Pietro De Rosa, the truffle master, are all automatically members of the council, while the one remaining place comes up for election every five years. As no one had stood against Umberto Cattaneo, the butcher, for the past fifteen years, the voters had almost forgotten how to conduct an election.

The Polizia Locale had consisted of a single officer, Luca Gentile, whose authority derived from the city of Naples, and Luca tried not to disturb them unnecessarily. This story concerns the one occasion when it was necessary.

-◦-

No one in the village could be certain where Dino Lombardi had come from but, like a black cloud, he appeared overnight, and was clearly more interested in thunderstorms than showers. Lombardi must have been around one metre ninety-three, with the build of a heavyweight boxer who didn't expect his bouts to last for more than a couple of rounds.

He began his reign of terror with the weaker inhabitants of the town, the shopkeepers, the local tradesmen and the restaurateur, whom he persuaded needed protection, even if they couldn't be sure from whom, as there hadn't been a serious crime in Cortoglia in living memory. Even the Germans hadn't bothered to climb that particular hill.

To be fair, Constable Gentile was due to retire in a few months' time, at the age of sixty-five, and the council hadn't got round to finding his replacement. But a further problem arose when the mayor, Salvatore Farinelli, died at the age of 102, and an election had to be held to replace him.

It was assumed that his son Lorenzo would succeed him. Mario Pellegrino would then become chairman of the council, and everyone else would move up a place, with the one vacancy being filled by Gian Lucio Altana, the local restaurateur. That was until Lombardi turned up at the town hall, and entered his name on the list for mayor. Of course, no one doubted Lorenzo Farinelli would win by a landslide, so it came as something of a surprise when the town clerk, on crutches, his left leg in plaster, announced from the steps of the Palazzo dei Municipio that Lombardi had polled 511 votes, to Farinelli's 486. On hearing the result, there was a gasp of disbelief from the crowd, not least because no one knew anyone who had voted for Lombardi.

Lombardi immediately took over the town hall, occupied the mayor's residence, and dismissed the council. He'd only been in office for a few days when the citizens were informed he would be imposing a sales tax on all three of the town's main companies, which was later extended to the shopkeepers and restaurateur. And if that wasn't enough, he began to demand a kickback from the buyers as well as the sellers.

Within a year, heaven on earth had been turned into hell on earth, with the mayor quite happy to be cast in the role of Beelzebub. So, frankly, it didn't come as a surprise to anyone when Lombardi was murdered.

Constable Gentile told the chairman of the council that as murder was out of his league, he would have to inform the authorities in Naples. He admitted in his report that there were 1,462 suspects, and he had absolutely no idea who had committed the crime.

Naples, a city that knows a thing or two about murder, sent one of its brightest young detectives to investigate the crime, arrest the culprit and bring them back to the city to stand trial.

Antonio Rossetti, who at the tender age of thirty-two had recently been promoted to lieutenant, was assigned to the case, although he considered it an inconvenience that would take him out of the front line – but surely not for long. He was already aware of Lombardi's past criminal record; extortion, bribery and corruption were but a few of his crimes, so the citizens of Cortoglia would be among

WHO KILLED THE MAYOR?

many who wouldn't mourn him. He had assured the chief of police that he would wrap up the case as quickly as possible, and return to Naples so he could deal with some real criminals.

However, it didn't help that Luca Gentile had disappeared even before Lieutenant Rossetti had set foot in Cortoglia. Some suggested Gentile was suffering from the strain of the whole affair, as the last murder in the town had been in 1846, when his great-great-great-grandfather had been the town's constable. But where had he disappeared to, and why, because Gentile was the only other person who knew how the mayor had been killed.

Rossetti was appalled to discover Lombardi had been cremated, and his ashes scattered on the far side of Mount Taburno within hours of his death, such was the locals' hatred of the man.

'So you, Gentile and the coroner are the only people who know how the murder was committed,' said the chief as he handed over the results of the autopsy to his lieutenant.

'And the murderer,' Rossetti reminded him.

-◦-

Lieutenant Antonio Rossetti arrived in Cortoglia later that morning, to be told that the council had decreed he should reside in the mayor's home until the murderer had been apprehended.

'After all,' the chairman said, 'let's get this over with so the young man can return to Naples as quickly as possible and leave us in peace.'

Antonio set up office in the local police station, which

consisted of one small room, one unoccupied cell and a lavatory. He took the relevant case files out of his bag and placed them on the desk. He looked at the large, empty board on the wall and pinned a photograph of Lombardi in the centre.

He then decided to leave his office and roam around the town, in the hope that someone might approach him, wanting to supply information. But even though he walked slowly, and smiled a lot, people crossed the road when they saw him as if he had some contagious disease. He was clearly not looked upon as the Good Samaritan.

After a fruitless morning, Antonio returned to his office and made a list of those people who had most to gain from Lombardi's death and came to the reluctant conclusion that he would have to start with the members of the Consiglio Comunale. He wrote Wine, Olive Oil and Truffles on his notepad and took the photographs of the five councillors from the case file, and pinned them around Lombardi's photograph. Rossetti decided to start with Truffles. He called at Signor De Rosa's office to make an appointment with the councillor at his shop later that afternoon.

◂◦▸

'Would you care for a glass of wine, Lieutenant?' said De Rosa, before the policeman had even sat down. 'The Cortoglia White is favoured by connoisseurs and 1947 was considered a vintage year.'

'No, thank you, sir. Not while I'm on duty.'

'Quite right,' said De Rosa. 'But forgive me if I do, as it may be my last for some time.' Rossetti looked surprised but didn't comment. De Rosa took a sip. 'So how can I help you?'

The policeman opened his notepad, and looked down at his prepared questions. 'As your family have lived in Cortoglia for over two hundred years—'

'Over three hundred years,' corrected the truffle master with a smile.

'I was rather hoping you might be able to shed some light on who killed Dino Lombardi?' continued Antonio.

De Rosa emptied his glass with a large gulp before saying, 'I most certainly can. You need look no further, Lieutenant, because I killed Lombardi.'

Antonio was taken by surprise but delighted to have a confession on his first day. He was already thinking about returning to Naples in triumph, and getting back to locking up some serious criminals.

'Are you willing to accompany me to the station and sign a written statement to that effect, Signor De Rosa?'

De Rosa nodded. 'Whenever it suits you.'

'You do realize, Signor De Rosa, that if you confess to the murder, I will have no choice but to arrest you, and take you to Naples, where you will stand trial, and could spend the rest of your life in the prison at Poggioreale?'

'I have thought of little else since the day I murdered the bastard. But I can't complain, I've had a good life.'

'Why did you kill Lombardi?' asked Antonio, who accepted that motive invariably accounted for any crime.

De Rosa filled his glass a second time. 'Dino Lombardi was an evil and ruthless man, Lieutenant, who preyed on everyone he came into contact with.' He paused and took a sip of his wine, before adding, 'He made their lives unbearable, mine included.'

'What do you mean by evil and ruthless, signor?'

'He intimidated the shopkeepers and the local trades-men, and even brought Gian Lucio, our local restaurateur, to his knees.'

Antonio kept on writing. 'How did he manage that?'

'He demanded protection money, even though he never made it clear who he was protecting us from as there hasn't been a serious crime in Cortoglia in living memory. And when he became mayor – a mystery in itself – he introduced a sales tax on all of our goods. If he had been allowed to continue for much longer, he would have put us all out of business. Last year my little company made a loss for the first time in three hundred years. So I took it upon myself to rid my fellow citizens of the fiend.' He put down his wine glass and smiled. 'I hear the council are planning to build a statue of me in the town square.'

'I only have one more question,' the detective said, looking up from his notebook. 'How did you kill Lom-bardi?'

'I stabbed him with my truffle knife,' said De Rosa without hesitation. 'It seemed appropriate at the time.'

'How many times did you stab him?'

'Six or seven,' he said, picking up a knife from his desk and giving a demonstration.

Antonio stopped writing and closed his notebook. 'I feel sure you know, Signor De Rosa, that it's a serious crime to waste police time.'

'Of course I do, Lieutenant,' said De Rosa, 'but now I

have confessed, you can arrest me, drag me off to Naples and throw me in jail.'

'Which I would be only too happy to do, signor,' said Antonio, 'if only Lombardi had been stabbed.'

The truffle master shrugged his shoulders. 'But how can you possibly know how he died when he has been cremated?'

'Because I have read the autopsy report,' said Antonio, 'so I know exactly how he was killed. What I don't know is who murdered him, but it certainly wasn't you.'

'Does it really matter?' said De Rosa. 'Just tell me how Lombardi was killed and I'll confess to the crime.'

This was the first time Antonio had ever known someone admit to a crime they hadn't committed.

'I'm going to leave, signor, before you get yourself into even more trouble.'

The truffle master looked disappointed.

Antonio closed his notepad, stood up, walked out of De Rosa's shop and back into the square without another word.

He tried not to laugh as he passed a pen full of the most contented pigs he'd ever seen, almost as if they knew they would never be slaughtered. He was on his way back to the police station when he spotted a pharmacy on the other side of the square, and remembered he needed a bar of soap and some toothpaste. A little bell above the door rang as he stepped inside. He stood by the counter for a few moments, before a young woman came through from the dispensary and said, 'Good morning, Signor Rossetti, how can I help you?'

Hardened criminals from the back streets of Naples

couldn't silence Antonio Rossetti, but a chemist from Cortoglia managed it with one sentence. She waited patiently for her customer to respond.

'I need a bar of soap,' he eventually managed.

'You'll find a good selection behind you on the third shelf down, Lieutenant.'

'Is it that obvious that I'm a policeman?' said Antonio.

'When you're the only person in town that nobody knows, everyone knows you,' she said.

Antonio selected a bar of soap but ignored the toothpaste, because he wanted an excuse to return as soon as possible. He placed the soap on the counter and tried not to stare at her.

'Will there be anything else, signor?'

'No, thank you.' Antonio picked up the bar of soap and headed for the door.

'Were you considering paying or don't the police in Naples bother with anything quite so mundane?' she asked, suppressing a smile.

'I'm so sorry,' said Antonio, quickly placing a note on the counter.

'Do call again if there is anything else I can help you with,' she said, passing him a small bag and his change.

'There is just one thing. You don't, by any chance, happen to know who killed the mayor?'

'I thought Signor De Rosa had already confessed to murdering Lombardi? I assumed by now you would have arrested him and locked him up.'

Antonio frowned, left the shop without another word and made his way back to the police station. He sat at his desk and began to write a report on his abortive meeting with De Rosa, but found it hard to concentrate. Once he'd completed it, he returned to the photographs on the board and put a large black cross through De Rosa.

Antonio decided he would have to pay a visit to Mario Pellegrino, the owner of the olive oil shop, next, but this time he wouldn't call to warn him.

◄○►

Rossetti left the police station just after breakfast the following morning, and set out for the olive oil shop in the square, pleased he would have to pass the pharmacy on his way. He slowed down as he approached the shop and glanced through the window. She was standing by the door, turning the closed sign to open, and looked up as he passed by. They exchanged a glance before he hurried on.

When Antonio arrived at the olive oil shop, Mario Pellegrino was waiting for him at the door.

'Good morning, Lieutenant,' he said, 'have you come to purchase a bottle of the finest olive oil on earth or is this a police raid?'

'I'm sorry I didn't call and make an appointment, Signor Pellegrino, but—' Antonio said as he followed him into the shop.

'You were hoping to take me by surprise,' said Pellegrino, 'but I have to tell you, Lieutenant, I am not at all surprised.'

'You were expecting me?' said Antonio as he stood beside the counter and took out his notepad and pen.

'Yes, everyone knows you've been sent from Naples to investigate the death of Lombardi, and I assumed I would be among the first people you would want to question.'

'But why you in particular, signor?'

'It's no secret that I detested the man. So if you were going to arrest me, the last thing you'd do is to call up and make an appointment, because that would give me enough time to escape.'

Antonio put down his pen. 'But why would you want to escape, Signor Pellegrino?'

'Because everyone knows I killed Lombardi, and I realized that it wouldn't take too long for a smart young detective like you to work out who the murderer was.'

'But why would you want to kill the mayor?' asked Antonio.

'He was ruining my business with his protection racket and added taxes. And if that wasn't enough, he was demanding kickbacks from my buyers, some of whom began to avoid the journey to Cortoglia as they feared they might be next. Another year and I would have had nothing to leave the children. I'm only thankful that my son Roberto is ready to take over the business while I'm locked up in prison.' Pellegrino stood up and stretched his arms across the counter as if expecting to be hand-cuffed.

'Before I arrest you, Signor Pellegrino,' said the police-man, 'I will need to know how you killed the mayor.'

Pellegrino didn't hesitate. 'I strangled the damn man,' he said.

'With what?'

This time he did hesitate. 'Does it matter?'

'No, not really—' said Antonio.

'Good, then let's get on with it,' Pellegrino said, once again stretching his arms across the counter.

'Just one minor problem,' Antonio continued. 'I'm afraid Lombardi wasn't strangled by you, or anyone else for that matter.'

'But as he was cremated, how can you be so sure?'

'Because, unlike you, I've studied the police report, and can assure you, Signor Pellegrino, that wasn't the way that Lombardi died.'

'What a pity. But as I would have liked to have strangled the man, can't you just charge me with attempted murder, and that will solve all our problems?'

'Except for the problem that the culprit will still be on the loose,' said Antonio. 'So if you'd be kind enough to advise your friends that I intend to catch the real murderer and put him behind bars, I'd be very grateful,' he added, as he slammed his notebook closed.

As Antonio turned to leave, he spotted a photograph behind the counter. Pellegrino smiled. 'My daughter's wedding,' he announced with pride. 'She married the son of my dear friend, Signor De Rosa. Oil and water may not mix, Lieutenant, but olive oil and truffles certainly do.' He laughed at a joke Antonio presumed he'd made many times before.

'And the chief bridesmaid?' said Antonio, pointing to a young woman who was standing behind the bride.

'Francesca Farinelli, the mayor's daughter. Lorenzo and I had assumed she would marry my second son, Bruno, but it was not to be.'

'Why not?' said Antonio. 'Wasn't there enough olive oil left over?'

'More than enough. But modern Italian women seem

to have minds of their own. I blame her father. He should never have let her go to university. It's not natural.'

Antonio would have laughed, but he suspected the old man meant it.

'I wonder if I might ask you for a small favour,' Pellegrino said, holding up a large bottle of olive oil.

'If it's in my power, signor, I'd be only too happy to do so.'

'I just wondered if you could let me know how the mayor was killed.'

The policeman ignored the offering and quickly left the shop.

◄◦►

Rossetti was on his way back to the police station to write up another abortive report but hesitated when he reached the pharmacy. He entered and found Francesca standing behind the counter, chatting to a customer.

'That should ease the pain, signora, but make sure that you only take one pill a day before going to bed. And if it doesn't get any better, come back and see me,' she said. Francesca turned to face Rossetti. 'Is it my turn to be arrested, Lieutenant?'

'No, something far simpler than that. I've run out of toothpaste.'

'You know, we do have customers who buy soap, toothpaste and razor blades all at the same time, or is this nothing more than subtle police tactics to wear the suspect down and make her admit she killed the mayor?'

Antonio laughed.

'However,' Francesca continued, 'if your plan was

simply to ask me out for a drink after I get off work this evening, I might just say yes.'

'Was it that obvious?' Antonio asked.

'Why don't we meet at Lucio's around six?'

'I'll look forward to it,' said Antonio as he turned to leave.

'Don't forget your toothpaste, Lieutenant.'

─◦─

When Antonio turned up at the police station, there was a large, burly man wearing a long white coat and a blue-and-white striped apron waiting for him outside the front door.

'Good morning, Inspector. My name is Umberto Cattaneo.'

'Lieutenant, Signor Cattaneo,' corrected Antonio.

'I feel confident, Lieutenant, that promotion will not be far away when you hear what I have to tell you.'

'Please don't tell me you killed the mayor?'

'Certainly not,' said the butcher as he lowered his voice. 'However, I can tell you who did kill Lombardi.'

At last, an informer, thought Antonio. He unlocked the door to the station and led Cattaneo through to his little office.

'But before I let you know who the murderer is,' continued Cattaneo as he sat down, 'I need to be sure that it won't be traced back to me.'

'You have my word on that,' said Antonio, opening his notepad. 'That's assuming we won't need you to act as a witness when the case comes to trial.'

'You won't need a witness,' said Cattaneo, 'because I can tell you where the gun is buried.'

Antonio snapped his notepad shut, and let out a deep sigh.

'But I haven't even told you who the murderer is,' Cattaneo protested.

'You needn't bother, Signor Cattaneo, because Lombardi wasn't shot.'

'But Gian Lucio told me he'd shot him. He even showed me the weapon,' insisted Cattaneo.

'Before I lock you both up for a couple of days, if for no other reason than to stop any more of you wasting my time, may I ask why you are so willing to get your friend arrested for a crime I can assure you he didn't commit?'

'Gian Lucio Altana is my oldest and dearest friend,' protested the butcher.

'Then why accuse him of murder?'

'Because I lost the toss,' said Cattaneo.

'You lost the toss?'

'Yes, we agreed that whoever won would give himself up and admit that he'd killed the mayor.'

'Then why hasn't he given himself up?' said Antonio, unable to hide his frustration.

'Signor De Rosa advised us against that. Said there had been far too many confessions already, and he felt Gian Lucio would have a better chance of being arrested if you thought I was an informer.'

'Just out of interest, Signor Cattaneo,' said Antonio, 'if you had won the toss, dare I ask how you would have killed the mayor?'

'I would have shot him as well, but unfortunately we only have one gun between us, so I had to bury the weapon in his garden, where you can still find it.'

'Again, just so that I understand his motive, may I ask why Gian Lucio was so willing to be charged with a murder that he didn't commit?'

'Oh, that's easy to explain, Lieutenant. Lombardi used to eat at Gian Lucio's restaurant three times a day and he never once paid the bill.'

'That's hardly a good enough reason to kill someone.'

'It is when you lose all your regular customers because none of them want to eat in the same restaurant as the mayor.'

'But that doesn't explain why you wanted to kill him.'

'Gian Lucio is my best customer, and he could no longer afford my finest cuts, so it wouldn't have been much longer before we were both out of business. By the way, Lieutenant, was Lombardi electrocuted by any chance?'

'Get out of here, Signor Cattaneo, before I get myself arrested for murder.'

Not a totally wasted morning, considered Antonio, because he was now confident only he, Constable Gentile and the murderer had any idea how Lombardi had been killed. But where was Gentile?

‒◦‒

Antonio arrived at Lucio's just before 6 p.m., looking forward to seeing Francesca. He sat at an outside table and placed a bunch of lilies on the chair next to him, smiling when Gian Lucio joined him.

'Can I get you a drink, Lieutenant?'

'No, thank you. I'll wait until my guest arrives. And Gian Lucio,' Antonio said as the restaurateur turned to leave, 'just to let you know your friend Signor Cattaneo failed to get you arrested for murder this morning.'

'I know, but then I did win the toss,' sighed Gian Lucio.

'My bet is that both of you know who killed Lombardi.'

'Can I get you a glass of wine while you're waiting, Lieutenant?' Gian Lucio said, quickly changing the subject. 'Francesca prefers the Cortoglia White.'

'Then why don't you make it two?'

Gian Lucio left quickly.

Antonio continued to look across the square to the pharmacy until he spotted Francesca locking up. He watched her crossing the square and immediately realized it was the first time he'd seen her not wearing a long white coat. She was dressed in a red silk blouse, a black skirt and a pair of high-heeled shoes that certainly hadn't been bought in Cortoglia. He tried not to stare at her. What else was different? Of course, she'd let her hair down. He hadn't thought it possible that she could be even more beautiful.

'As you're a highly trained detective,' Francesca said when she sat down next to him, 'you will know that my name is Francesca, while I'm not sure if you are Antonio or Toni?'

'My mother calls me Antonio, but my friends call me Toni.'

'Do your family also come from Naples?'

'Yes,' said Antonio. 'My parents are both schoolteachers. My father is the headmaster of the Michelangelo Illioneo School, where my mother teaches history, but no one is in any doubt who runs the place.'

Francesca laughed. 'Any brothers or sisters?'

'Just one brother, Darius. He's a lawyer. So once I've locked any criminals up, he puts on a long black gown and defends them. That way we keep it all in the family.'

Francesca laughed again. 'Did you always want to be a policeman?' she asked, as Gian Lucio handed them both a glass of wine.

'From the age of six when someone stole my sweets. But to be fair, if you're brought up in Naples, you have to decide at an early age which side of the law you're going to be on. Did you always want to be a pharmacist?'

'I first worked in the shop at the age of twelve,' she said, looking across the square, 'and with the exception of four years at Milan University studying chemistry, it's been my second home. So when the owner retired, I took over.'

'How did your father feel about that?'

'He was too busy fighting the mayoral election at the time, and I do mean fighting, to have even noticed.'

'Which everyone assumed your father would win.'

'By a landslide. So it came as something of a surprise when the town clerk announced that Lombardi had won.'

'But I haven't come across anyone who voted for Lombardi,' said Antonio.

'In that election, it didn't matter how you voted, Toni, only who was counting the votes.'

'But your father became mayor soon after Lombardi was murdered?'

'No one even stood against him the second time, so I hope you'll attend his inauguration on Saturday?'

'I wouldn't miss it,' said Antonio, raising his glass.

'That's assuming I haven't arrested Lombardi's murderer before then.'

'How many people admitted to killing the mayor today?'

'Two. Pellegrino and the florist, Signor Burgoni.'

'So how did he bump off Lombardi?' Francesca asked.

'Claimed he ran him down in his Ferrari, and then reversed over him to make sure he was dead. Right here in the town square.'

'Sounds pretty convincing to me, so why didn't you arrest him?'

'Because he doesn't own a Fiat, let alone a Ferrari, and what's more, doesn't even have a driving licence,' said Antonio, as he handed Francesca the lilies. 'So he'll be able to continue selling his flowers.'

Francesca laughed, just as Gian Lucio appeared and suggested another glass of wine.

'No, no, Gian Lucio,' said Francesca, 'I must get home. There's so much I have to do before Saturday.'

'When your father will take up his rightful position as mayor of Cortoglia. But I do hope that we'll see you both before then,' said Gian Lucio as he offered a slight bow.

'If I'm given a second chance,' said Antonio as Francesca stood up, and they began to walk across the square towards the pharmacy. Francesca explained that she lived in an apartment above the shop.

'Where are you staying?' said Francesca.

'They've put me in Lombardi's old home while I'm here. I've never lived in such luxury, and I'm trying not to get used to it as it won't be long before I have to return to my little flat in Naples.'

'Not if you don't catch the killer,' she teased.

'Nice idea, but my chief's becoming restless. He's made it clear he expects me back at my desk within a fortnight, with or without the murderer.'

When they reached Francesca's door, she took out a key, but before she could put it in the lock Antonio bent down and kissed her.

'I look forward to seeing you tomorrow, Toni.'

Antonio looked puzzled until Francesca added, 'I have a feeling that it can't be too long before you'll need another bar of soap. By the way, Toni, some of our customers buy them in boxes of three, even six.'

Francesca opened the door and disappeared inside. Antonio walked across to the other side of the square to find several of the locals were grinning.

◄○►

The following day started badly for Antonio. He was studying the pinboard, now covered in photographs, several with crosses through them. His thoughts were interrupted by Riccardo Forte, the local postman, who marched in and even before delivering the morning mail said, 'I can't bear the strain any longer, Lieutenant. I've decided to give myself up and admit that it was me who murdered the mayor.'

'I was just making a cup of coffee, Riccardo, would you like one?'

'Not before you arrest me and beat me up.'

'Later perhaps, but first a few questions.'

'Of course.'

'Black or white?'

'Black, no sugar.'

Toni poured a cup of coffee and handed it to the post-man. 'How did you kill the mayor, Riccardo?' he asked, no longer wasting any time with preliminaries.

'I drowned him,' said the postman.

'In the sea?' suggested Antonio, raising an eyebrow.

'No, in his bath. I took him by surprise.'

'It must have come as quite a surprise,' said Antonio, opening his notebook. 'But before I charge you, Riccardo, I still have one or two more questions.'

'I'll admit to anything,' he said.

'I'm sure you will, but first, how old are you?'

'Sixty-three.'

'And your height?'

'One metre sixty-two.'

'And your weight?'

'Around seventy-six kilos.'

'And you want me to believe, Riccardo, that you over-powered a man who was almost two metres tall and weighed around a hundred kilos. A man who some sug-gested never took a bath. Tell me, Riccardo, was Lombardi asleep at the time?'

'No,' said the postman, 'but he was drunk.'

'Ah, that would explain it,' said Antonio. 'Although, frankly, if he'd passed out before you attempted to drown him, it would still have been a close-run thing.' The post-man tried to look offended. 'In any case, there's something else you've overlooked.'

'What's that?'

'Lombardi couldn't have been drowned in a bath, because there's only a shower in the house.'

'In the sea?' said the postman hopefully.

'Not an option. Not least because eleven other younger men have already confessed to drowning him in the sea.' Antonio closed his notebook. 'But a good try, Riccardo. More importantly, have I got any letters this morning?'

'Yes, three,' said the postman, putting the opened envelopes on the table. 'One from your mother, who wonders if you will be back in time for lunch on Sunday. The second is from the chief of police in Naples who wants to know why you haven't arrested anyone yet, and a third from your brother.'

'And what does he want?' Antonio asked, ignoring the fact that the postman had illegally tampered with the mail.

'Could you let him know as soon as you have arrested someone, and if they've got any money, would you remember to recommend him?'

'Are there any secrets in this town?'

'Just one,' said the postman.

◄○►

Dinner with Francesca at Lucio's restaurant was about as public as an execution. If Antonio had even thought about holding her hand, it would have been front-page news in the *Cortoglia Gazzetta*.

'Don't you ever get bored living in a small town?' he asked her after a waiter had whisked away their plates.

'Never, I have the best of both worlds,' she replied. 'I can read the same books as you, watch the same television programmes, eat the same food and even enjoy the same wine but at half the price. And if I want to go to the opera, visit an art gallery or buy some new clothes, I can always spend the day in Naples and be back in Cortoglia before the sun sets. And perhaps you haven't noticed, Toni, the magnificent rolling hills or how fresh the air is, and when people pass you in the street they smile and know your name.'

'But the bustle, the excitement, the variety of everyday life?'

'The traffic, the pollution, the graffiti, not to mention the manners of some of your fellow Neapolitans who consider women should only be seen in the kitchen or the bedroom, and then not necessarily the same woman.'

Antonio leant across the table and took her hand. 'I couldn't tempt you to come back to Naples with me?'

'For the day, yes,' said Francesca. 'But then I'd want us to be back in Cortoglia by nightfall.'

'Then you'll have to go on murdering some more of the locals.'

'Certainly not. One will be quite enough for the next hundred years. So who's the latest person who tried to convince you they disposed of Lombardi?'

'Paolo Carrafini.'

'Whose wine we are both enjoying,' said Francesca, raising her glass.

'And will continue to do so,' said Antonio, 'as Signor Carrafini's attempt to prove he murdered the mayor turned out to be the least convincing so far.'

'What was wrong with Lombardi falling through a trap door into the wine cellar and breaking his neck?'

'Nothing wrong with the idea,' said Antonio, 'it's just a pity Signor Carrafini would have had to lift up the trap door before he could push Lombardi through. You should tell any other potential murderers that they must be prepared for something to go wrong even when they're innocent.'

'So who's next on your list?'

'I'm afraid it's your father's turn and he's the last person I want to arrest. Although when it comes to motive, he's an obvious candidate.'

'Why?'

'Because we know Lombardi removed him as mayor and within days of the murder, your father was back in the town hall.'

'Along with his friends,' Francesca reminded him.

'Who we now know are all innocent, so I can't wait to find out how your father killed Lombardi.'

Francesca leant across the table and touched his cheek. 'Don't worry, my father isn't going to admit to the murder.'

'All the more reason to believe he did it.'

'Except in his case he has a cast-iron alibi. He was in Florence at the time, attending a local government conference.'

'That's a relief, assuming there are witnesses.'

'Over a hundred.'

'More than enough. But if it wasn't your father who killed Lombardi, I'm fast running out of suspects. Although there still remains the mystery of the missing policeman, because Luca Gentile hasn't been seen in Cortoglia since the day Lombardi was murdered, which is suspicious in and of itself.'

'Luca isn't capable of murder,' said Francesca. 'Although I suspect he knows who did it, which is why he won't be returning to Cortoglia and resuming his former duties until you're safely back in Naples.'

'Then I've still got a few more days left to surprise you all,' said Antonio.

'I think you'll find there are at least three more potential murderers who can't wait to give themselves up.'

'Surely they must be running out of ideas by now?'

'I think you'll enjoy tomorrow's, which is a great improvement on trap doors, truffle knives or being shot.'

'Tell them not to bother tomorrow,' said Antonio. 'I'm taking the day off to watch your father being inaugurated as mayor. Why don't I get the bill?'

'There won't be a bill, Toni, however long you decide to stay,' said Francesca. 'Gian Lucio is telling everyone that although he confessed to shooting Lombardi, even producing the gun, you still refused to lock him up.'

'Because he wasn't guilty,' protested an exasperated Antonio, 'and if we hadn't been having dinner here tonight, I would have locked him up for the possession of a firearm.'

'But it wasn't even his.'

'Ah, but he won the toss,' said Antonio.

'Won the toss?'

'At last I have found something you don't know about,' he said as he stood up to leave. Antonio took her hand as they crossed the square to Francesca's home.

When she opened the door this time Antonio followed her inside.

◄○►

The Naples chief of police called Antonio a few days later, and asked if he was making any progress.

'I can't pretend I am, chief,' admitted Antonio. 'To date,' he said, opening a thick file, 'forty-four people have confessed to killing the mayor, and I'm fairly sure none of them are guilty. And worse, I think they all know who did murder Lombardi.'

'Someone will crack,' said the chief. 'They always do.'

'This isn't Naples, chief,' Antonio heard himself saying.

'So who's the latest one to confess?'

'Not one, but eleven. The local football team claim they pushed Lombardi over a cliff and he drowned in the sea.'

'And what makes you so sure they didn't?'

'I interviewed all eleven of them. The nearest coastline is over forty miles away, and they couldn't even agree on which cliff they pushed him over, where they pulled him out of the water, or how they managed to get him back to Cortoglia and tuck him up in bed. And in any case, I'm not convinced that lot could have murdered Lombardi between them.'

'What makes you say that?'

'They haven't won a football match in the past fifteen years and, don't forget, this was an away game. Frankly, I think it's more likely Lombardi would have pushed all eleven of them over a cliff before they laid a hand on him.'

'All the more reason for you to come back,' said the chief. 'Lombardi's clearly not going to be missed by anyone in Cortoglia, because I've just received a confidential report from the Guardia di Finanza to let me know even the Mafia expelled him. They felt he was too violent. So if you haven't discovered who murdered him by the end of next week, I want you back in Naples where real criminals are still roaming the streets.'

Antonio wasn't given a chance to respond.

◄○►

Everyone took the day off, Antonio included, to celebrate the installation of the new mayor. Lorenzo Farinelli had been elected unopposed, which didn't come as a surprise to anyone, and the council of six remained in place. Dancing and drinking in the town square went on until the early hours, right outside Antonio's bedroom window, and that wasn't the only reason he couldn't get to sleep.

The next morning he called his mother to tell her he'd met the woman he was going to marry, and she would be captivated, and not just by her beauty.

'I can't wait to meet her,' said his mother. 'Why don't you bring her to Naples for the weekend?'

'Why don't you and Papa come to Cortoglia?'

—◦—

During the next few days, the number of citizens who confessed to killing Lombardi rose from forty-four to fifty-one, and when the chief called again from Naples to tell him to wrap up the case, Antonio had to admit that the locals had defeated him, and he accepted that perhaps the time had come to head back to the real world.

Indeed, Antonio might have done so if the new mayor hadn't phoned and asked to see him on a private matter.

As the young detective walked across the square to the town hall, he assumed that the number of murderers in the town was about to rise from fifty-one to fifty-two, as Farinelli was now the only person on the council who hadn't confessed to murdering Lombardi, and Antonio had recently discovered he hadn't been at a conference in Florence on the day of the murder. But he did know who had been.

—◦—

'Those in favour?' said the mayor, looking around the council chamber that he and his fellow members of the Consiglio Comunale had recaptured.

The five other members of the council – Pellegrino, De Rosa, Carrafini, Cattaneo and Altana – all raised their hands.

'And are we also agreed on the sum of money we should offer him?'

The five hands were raised once again, without a murmur of dissent.

'But do you think it will be enough?' asked Pellegrino, as there was a knock on the door.

'I suspect we're about to find out,' said the mayor as Antonio entered the room, surprised to find the whole council awaiting him. Farinelli nodded towards the empty seat at the other end of the table.

Once Antonio had poured himself a glass of water and sat back, the mayor said, 'We've just finished our first meeting of the new council, and wondered if you would bring us up to date on how your investigation is progressing.'

'Although I don't have sufficient proof, Mr Mayor, I'm fairly sure I now know who killed Lombardi.' His eyes remained fixed on the person seated at the other end of the table. 'However, despite my suspicions, I've been instructed by my chief to close the case and return to Naples.'

Antonio couldn't have missed the collective sigh of relief from those seated around the table.

'I am sure your chief has made a wise decision,' said the mayor. 'However, I confess,' he paused as Antonio continued to stare at him, 'that wasn't the reason we wanted to see you. As you probably know, Lieutenant, Luca Gentile has recently been in touch to let us know that he will not be returning to Cortoglia for personal reasons, and the Consiglio voted unanimously to offer you the position of chief of police.'

'But the town has only ever had one policeman.'

'Yes,' said De Rosa, 'but we all also felt with so many murderers on the loose, you ought to have a deputy.'

'But there's barely enough space for one officer in the police station. There's only one desk and there isn't even a lock on the cell door.'

'True, but then we've never needed one in the past,' said Pellegrino. 'However, the council have agreed we should build a new police station, worthy of your status.'

'But—'

'We'd also be happy for you to go on living in your present accommodation,' Cattaneo interjected.

'That's incredibly generous, but I still feel—'

'And we'd pay you the same amount as the chief of police in Naples,' Farinelli said, hoping to close the deal.

'That's more than generous—' began Antonio.

'However,' the mayor continued, 'although we didn't put it to a vote, there is one thing we all felt strongly about. If you were able to marry a local girl . . .'

—◦—

Several guests, including Antonio's parents and brother, arrived from Naples on the morning of Antonio Rossetti and Francesca Farinelli's wedding. However, Antonio assured the mayor they would all be leaving the next day.

The whole town turned out to witness the vows of eternal love sworn by the couple, including several locals who hadn't been invited. When il Signor and la Signora Rossetti left the wedding celebrations to set off for Venice, Antonio suspected the festivities would still be going on when they returned home in a fortnight's time.

The newly-weds spent their honeymoon in Venice, eating too much spaghetti alle vongole, and drinking too much wine, while still finding a way of not putting on too much weight.

On the final night Antonio sat up in bed and watched his wife undress. When she slipped under the covers to join him, he took her in his arms.

'It's been the most wonderful fortnight, my darling,' Francesca said. 'So many memories to share with everyone when we get back home.'

'Including your feeble effort to climb St Mark's, while pretending you weren't out of breath when you finally reached the top.'

'That hardly compares to your pathetic attempt to manoeuvre a gondola under the Bridge of Sighs, despite the gondolier pointing out that it was the widest stretch of water on the canal.'

'Don't tell anyone!'

'I have photographs,' Francesca teased.

'But I confess the highlight was this evening's candle-lit dinner at Harry's Bar overlooking the Rialto.'

'Memorable,' sighed Francesca as she kissed him, 'but if Gian Lucio was to open a restaurant in Venice, they'd have a genuine rival.'

'If you'd only come to Naples, Francesca, I would

introduce you to one or two restaurants you might enjoy just as much.'

'Perhaps I'll come for lunch one day. Although I confess I'm looking forward to getting back to Cortoglia.'

'Me too,' admitted Toni. 'And I wouldn't be surprised to find they're all still in the market square celebrating.'

'Let's just hope no one's murdered my father.'

'Not least because I still haven't solved the mystery of who killed the last mayor. Come to think of it, you're about the only person who didn't confess to murdering Lombardi.'

'I was going to when you first visited the pharmacy. But you seemed more interested in trying to pick me up.'

Toni laughed. 'Then all I need to know, my darling, is how you killed Lombardi?'

'A spoonful of cyanide dropped into his coffee after dinner, just before he went to bed. A slow and painful death, but no more than he deserved.'

Antonio sat bolt upright and stared at his wife.

'And I don't have to remind you, my darling,' continued Francesca, 'that in Italy, a man cannot give evidence against his wife.'

THE PERFECT MURDER

Coincidences are frowned upon in a novel, whereas in real life they regularly occur.

I had already read the proofs of *Tell Tale*, and returned them to my publisher, when *Reader's Digest* announced they would be relaunching their 100-word short story competition later this year.

The commissioning editor of *Reader's Digest* invited me to take up the challenge a second time, and produce a 100-word tale within twenty-four hours.

Result? 'The Perfect Murder'. I hope you enjoy my latest effort, and if you are a closet author yourself, perhaps you should finally come out, and also take up the challenge.

This is also a hundred words.

ALBERT STARED AT the prisoner standing in the dock, well aware he hadn't committed the murder.

Albert had struck the fatal blow moments after Yvonne admitted she was seeing another man. He slipped out of her flat and into a telephone box on the other side of the road. When his rival appeared, he dialled 999.

Twenty minutes later two detectives dragged the innocent man out of her apartment, threw him into the back of a police car and, sirens blazing, sped off.

'Do you find the defendant guilty or not guilty of murder?'

The foreman rose.

'Guilty,' said Albert.

FOREWORD TO *HEADS YOU WIN*

Dear Reader,

It was fun compiling these short stories after the challenge of writing seven volumes of the Clifton Chronicles.

What I hadn't anticipated would happen during that time is that I would come up with an idea for a stand-alone novel every bit as demanding and exciting as anything I have ever written in the past.

For those of you who have already read the final volume of the Chronicles, *This Was a Man*, none of this will come as a surprise because Harry Clifton outlined the plot for you in the last chapter of that book.

However, I thought I'd go one step further than Harry, and share with you the first three chapters of *Heads You Win*, which will be published in November 2018.

I hope you enjoy it.

Jeffrey Archer,
March 2018

1

ALEXANDER

Leningrad, 1968

'WHAT ARE YOU going to do when you leave school?' asked Alexander.

'I'm hoping to join the KGB,' Vladimir replied, 'but they won't even consider me if I don't get a place at the state university. How about you?'

'I intend to be the first democratically elected president of Russia,' said Alexander, laughing.

'And if you make it,' said Vladimir, who didn't laugh, 'you can appoint me as head of the KGB.'

'I don't approve of nepotism,' said Alexander, as they strolled across the schoolyard and out onto the street.

'Nepotism?' said Vladimir, as they began to walk home.

'It derives from the Italian word for nephew, and dates back to the popes of the seventeenth century, who often handed out patronage to their relations and close friends.'

'What's wrong with that?' said Vladimir. 'You just exchange the popes for the KGB.'

'Are you going to the match on Saturday?' asked Alexander, wanting to change the subject.

'No. Once Leningrad reached the semi-finals, there

was never any chance of someone like me getting a ticket. But surely as your father's the docks' supervisor, you'll automatically be allocated a couple of seats in the reserved stand for party members.'

'Not while he still refuses to join the Communist Party,' said Alexander. 'And when I last asked him, he didn't sound at all optimistic about getting a ticket, so Uncle Niko is now my only hope.'

As they continued walking, Alexander realized they were both avoiding the one subject that was never far from their minds.

'When do you think we'll find out?'

'I've no idea,' said Alexander. 'I suspect our teachers enjoy watching us suffering, well aware it will be the last time they have any power over us.'

'You have nothing to worry about,' said Vladimir. 'The only discussion in your case is whether you'll win the Lenin Scholarship to the foreign language school in Moscow, or be offered a place at the state university to study mathematics. Whereas I can't be sure of getting into any university, and if I don't, my chances of joining the KGB are kaput.' He sighed. 'I'll probably end up working on the docks for the rest of my life, with your father as my boss.'

Alexander didn't offer an opinion as the two of them entered the tenement block where they lived, and began to climb the worn stone steps to their flats.

'I wish I lived on the first floor, and not the fourteenth.'

'You know as well as I do that only party members live on the first three floors, Vladimir. But I'm sure that once you've joined the KGB, you'll come down in the world.'

'See you in the morning,' said Vladimir, ignoring his friend's jibe as he began to climb the remaining six flights.

As Alexander opened the door to his family's tiny flat on the eighth floor, he recalled an article he'd recently read in a state magazine reporting that America was so overrun with criminals that everyone had at least two locks on their front door. Perhaps the only reason they didn't in the Soviet Union, he thought, was because no one had anything worth stealing.

He went straight to his bedroom, aware that his mother wouldn't be back until she'd finished her shift at the docks. He took several sheets of lined paper, a pencil and a well-thumbed book out of his satchel, and placed them on the tiny table in the corner of his room, before opening *War and Peace* at page 179 and continuing to translate Tolstoy's words into English. *When the Rostov family sat down for supper that night, Nikolai appeared distracted, and not just because . . .*

Alexander was double-checking each line for spelling mistakes, and to see if he could think of a more appropriate English word, when he heard the front door open. His tummy began to rumble, and he wondered if his mother had been able to smuggle any titbits out of the officers' club, where she was the cook. He closed his book and went to join her in the kitchen.

Elena gave him a warm smile as he sat down on a wooden bench at the table.

'Anything special tonight, Mama?' Alexander asked hopefully.

She smiled again, and began to empty her pockets,

producing a large potato, two parsnips, half a loaf of stale bread and this evening's prize, half a sausage that had probably been left on an officer's plate after lunch. A veritable feast, thought Alexander, compared to what his friend Vladimir would be eating tonight. There's always someone worse off than you.

'Any news?' Elena asked as she began to peel the potato.

'You ask me the same question every night, Mama, and I keep telling you that I don't expect to hear anything for at least another month, possibly longer.'

'It's just that your father would be so proud if you won the Lenin Scholarship.' She put down the potato and placed the peel to one side. Nothing would be wasted. 'You know, if it hadn't been for the war, your father would have gone to university.'

Alexander knew only too well, but he was always happy to be reminded how Papa had been stationed on the Eastern Front as a young corporal during the Siege of Leningrad, and although a crack Panzer division had attacked his section continuously for ninety-three days, he'd never left his post until the Germans had been repelled and retreated to their own country.

'For which he was awarded the Defence of Leningrad medal,' said Alexander on cue.

His mother must have told him the story a hundred times, but Alexander didn't tire of it, although his father never raised the subject. And now, almost twenty-five years later, after returning to the docks he'd risen to Comrade Chief Supervisor, with 3,000 workers under his command. Although he wasn't a party member, even the KGB acknowledged that he was the right man for the job.

The front door opened and closed with a bang, announcing that his father was home. Alexander smiled as he strode into the kitchen. Tall and heavily built, Konstantin Karpenko was a handsome man who could still make a young woman turn and take a second look. His weather-beaten face was dominated by a luxuriantly bushy moustache that Alexander remembered stroking as a child, something he hadn't dared to do for several years. Konstantin slumped down onto the bench opposite his son.

'Supper won't be ready for another half-hour,' said Elena as she diced the potato.

'We must speak only English whenever we are alone,' said Konstantin.

'Why?' asked Elena in her native tongue. 'I've never met an Englishman in my life, and I don't suppose I ever will.'

'Because if Alexander is to win that scholarship and go to Moscow, he will have to be fluent in the language of our enemies.'

'But the British and Americans fought on the same side as us during the war, Papa.'

'On the same side, yes,' said his father, 'but only because they considered us the lesser of two evils.' Alexander gave this some thought as his father stood up. 'Shall we have a game of chess while we're waiting?' he asked. Alexander nodded. His favourite part of the day. 'You set up the board while I go and wash my hands.'

Once Konstantin had left the room, Elena whispered, 'Why not let him win for a change?'

'Never,' said Alexander. 'In any case, he'd know if I wasn't trying, and leather me.' He pulled open the drawer below the kitchen table and took out an old wooden board and a box containing a set of chess pieces, one of which was missing, so each night a plastic salt cellar had to substitute for a bishop.

Alexander moved his king's pawn two squares forward, before his father returned. Konstantin responded immediately, moving his queen's pawn one square forward.

'How did you do in the match?' he asked.

'We won three nil,' said Alexander, moving his queen's knight.

'Another clean sheet, well done,' said Konstantin. 'But it's more important you win that scholarship. I assume you still haven't heard anything?'

'Nothing,' said Alexander, as he made his next move. It was a few moments before his father countered. 'Papa, can I ask if you've managed to get a ticket for the match on Saturday?'

'No,' admitted his father, his eyes never leaving the board. 'They're rarer than a virgin on Nevsky Prospect.'

'Konstantin!' said Elena. 'You can behave like a docker at work, but not when you're at home.'

Konstantin grinned at his son. 'But your uncle Niko has been promised a couple of tickets on the terraces, and as I have no interest in going . . .' Alexander leapt in the air as his father made his next move, pleased to have distracted his son.

'You could have had as many tickets as you wanted,' said Elena, 'if only you'd agree to become a party member.'

'That's not something I'm willing to do, as you well

6

know. Quid pro quo. An expression you taught me,' said Konstantin, looking across the table at his son. 'Never forget, that lot will always expect something in return, and I'm not going to sell my friends down the river for a couple of tickets to a football match.'

'But we haven't reached the semi-final of the cup for years,' said Alexander.

'And probably won't again in my lifetime. But it will take far more than that to get me to join the Communist Party.'

'Vladimir's already a pioneer and signed up for the Komsomol,' said Alexander, after he'd made his next move.

'Hardly surprising,' said Konstantin. 'Otherwise he'd have no hope of eventually joining the KGB, which is the natural habitat for that particular piece of pond life.'

Once again, Alexander was distracted. 'Why are you always so hard on him, Papa?'

'Because he's a shifty little bastard, just like his father. Be sure you never trust him with a secret, because it will have been passed on to the KGB before you've reached home.'

'He's not that bright,' said Alexander. 'Frankly, he'll be lucky to be offered a place at the state university.'

'He may not be bright, but he's cunning and ruthless, a dangerous combination. Believe me, he'd shop his mother for a ticket to the cup final, probably even the semi-final.'

'Supper's ready,' said Elena.

'Shall we call it a draw?' said Konstantin.

'No, Papa. I'm six moves away from checkmate, and you know it.'

'Stop squabbling, you two,' said Elena, 'and lay the table.'

'When did I last manage to beat you?' asked Konstantin as he placed his king on its side.

'November the nineteenth, 1967,' said Alexander, as the two of them stood up and shook hands.

Alexander put the salt cellar back on the table and returned the chess pieces to the box while his father took down three plates from the shelf above the sink. Alexander opened the kitchen drawer and took out three knives and three forks of different vintages. He recalled a paragraph in *War and Peace* that he'd just translated. The Rostovs regularly enjoyed a five-course dinner (better word than supper – he would change it when he returned to his room), and a different set of silver cutlery accompanied each dish. The family also had a dozen liveried servants who stood behind each chair to serve the meals that had been prepared by three cooks, who never seemed to leave the kitchen. But Alexander was sure that the Rostovs couldn't have had a better cook than his mother, otherwise she wouldn't be working in the officers' club.

One day . . . he told himself, as he finished laying the table and sat back down on the bench opposite his father. Elena joined them with that evening's offering, which she divided between the three of them, but not equally. The remains of the sausage had been cut into two pieces, the potato diced, and the peelings fried and made to look like a delicacy. Both of her men also had a parsnip, along with a thick slab of black bread and lard.

'I've got a church meeting this evening,' said Konstantin as he picked up his fork. 'But I shouldn't be back too late.'

Alexander cut his sausage into four pieces, chewing each morsel slowly, between mouthfuls of bread and sips of water. He saved the parsnip till last. Its bland taste lingered in his mouth. He wasn't sure if he even liked it. In *War and Peace* parsnips were only eaten by the servants. Despite taking their time, and talking constantly, the meal was over in a few minutes.

Konstantin emptied his glass of water, wiped his mouth on the sleeve of his jacket, stood up and left the room without another word.

'You can go back to your books, Alexander. This shouldn't take me too long,' his mother said with a wave of her hand.

Alexander happily obeyed her. Back in his room, he replaced the word 'supper' with 'dinner', before turning to the next page and continuing with his translation of Tolstoy's masterpiece. *The French were advancing on Moscow* . . .

As Konstantin left the apartment block and walked out onto the street, he was unaware of a pair of eyes staring down at him.

Vladimir had been gazing aimlessly out of the window, unable to concentrate on his school work, when he saw Comrade Karpenko leaving the building. It was the third time that week. Where was he going at this time of night? Perhaps he should find out. He quickly left his room and tiptoed down the corridor. He could hear loud snoring coming from the front room, and peeped in to see his father slumped in a horsehair chair, an empty bottle of vodka lying on the floor by his side. He opened and closed the front door quietly, then bolted down the stone steps and out onto the street. Glancing to his left he spotted Mr Karpenko turning the corner and ran after him, slowing down before he reached the end of the road.

He peered around the corner, and watched as Comrade Karpenko went into the Church of the Apostle Andrew. What a complete waste of time, thought Vladimir. The Orthodox Church may have been frowned on by the KGB, but it wasn't actually banned. He was about to turn back and go home when another man appeared out of the shadows, who he'd never seen at church on Sundays.

Vladimir was careful to remain out of sight as he edged his way slowly towards the church. He watched as two more men came from the other direction and quickly made their way inside, then froze when he heard footsteps behind him. He slipped over the wall and lay on the ground, waiting until the man had passed before he crept between the gravestones to the back of the church and an entrance that only the choristers ever used. He turned the door knob and cursed when it didn't open.

Looking around, he spotted a half-open window above him. He couldn't quite reach it, so using a rough stone slab as a step, pushed himself up off the ground. On his third attempt, he managed to grab the window ledge, and with a supreme effort pulled himself up and squeezed his slim body through the window before dropping to the floor on the other side.

Vladimir tiptoed silently through the back of the

church until he reached the sanctuary, where he hid behind the altar. Once his heartbeat had returned to almost normal, he peered around the side of the altar to see a dozen men seated in the choir stalls, deep in conversation.

'So when will you share your idea with the rest of the workforce?' one of them was asking.

'Next Saturday, Stefan,' said Konstantin, 'when all our comrades come together for the monthly works meeting. I'll never have a better opportunity to convince them to join us.'

'Not even a hint to some of the older hands about what you have in mind?' asked another.

'No. Our only chance of success is surprise. We don't need to alert the KGB to what we're up to.'

'But they're certain to have spies in the room, listening to your every word.'

'I'm aware of that, Mikhail. But by then the only thing they'll be able to report back to their masters will be the strength of our support for forming an independent trade union.'

'Although I have no doubt the men will back you,' said a fourth voice, 'no amount of rousing oratory can stop a bullet in its tracks.' Several of the men nodded.

'Once I've delivered my speech on Saturday,' said Konstantin, 'the KGB will be wary of doing anything quite that stupid, because if they did, the men would rise as one, and they'd never be able to squeeze the genie back into the bottle. But Yuri is right,' he continued. 'You're all taking a considerable risk for a cause I've long believed in, so if anyone wants to change their mind and leave the group, now is the time to do so.'

'You won't find a Judas among us,' said another voice, as Vladimir stifled a cough. The men all stood as one to acknowledge Karpenko as their leader.

'Then we'll meet again on Saturday morning. Until then we must remain silent, and keep our counsel.'

Vladimir's heart was thumping as the men shook hands with each other, one by one, before leaving the church. He didn't move until he finally heard the great west door slam shut, and a key turn in the lock. Then he scurried back to the vestry, and with the help of a stool, wriggled back out of the window, clinging to the ledge before dropping to the ground like a seasoned wrestler. The one discipline where Alexander wasn't in his class.

Knowing he didn't have a moment to lose, Vladimir ran in the opposite direction to Mr Karpenko, towards a street that didn't need a NO ENTRY sign, as only party officials ever considered entering Stalin Prospect. He knew exactly where Major Polyakov lived, but wondered if he had the nerve to knock on his door at that time of night. At any time of the day or night, for that matter.

When he reached the street with its leafy trees and neat cobblestone pavement, Vladimir stood and stared at the house, losing his nerve with every second that passed. He finally summoned up enough courage to approach the front door, and was about to knock when it was flung open by a man who didn't like to be taken by surprise.

'What do you want, boy?' the man demanded, grabbing his unwelcome visitor by the ear.

'I have information,' said Vladimir, 'and you told us

12

when you visited our school last year looking for recruits, that information was golden.'

'This had better be good,' said Polyakov, who didn't let go of the boy's ear as he dragged him inside. He slammed the door behind him. 'Start talking.'

Vladimir faithfully reported everything he'd overheard in the church. By the time he'd come to the end, the pressure on his ear had been replaced by an arm around his shoulder.

'Did you recognize anyone other than Karpenko?' Polyakov asked.

'No, sir, but he mentioned the names Yuri, Mikhail, and Stefan.'

Polyakov wrote down the names, then said, 'Are you going to the match on Saturday?'

'No, sir, it's sold out, and my father wasn't able to—'

Like a conjurer, the KGB chief produced a ticket from an inside pocket and handed it to his latest recruit.

◄○►

Konstantin closed the bedroom door quietly, not wanting to wake his wife. He took off his heavy boots, undressed and climbed into bed. If he left early enough in the morning, he wouldn't have to explain to Elena what he and his disciples had been up to, and even more important, what he had planned for Saturday's meeting. Better she thought he'd been out drinking, even that there was another woman, than burden her with the truth. He knew she would only try to convince him not to go ahead with the prepared speech.

After all, they didn't have too bad a life, he could hear

her reminding him. They lived in an apartment block that had electricity and running water. She had her job as a cook at the officers' club, and Alexander was waiting to hear if he'd won a scholarship to the prestigious foreign language school in Moscow. What more could they ask for?

That one day everyone could take privileges like that for granted, Konstantin would have told her.

He lay awake all night, composing a speech in his mind that he couldn't risk committing to paper. He rose at five thirty, and once again took care not to wake his wife. He doused his face in freezing water, but didn't shave, then dressed in overalls and a rough, open-neck shirt before finally pulling on his well-worn hobnailed boots. He crept out of the bedroom and collected his lunch box from the kitchen: a hard-boiled egg, an onion, and two slices of bread and cheese. Only members of the KGB would eat better.

He closed the front door quietly behind him and made his way down the well-worn stone stairs before stepping out onto the empty street. He always walked the six kilometres to work, eschewing the overloaded bus that ferried the workers to and from the docks. If he hoped to survive beyond Saturday, he needed to be fit, like a highly trained soldier in the field.

Whenever he passed a fellow worker in the street, Konstantin always acknowledged him with a mock salute. Some returned his salutation, others nodded, while a few, like bad Samaritans, looked the other way. They may as well have had their party numbers tattooed on their foreheads.

Konstantin arrived outside the dock gates an hour later, and clocked on. As works supervisor, he liked to be the first to arrive and the last to leave. He walked along the dockside while he considered his first assignment of the day. A submarine destined for Odessa on the Black Sea had just berthed at dock 11 for refuelling and to pick up provisions, before continuing on its way, but that wouldn't be for at least another hour. Only the most trusted men would be allowed anywhere near dock 11 that morning.

Konstantin's mind drifted back to the previous night's meeting. Something wasn't quite right, but he couldn't put a finger on it. Was it someone and not something, he wondered, as a vast crane at the far end of the dock began to lift its heavy load and swing slowly towards the waiting submarine on dock 11.

The operator seated in the crane's cab had been chosen carefully. He could unload a tank into a ship's hold with only inches to spare on either side. But not today. Today he was transferring barrels of oil to a submarine that needed to remain submerged for days at a time, but the task also demanded pin-point accuracy. One piece of luck – no wind that morning.

Konstantin tried to concentrate as he went over his speech once again. As long as none of his colleagues opened their mouths, he was confident everything would fall neatly into place. He smiled to himself.

The crane operator was satisfied that he had judged it to an inch. The load was perfectly balanced and still. He waited just one more moment before he eased a long heavy lever gently forward. The large clamp sprang open and three barrels of oil were released. They crashed down onto the dockside moments later. Inch perfect. Konstantin Karpenko had looked up, but it was too late. He was killed instantly. A dreadful accident, for which no one was to blame. The man in the cab knew he had to disappear before the early shift clocked on. He swung the crane's arm back into place, turned off the engine, climbed out of the cab and began to make his way down the ladder to the ground.

Three fellow workers were waiting for him as he stepped onto the dockside. He smiled at his comrades, not spotting the six-inch serrated blade until it was thrust deep into his stomach and then twisted several times. The other two men held him down until he finally stopped whimpering. They bound his arms and legs together before pushing him over the side of the dock and into the water. He reappeared three times, before finally disappearing below the surface. He hadn't officially signed on that morning, so it would be some time before anyone noticed he was missing.

--◦--

Konstantin Karpenko's funeral was held at the Church of the Apostle Andrew. The turnout was so large that the congregation spilled out onto the street, long before the choir had entered the nave.

The bishop who delivered the eulogy described Konstantin's death as a tragic accident. But then, he was probably one of the few people who believed the official communiqué issued by the dock commandant, and only then after it had been sanctioned by Moscow.

Seated near the front were twelve men who knew it

hadn't been an accident. They had lost their leader, and the promise of a thorough investigation by the KGB wouldn't help their cause, because state inquiries usually took at least a couple of years to report their findings, by which time their moment would have passed.

Only family and close friends stood beside the grave to pay their last respects. Elena wept as the body of her husband was lowered slowly into the ground. Alexander forced himself to hold back the tears as he held his mother's hand, something he hadn't done for years. He was suddenly aware that, despite his youth, he was now the head of the family.

He looked up to see Vladimir, who he hadn't spoken to since his father's death, half hidden at the back of the gathering. When their eyes met, his best friend quickly looked away. His father's words flashed into Alexander's mind. *He's cunning and ruthless. Believe me, he'd shop his mother for a ticket to the cup final, probably even the semi-final.* Vladimir hadn't been able to resist telling Alexander that he'd got a stand seat for the match on Saturday, although he wouldn't say who had given it to him, or what he'd had to do to get it.

Alexander could only wonder just how far Vladimir would go to make sure he was offered a place at the state university, his only chance of being recruited by the KGB. He realized in that instant they were no longer friends. After a few minutes Vladimir scurried away, like Judas in the night. He'd done everything except kiss Alexander's father on the cheek.

Elena and Alexander remained kneeling by the graveside long after everyone else had departed. When she finally rose, Elena couldn't help wondering what Konstantin could have done to cause such wrath. Only the most brainwashed party member could have accepted the official line that after the tragic accident the crane operator had committed suicide. Even Leonid Brezhnev, the party's General Secretary, had joined in the deception, with a Kremlin spokesman announcing that Comrade Konstantin Karpenko had been made a Hero of the Soviet Union, and his widow would receive a full state pension.

Elena had already turned her attention to the other man in her life. She had decided she would move to Moscow, find a job, and do everything in her power to advance her son's career. But after a long discussion with her brother Niko, she reluctantly accepted that she would have to remain in Leningrad, and try to carry on as if nothing had happened. She would be lucky even to hold on to her present job, because the KGB had tentacles that stretched far beyond her irrelevant existence.

On Saturday, in the semi-final of the Soviet Cup, Leningrad beat Odessa 2–1, and qualified to play Torpedo Moscow in the final.

Vladimir was already trying to work out what he needed to do to get a ticket.

2

ALEXANDER

ELENA WOKE early, still not used to sleeping alone. Once she'd given Alexander his breakfast and packed him off to school, she tidied the flat, put on her coat and left for work. Like Konstantin, she preferred to walk to the docks, and not have to repeat a thousand times, *how kind of you*.

She thought about the death of the only man she'd ever loved. What were they hiding from her? Why wouldn't anyone tell her the truth? She would have to pick the right moment and ask her brother, who she was sure knew far more than he was willing to admit. And then she thought about her son, whose exam results were due any day now.

She finally thought about her job, which she couldn't afford to lose while Alexander was still at school. Was the state pension a hint that they no longer wanted her around? Did her presence continually remind everyone how her husband had died? But she was good at her job, which was why she worked in the officers' club, and not in the docks' canteen.

'Welcome back, Mrs Karpenko,' said the guard on the gate when she clocked in.

'Thank you,' said Elena.

As she walked through the docks several workers doffed their caps and greeted her with a 'Good morning', reminding her just how popular Konstantin had been.

Once she had entered the back door of the officers' club, she hung up her coat, put on an apron and went through to the kitchen. She checked the lunch menu, the first thing she did every morning. Vegetable soup and rabbit pie. It must be Friday. She began to prepare the dishes, just as she did every day. First she inspected the meat, three rabbits that would need to be skinned, and then there were vegetables to be sliced and potatoes to be peeled.

A gentle hand rested on her shoulder. She turned to see Comrade Novak, a sympathetic smile on his face.

'It was a wonderful service,' her supervisor said. 'But no more than Konstantin deserved.' Someone else who obviously knew the truth, but wasn't willing to voice it. Elena thanked him, and didn't stop working until the siren sounded to announce the mid-morning break. She hung up her apron and joined Olga in the yard. Her friend was enjoying the other half of yesterday's cigarette, and passed the stub to Elena.

'It's been one hell of a week,' said Olga, 'but we all played our part in making sure you didn't lose your job. I was personally responsible for yesterday's lunch being a disaster,' she added after inhaling deeply. 'The soup was cold, the meat was overcooked, the vegetables were soggy, and someone forgot to make any gravy. The officers were all asking when you'd be back.'

'Thank you,' said Elena, wanting to hug her friend, but the siren sounded again.

—◆—

Alexander hadn't cried at his father's funeral. So when Elena arrived home after work that night and found him sobbing, she realized it could only be one thing.

She sat down on the kitchen bench next to him and put an arm around his shoulder.

'Winning the scholarship was never that important,' she said. 'Just being offered a place at the foreign language school is a great honour in itself.'

'But I haven't been offered a place anywhere,' said Alexander.

'Not even to study mathematics at the state university?'

Alexander shook his head. 'I've been ordered to report to the docks on Monday morning, when I'll be allocated to a gang.'

'Never!' said Elena. 'I'll protest.'

'It will fall on deaf ears, Mama. They've made it clear that I don't have any choice.'

'What about your friend Vladimir? Will he also be joining you on the docks?'

'No. He's been offered a place at the state university. He starts in September.'

'But you beat him in every subject.'

'Except treachery,' said Alexander.

—◆—

When Major Polyakov strolled into the kitchen just before lunch the following Monday, he leered at Elena as if she were on the menu. The major was no taller than her, but must have been twice her weight, which was, Olga joked, a tribute to her cooking. Polyakov held the title of Head of Security, but everyone knew he was KGB and didn't report to the dock commandant, but directly to Moscow, so even his fellow officers were wary of him.

It wasn't long before the leer turned into a close inspection of Elena's latest dish. While other officers would occasionally come into the kitchen to sample a titbit, Polyakov's hands ran down her back, coming to rest on her bottom. He pressed himself up against her. 'See you after lunch,' he whispered before leaving to join his fellow officers in the dining room. Elena was relieved to see him rushing out of the building an hour later. He didn't return before she clocked off, but she feared it could only be a matter of time.

◄◦►

Niko dropped into the kitchen to see his sister at the end of the day, and she gave him a blow-by-blow account of what she'd had to endure that afternoon.

'There's nothing any of us can do about Polyakov,' said Niko. 'Not if we want to keep our jobs. While Konstantin was alive he wouldn't have dared lay a hand on you, but now . . . there's nothing to stop him adding you to a long list of conquests who'll never complain. You only have to ask your friend Olga.'

'I don't need to. But something Olga let slip today made me realize she knows why Konstantin was killed, and who was responsible. She's obviously too frightened to say a word, so perhaps it's time you told me the truth. Were you at that meeting?'

'It was a tragic accident,' said Niko, putting a finger to his lips.

Elena turned on all the taps before she whispered, 'Is your life in danger too?' Her brother nodded, and left the kitchen without another word.

-<o>-

Elena lay in bed that night thinking about her husband. Part of her was still unwilling to accept he wasn't alive. It didn't help that Alexander had worshipped his father, and had always tried so hard to live up to his impossible standards. Standards that must have been the reason Konstantin had sacrificed his life, and at the same time condemned his son to spend the rest of his days as a dock labourer.

Elena had hoped their son would join the Ministry of Foreign Affairs, and that she would live long enough to see him become an ambassador. But it was not to be. *If brave men aren't willing to take risks for what they believe in*, Konstantin had once told her, *nothing will ever change*. Elena only wished her husband had been more of a coward. But then, if he had been, perhaps she wouldn't have fallen so helplessly in love with him.

Elena's brother Niko had been his third in command at the docks, but Polyakov clearly didn't consider him a threat, because he kept his job as chief loader after Konstantin's 'tragic accident'. What Polyakov couldn't know was that Niko hated the KGB even more than his brother-in-law had, and although he appeared to have fallen into line, he was already planning his revenge, which wouldn't involve making impassioned speeches, although it would take every bit as much courage.

—◦—

Elena was surprised to see her brother waiting for her outside the dock gates when she clocked off on Tuesday afternoon.

'This is a pleasant surprise,' she said, as they began to walk home.

'You may not think so when you hear what I've got to say.'

'Does it concern Alexander?' asked Elena anxiously.

'I'm afraid it does. He's begun badly. Refuses to take orders, and is openly contemptuous of the KGB. Today he told a junior officer, and they're always the worst, to fuck off.' Elena shuddered. 'You must tell him to knuckle down, because I won't be able to cover for him much longer.'

'I'm afraid he has his father's fierce independent streak,' said Elena, 'without any of his discretion or wisdom.'

'And it doesn't help that he's brighter than everyone else around him, including the KGB officers,' said Niko. 'And they know it.'

'But what can I do, when he doesn't listen to me any longer?'

They walked in silence for a while before Niko spoke again, and then not until he was certain they were on their own. 'I may have come up with a solution. But I can't pull

it off without your full cooperation.' He paused. 'And Alexander's.'

—◦—

As if Elena's problems at home weren't bad enough,
things were becoming worse at work, as the major's
advances became less and less subtle. She had considered
pouring boiling water over his wandering hands, but the
consequences didn't bear thinking about.

It must have been about a week later, as she was tidy-
ing up the kitchen before returning home, that Polyakov
staggered in, clearly drunk, and began to unbutton his
trousers as he advanced towards her. Just as he was about
to place a sweaty hand on her breast, a junior officer
rushed in, and said that the commandant needed to see
him urgently. Polyakov couldn't hide his frustration, and
as he left, hissed at Elena, 'Don't go anywhere. I'll be back
later.' Elena was so terrified, she didn't move for over an
hour. But the moment the siren finally sounded, she
pulled on her coat and was among the first to clock off.

When her brother joined her for supper that evening,
she begged him to tell her his plan.

'I thought you said it was far too great a risk.'

'I did, but that was before I realized I can't avoid
Polyakov's advances any longer.'

'You told me you could even bear that, as long as Alexander never found out.'

'But if he did,' said Elena quietly, 'can you imagine the
repercussions? So tell me what you have in mind, because
I'll consider anything.'

Niko leant forward and poured himself a shot of vodka

25

before he began to take her slowly through his plan. 'As you know, several foreign vessels unload their cargo at the docks every week, and we have to turn them round as quickly as possible, so any waiting ships can take their place. That's my job.'

'But how will that help us?' asked Elena.

'Once a ship has been unloaded, the loading process begins. Because not everyone wants bags of salt or cases of vodka, some vessels leave the port empty.' Elena remained silent while her brother continued. 'There are two ships due in on Friday, which after they've discharged their cargo will leave on the Saturday afternoon tide with empty holds. You and Alexander could be hidden on one of them.'

'But if we're caught we could end up on a cattle train to Siberia.'

'That's why it's so important to take our chance this Saturday, because for once the odds will be stacked in our favour.'

'Why?' asked Elena.

'Leningrad are playing Torpedo Moscow in the final of the Soviet Cup, and almost all of the officers will be sitting in a box at the stadium supporting Moscow, while most of the workers will be cheering on the home side from the terraces. So there'll be a three-hour window we could take advantage of, and by the time the final whistle blows, you and Alexander could be on your way to a new life in London or New York.'

'Or Siberia?'

3

ALEXANDER

Leningrad, 1968

Niko and Elena never left for the docks in the morning at the same time, and they didn't return home together at night. When they were at work, there was no reason for their paths to cross, and they were careful to make sure they never did. Niko came down from his flat on the next floor every evening, but they didn't discuss what they were planning until after Alexander had gone to bed, when they talked of little else.

By Friday evening, they'd gone over everything they imagined could go wrong again and again, although Elena remained convinced something would trip them up at the last moment. She didn't sleep that night, but then she hadn't slept for more than a couple of hours a night for the past month.

Niko told her that because of the cup final, almost all the dockers had opted for the early shift on Saturday morning – six until midday – so once the noon siren blasted the docks would only be manned by a skeleton crew.

'And I've already told Alexander I wasn't able to get him a ticket, so he's reluctantly signed up for the afternoon shift.'

'When will you tell him?' asked Elena.

'Not until the last moment. Think like the KGB. They don't even tell themselves.'

Comrade Novak had already told Elena that she could take Saturday off, because he doubted if any of the officers would bother to come in for lunch, as they wouldn't want to miss the kick-off.

'I'll just pop in during the morning,' she told him. 'After all, they might not all be football fans. But I'll leave around midday if no one turns up.'

Uncle Niko had managed to pick up a couple of spare tickets on the terraces, but he didn't tell Alexander that he'd sacrificed them to make sure his deputy loader and the chief crane operator wouldn't be around on Saturday afternoon.

◄o►

When Alexander came into the kitchen for breakfast the following morning, he was surprised to find his uncle had joined them, and wondered if he'd managed to get hold of a spare ticket at the last moment. When he asked him, Alexander was puzzled by his reply.

'You could be playing in a far more important match this afternoon,' said Niko. 'It's also against Moscow, and one you can't afford to lose.'

The young man sat in silence as his uncle took him through what he and his mother had been planning for the past month. Elena had already told her brother that if Alexander didn't want to be involved, for whatever reason, the whole enterprise would have to be called off. She needed to be certain that he wasn't in any doubt about the risks they were taking. Niko even offered him a bribe to make sure he was fully committed.

'I did manage to get a ticket for the match,' he said, waving it in the air, 'so if you'd rather—'

He and Elena watched the young man carefully to see how he would react. 'To hell with the match,' he said.

'But it will mean you having to leave Russia, perhaps never to return,' said Niko.

'That won't stop me being a Russian. And we may never get a better chance to escape from those bastards who killed my father.'

'Then that's settled,' said Niko. 'But you have to understand I won't be coming with you.'

'Then we won't be going,' said Alexander, jumping up from his father's old chair. 'I won't risk leaving you behind to face the music.'

'I'm afraid you'll have to. If you and your mother are to have any chance of getting away, I'll have to stay behind and cover your tracks. It's no more than your father would have wanted.'

'But—' began Alexander.

'No buts. Now I must get going and join the morning shift so I can supervise the loading of both ships and everyone will assume that, like them, I'll be at the football this afternoon.'

'But won't they become suspicious when no one remembers seeing you at the match?'

'Not if I get my timing right,' said Niko. 'The second half should begin around four o'clock, by which time I'll be watching the match with the rest of the lads, and with a bit of luck, by the time the final whistle blows, you'll be outside territorial waters. Just make sure you report for the afternoon shift on time, and for a change, do whatever your supervisor tells you.' Alexander grinned as his uncle stood up and gave him a bear hug. 'Make your father proud of you,' he said before leaving.

As Niko stepped out of the flat he met Alexander's friend coming down the stairs.

'Have you got a ticket for the match, Mr Obolsky?' he asked.

'I have,' said Niko. 'In the north end terrace with the rest of the lads. So I'll see you there.'

'Afraid not,' said Vladimir. 'I'm in the west stand.'

'Lucky boy,' said Niko, and although he was tempted, he didn't ask what he'd had to do in return for his ticket. 'What about Alexander, will he be with you?'

'Sadly not. He's having to work the afternoon shift, and I can tell you, he's pretty pissed off.'

'Tell him I'll drop by this evening and give him a blow-by-blow account.'

'That's good of you, Vladimir. I'm sure he'll appreciate it. Enjoy the game,' he added as they went their separate ways.

◄○►

Once Niko had left for the docks, Alexander still had a dozen more questions for his mother, some of which she couldn't answer, including which country they would be going to.

'Two ships will be sailing on the afternoon tide around three o'clock,' said Elena, 'but we won't know which one Uncle Niko has chosen until the last moment.'

It was clear to Elena that Alexander had already forgotten about the football match, as he paced excitedly around the room, preoccupied only by the thought of escaping. She looked anxiously on. 'This isn't a game, Alexander,' she said firmly. 'If we were caught, your uncle would be shot, and we'll be transported to a labour camp, where you'll spend the rest of your life wishing you'd gone to the match. It's not too late for you to change your mind.'

'I know what my father would have done,' said Alexander.

'Then you'd better go and get ready,' said his mother.

Alexander returned to his room without another word while his mother packed the lunch box he took to work every morning. On this occasion it wasn't filled with food, but with all the notes and coins she and Konstantin had scraped together over the years, a few pieces of jewellery of little value, other than her mother's engagement ring, which she hoped could be sold once they landed in a strange country, and finally a Russian–English dictionary. How Elena now wished she'd spent more time concentrating when Konstantin and Alexander had spoken English every evening. She then packed her own small suitcase, hoping it wouldn't attract attention when she turned up for work later that morning. The problem was deciding what to pack and what to leave behind. Her photos of Konstantin and the family were her first priority, followed by one change of clothes and a bar of soap. She also managed to squeeze in a hairbrush and a comb before forcing the lid closed. Alexander had wanted to take his copy of *War and Peace*, but she had assured him he'd be able to get another copy wherever they landed.

Alexander was desperate to get going, but his mother wasn't willing to leave before the agreed time. Niko had warned her they couldn't afford to draw attention to themselves by arriving at the dock gates before the siren sounded at twelve. They finally left the flat just after eleven, taking a circuitous route to the dockyard where it was unlikely they would run into anyone they knew. They arrived outside the entrance at a few minutes past twelve, to face a stampede of workers heading in the opposite direction.

Alexander battled his way through the advancing army, while his mother, head bowed, followed in his wake. Once they'd clocked in, Elena reminded him: 'The siren will go at two for the mid-afternoon break, then we'll have twenty minutes, no more, so make sure you join me at the officers' club as quickly as possible.'

Alexander nodded, and headed for dock number 6 to begin his shift, Elena in the opposite direction. Once Elena reached the back door of the club, she opened it cautiously, poked her head inside and listened intently. Not a sound.

She hung up her coat and made her way through to the kitchen. She was surprised to find Olga sitting at the table smoking, something she would never have done if an officer had been on the premises. Olga told her that even Comrade Novak had left moments after the siren had sounded at midday. She blew out a cloud of smoke, her idea of rebellion.

'Why don't I cook us both a meal?' said Elena, putting on her apron. 'Then we can eat our lunch sitting down for a change, as if we were officers.'

'And there's half a bottle of that Albanian red left over from yesterday's lunch,' said Olga, 'so we can even drink the bastards' health.'

Elena laughed for the first time that day, and then set about preparing what she hoped would be her last meal in Leningrad.

At one o'clock, Olga and Elena went into the dining room and laid the table, putting out the best cutlery and linen napkins. Olga poured two glasses of red wine, and was about to take a sip from her glass when the door burst open and Major Polyakov strode in.

'Your lunch is prepared, Comrade Major,' she said, not missing a beat. He looked at the two wine glasses suspiciously. 'Will anyone be joining you?' she added quickly.

'No, they're all at the match so I will be dining alone,' said Polyakov before turning to Elena. 'Be sure you don't leave before I've finished my lunch, Comrade Karpenkova.'

'Of course not, Comrade Major,' Elena replied.

The two women scurried back into the kitchen. 'That can only mean one thing,' said Olga as Elena filled a bowl with hot fish soup.

Olga took the first course through to Polyakov and placed it on the table. As she turned to leave, he said, 'Once you've served the main course, you can take the rest of the day off.'

'Thank you, Comrade Major, but one of my duties after you've left is to clear up—'

'Immediately after you've served the main course,' he repeated. 'Do I make myself clear?'

'Yes, Comrade Major.' Olga returned to the kitchen,

33

and once the door was closed she told Elena what Polyakov had demanded. 'I'd do anything I can to help,' she added, 'but I daren't cross the bastard.' Elena said nothing as she filled a plate with rabbit stew, turnips and mashed potato. 'You could always go home now,' said Olga. 'I'll tell him you weren't feeling well.'

'I can't,' said Elena, noticing that Olga was undoing the top two buttons of her blouse. 'Thank you,' she said. 'You're a good friend, but I fear he wants to sample a new dish.' She handed the plate to Olga.

'I'd happily kill him,' said Olga, before returning to the dining room.

The major pushed his empty soup bowl to one side, as Olga placed the plate of hot stew in front of him.

'If you're still on the premises by the time I've finished,' he said, 'you'll be back serving those scum in the works canteen on Monday.'

Olga picked up the soup bowl and returned to the kitchen, surprised by how calm her friend appeared to be, even though she couldn't have been in any doubt as to what was about to happen. But then, Elena couldn't tell her why she was willing to endure even that, if it meant that she and her son would finally escape Polyakov's clutches.

'I'm so sorry,' said Olga, as she slipped on her coat, 'but I can't afford to lose my job. See you on Monday,' she added, before giving Elena a longer than usual hug.

'Let's hope not,' whispered Elena as Olga closed the door behind her. She was just about to turn off the stove when she heard the dining room door open. She turned to see Polyakov walking slowly towards her, still chewing a last mouthful of stew. He wiped his mouth on his sleeve before unbuttoning a jacket covered in medals that hadn't been won on a battlefield. He unbuckled his belt and placed it on the table beside his pistol, then kicked off his boots before starting to unbutton his trousers, which fell to the floor. He stood there, no longer able to hide the rolls of surplus flesh that were usually disguised beneath a well-tailored uniform.

'There are two ways we can do this,' said the KGB chief as he continued walking towards her until their bodies were almost touching. 'I'll leave the choice to you.'

Elena forced a smile, wanting to get the whole thing over with as quickly as possible. She took off her apron and began to unbutton her blouse.

Polyakov smirked as he clumsily fondled her breasts. 'You're just like the rest of them,' he said, pushing her towards the table while trying to kiss her at the same time. Elena could smell his stinking breath, and turned her head so their lips didn't touch. She felt his stubby fingers fumbling under her skirt, but this time she didn't resist, just stared blankly over his shoulder as a sweaty hand moved up the inside of her thigh.

He shoved her up against the table, lifted her skirt and thrust her legs apart. Elena closed her eyes and clenched her teeth. She could feel him panting on her neck as he lurched forward, and prayed it would be over quickly.

The two o'clock siren sounded.

Elena looked up when she heard the door on the far side of the room open, and stared in horror as Alexander came charging towards them. Polyakov turned around, quickly pushed Elena to one side and reached for his gun, but the young man was now only a yard away. Alexander lifted the pot from the stove, and hurled the remains of the hot stew in Polyakov's face. The major staggered back and fell to the floor, delivering a stream of invective that Elena feared would be heard on the far side of the yard.

'You'll hang for this!' Polyakov yelled as he grabbed the edge of the table and tried to pull himself up. But before he could utter another word, Alexander swung the heavy iron pot into his face. Polyakov collapsed to the floor like a puppet whose strings have been cut, blood pouring from his nose and mouth. Mother and son didn't move as they stared at their fallen adversary.

Alexander was the first to recover. He picked up Polyakov's tie from the floor and quickly bound his hands behind his back, then grabbed a napkin from the table and stuffed it in his mouth. Elena hadn't moved. She was just staring ahead, as if paralysed.

'Be ready to leave the moment I get back,' said Alexander, grabbing Polyakov by the ankles. He dragged him out of the kitchen and down the corridor, not stopping until he reached the lavatories, where he crammed the major into the end cubicle. It took all his strength to lift him onto the toilet, and then tie him to the pipe. He locked the door from the inside, and climbing up onto the major's legs, pulled himself over the top and lowered himself to the floor. He ran back to the kitchen to find his mother on her knees, sobbing.

He knelt down beside her. 'No time for tears, Mama,' he said gently. 'We have to get going before the bastard has the chance to come after us.' He helped her slowly to her feet, and while she put on her coat and collected her small suitcase from the larder, he gathered up Polyakov's uniform, belt and gun and dumped them in the nearest waste bin. Taking Elena firmly by the hand, he led her out of the kitchen to the back door. He opened it tentatively, stepped outside and checked in every direction before standing aside to allow her to join him.

'Where did you agree to meet Uncle Niko?' he asked, responsibility once again changing hands.

'Head towards those two cranes,' said Elena, pointing to the far end of the dock. 'Whatever you do, Alexander, don't mention what just happened to your uncle. It's better that he doesn't know, because as long as everyone thinks he was at the match, there will be no way of connecting him with us.'

As Alexander led his mother towards dock 3, her legs felt so weak she could hardly place one foot in front of the other. Even if she had considered changing her mind at the last moment, she now realized they had no choice but to try and escape. The alternative didn't bear thinking about. She kept her eyes on the two idle cranes that Niko had said would be their signpost, and as they drew nearer, they saw a lone figure step out from behind two large wooden crates by the entrance of a deserted warehouse.

'What kept you?' Niko demanded anxiously, his eyes darting in every direction like a cornered animal.

'We came as quickly as we could,' said Elena, without explanation.

Alexander stared down into the crates to see half a dozen cases of vodka neatly stacked in each one. The agreed tariff for a one-way trip to . . .

'All you have to do now,' said Niko, 'is decide whether you want to go to America or England.'

'Why don't we let fate decide?' said Alexander. He took a kopek from his pocket, and balanced it on the end of a thumb. 'Heads America, tails England,' he said, and flipped it high into the air. The coin bounced on the dock-side before coming to rest at his feet. Alexander bent down and looked at it for a moment, then picked up his mother's suitcase and his lunch box and put them in the bottom of the chosen crate. Elena then climbed inside, and waited for her son to join her.

They crouched down and clung to each other as Niko placed the lid firmly back on top of the crate. Although it took him only a few moments to hammer a dozen nails into the lid, Elena was already listening for another sound. The sound of boots running towards them, the lid of the crate being ripped off, and the two of them being dragged out to face a triumphant Major Polyakov.

Niko tapped the side of the crate with the palm of his hand, and suddenly they felt themselves being yanked off the ground. The crate swung gently from side to side as they were lifted higher and higher into the air, before it began its slow descent towards the hold of one of the ships. Then, without warning, the crate landed with a thud.

Elena could only wonder if they would spend the rest of their lives regretting not climbing into the other crate.

extracts reading groups
competitions books new
discounts extracts extracts
competitions events
books reading groups
new extracts events
events books
new reading groups
interviews
books events extracts
events extracts
discounts books
new books events events new books extracts
events new interviews new books extracts
discounts extracts discounts
www.panmacmillan.com
extracts events reading groups books
competitions books extracts new